The Navigator's Wife

The Navigator's Wife

Jane Galer

LNP
Long Nights Press
an imprint of *Poiêsis Press*
Mendocino MenloPark London

While this work is based upon a historical event and I have followed the primary people involved with as much faithful recounting of the narrative as is available, some characters are entirely fictitious, and others are given personalities and life details which are of my own imaginings. An appendix is provided with historical detail for those who wish to suss out the difference.

Published in the United States by:
Long Nights Press
An imprint of Poiêsis Press
Mendocino, California   www.poiesispress.com

17 16 15 14 13 12   1 2 3 4 5

Frontiersman for the Tsar: Timofei Tarakanov and the Expansion of Russian America (Montana, The Magazine of Western History, Autumn 2006, vol. 56, number 3) reprinted by permission of the author.

ISBN 978-0-9845697-3-1

Cover illustration: Surikov, Vasily, 1848-1916. *Portrait of L.T. Matorina / Cossack Woman.* 1892. Tretyakov Gallery, Moscow, Russia, public domain, electronic source www.wikipaintings.org.

Cover design: Jung Design (www.jungdesign.net)
Long Nights Press logo image: Copyright © 1999 Julie Higgins

Set in Minion Pro, Adobe Garamond Pro, and Antiquarian Scribe™. Antiquarian Scribe™ was designed in 2009 by Brian Willson of Three Islands Press (3IP).

Printed on acid free paper.

Also by Jane Galer

Non-Fiction

Becoming Hummingbird:
Charting Your Life Journey the
Shaman's Way

Poetry

Too Deep for Tears
The Spirit Birds

Memoir

How I Learned to Smoke:
An American Girl in Iran

1808
Latitude 48° N
Near Destruction Island
Off the Olympic Coast

Part I

Shipwreck

1

Aground

Anna

Anna wondered at her insistence on this tea service. The samovar, an ornate and large construction of hammered, tinkling brass, threatened to tip and slide, port to starboard with each pitch and roll of the ship; sloshing tea, hot and pale, became a point of contention with him. The more he emphasized the stupidity of such a convention as tea, and the absurdity, the drama, of social intercourse, the more she clung to it. (It was, for her, a matter of survival—many things might be sacrificed on this voyage to the land of aboriginals and furs and cold, but not tea.) And so each day, she ostentatiously prepared it, knowing how the rustling of her skirts back and forth across the small cabin, her rigid leather boots tapping hard on the wooden deck, her small feet caught tightly within, how these things irritated him and how she persisted in her ritual because they did. How the fact of irritating him became a calendar of their voyage. In consequence, she often looked into the bottom of her teacup to read the leaves stranded there, the thin flecks of black leaf showing her a future she could not yet imagine, but felt somehow must change.

She passed her hand over the thick dark curls already escaping from the knot of long hair at her back—a gesture, a habit of nerves—and turned to watch him drink down his cooling tea, his eyes narrowly fixed on her over the creamy, china rim, and she rubbed her knuckles, lightly and unconsciously, across her mouth. She had not been slapped, but his look of annoyance felt like one. Was he even thinking of her, or was this fierceness directed at the roiling ocean, his very real enemy. She lifted her head to meet his gaze straight on, lowering her hand. For a moment she thought about trying to breach this void, begin a conversation that might take them back. How far would it be? Back to Russian earth certainly, when the excitement of this enterprise, then so clearly buffered by ignorance, virginal ignorance, made her hang on his every word.

The crew called him the navigator, as if making the point that he lacked the skills to be their Captain by rank or by means, and they regretted shipping with him on this voyage almost as much as they were wary of her presence. They found her young, slim womanliness imposing, and such imposition hindered her in ways that brought an isolation to her more, perhaps, than even the lack of female companionship equal to her own social status would do. (Yes, there were other women aboard, four Hawaiians, coarse, dark, perhaps morally loose, yes, certainly loose, serving women. Their command of Russian vocabulary is mostly sexual in nature. Were it not for their common bond as women, they would simply be crew members whom she might or might not recognize by name.) Anna knew her place well enough, just as they knew theirs. She was no queen, but with her station as a woman of small education married to a military officer, she knew to what she was entitled. And yes, she understood to a fine degree what she was trading in her marriage bed. And yet she had not understood at all, and thinking about it made her chest tighten and her breath catch. To have no companions would seem less oppressive than to have these men of the sea ebbing around her, their hushed rough talk, their eyes wanting. At night, when her husband joined her in their small cabin and took his rightful needs from her, she felt the humiliation of knowing that the crew heard him, his rhythm taking advantage of the crashing bow wave, so that he hardly need work at all to achieve his release, his gasp of excess like the whale's blow she has heard often on this voyage. She liked to use this image in her head; waiting for him to finish she would imagine the great whale coming to the surface for air, imagine how unlike her husband the whale would be, weightless and fluid, and then with a burst of energy, a thrust of the great tail to bring all that weight quite spectacularly out of the water. The navigator would finish and roll away, stumbling the few steps to his own bunk, and she would wish herself, will herself, out at the rail in the crepuscular light, the great whale before her.

The navigator, her husband, their Captain, does not shoot

with a practiced eye, does not inspire his men, and now, it
seems, cannot captain his ship. His brow furrowed as he
cursed in the coarse Russian she takes as a personal reminder
that she has married just slightly too far on the wrong side of
her station and expectations.

Why is that? She has plenty of time to think about this,
to wonder, on this month-long voyage. What blindness has
allowed it to come to this? In Russia, why had he seemed the
man for her? She cannot recall now, not a smell of him that
drew her breath, not a look in his eyes, though she knows
it must have been there: some instinctive, unconscious response blooming in her heart. What was it that brought her
willingly to the altar where she spoke clearly? She remembered her color rising, a bright rose in her cheeks when
asked to declare that her body and soul would be his forever
to command and to hold. Then, when his uniform was new
and white and trimmed with gold, and he was certain. That
was it. He was certain; he had won her with his certainty. The
tales of adventure, of wild threatening natives, of the beautiful furs he would give her because that was what they were
after, their version of gold, these bales and bales of furs, and
she would have the ones of her choosing. She would be queen
of furs. Pelts too luxurious for any but true queens would
pass through her hands. She had imagined piles of them to
sleep among, imagined, even though it made her blush, wig-
gling down naked, caressed in layers of seal and otter pelt, as
many as she chose. They would be wealthy, world wise, and
they would bring that wealth home to Russia again, and their
status would shine above either of their ranks. His certainty
brought her to the altar, to his bed, and to this, his ship. He

had been certain that this would be a genteel adventure, garner him with wealth and attention when at last he made his way back to Russian soil, real Russian soil, not these outposts of lost souls, pretenders and their greedy deliberate commerce. Anna did not fancy herself an explorer, even in her most exuberantly naïve moments. She knew she wasn't silly or weak, certainly, but she wasn't a brute, an ox, nor a milk cow either. Being fearless or brave was not something she asked of herself. She straightened her back.

"Anna! I must have quiet!" He struck his fist on the parchment map and glared at her.

She had been tapping her spoon absently on the cup edge. His voice strangled her reverie, the spoon jumped and clattered to the floor. He knew she had nowhere to go to give him privacy with his maps. He could leave this cabin, she could not. Not without his order, and not in this storm. He glared at her anyway. She is the conduit for his frustration, and she knows she will feel more of it later.

Suddenly, the ship rolled and skipped as the hull, checked in its way, hopped across doubled waves. The navigator leapt for the cabin door, throwing his heavy dark coat over his shoulders, its wide full cape flapping momentarily as if he would take flight like a great fat bird, and shouting orders as he left the cabin. They could hear the crew already in the throes of removal and replacement, changing sails, correcting course, screaming observations and directions in organized, frenetic chaos. The navigator himself may well be in the way, but he is determined to control the ocean and his ship upon her. Through the port lights Anna can see that while somewhere far away the sun surely shines brightly, here it might as well be night. Anna pitched forward momentarily and her teacup proceeded with the trajectory, spraying tea, speckled with dark leaves, across the precious maps. She did not fall to the floor, but tangled in her own sweep of skirt she hovered for a moment while a giddy momentum of the ship danced her toward and then away from her bunk. Her breath constricted, fear and excitement and the simple confinement of her garment depriving her for a moment of life, and then she sat, hard, on the floor in a balloon of dress, her face in her hands.

She began to pray, and yet, instead of prayer—the regular chant of words she knew by rote but which could at times lull her senses by the mere breathing of them—she felt despair welling up. Counting the many reasons she had to fear, like the tiny buttons on her jacket, fears that constrained her no less tightly, and now a new one, the very real notion that today she might drown. She could see it clearly. A sudden plunge off a pitched deck. Perhaps she would stumble and lose her hold, tripped by her own skirts so that later, she imagines, they would shake their heads and purse their lips and blame her clumsiness for her own death. Wadded between her legs, acres of linen and thick wool would congeal and tangle her, and she would wait, helpless in a final roll of ocean swell, watching her own horrible fate unfold, watching her husband and a shocked crew perched on the safety of the high end of pitch, working their mouths to move words toward her through the squall. But she cannot hear because the deck submerges beneath her body and she floats like a jellyfish, calmly ballooning across the deck rail out into open ocean.

"Anna! Anna!"

She coughed in response as if to clear the imaginary water from her lungs.

"Get up! Dress yourself at once in as many clothes as you can wear! We have lost both our anchors; our foremast is split in two. Dear God, Anna, quick now! We must surely abandon this ship or be lost to the rocks." He crossed himself and then reached for her, picking at her sleeve, waving his other hand.

The Navigator

The *Sv. Nikolai* ran all night along a leeward shore that, when he could catch a glimpse of dark outline here and there, bore very little resemblance to his maps, so little that he began to suspect he did not know accurately where they were, but he could not be sure. He had pricked his chart carefully enough when he was able to make a clean observation of the night sky, but by God, that had been a week past and when the storm came upon them he had hugged the coastline. The wind at his back as it always was on the southerly route meant he could keep a south-southwesterly line, keep the dense trees of the coast in sight, a mile or so off; and yet when the gale came up behind them from the northwest like an angry ghost he was acutely aware of the huge jagged rocky stacks clustered offshore, and the white foam of treacherous shallows made his mouth go dry. Now they had to push hard against a wind that pushed back, moving them always closer to the shore, always more out of control. The desperate darkness of the dirty weather made him feel as though they were in the bottom of a cauldron being stirred. No one on board could ignore Death so close by. This two-masted, square-rigged schooner seemed like a fragile canoe against the swells of the sea.

In the storm he had attempted the only two sailing tricks he knew to bring control back to his ship and out of the hands of the gale that blew with such erratic intensity, never affording him the opportunity to reduce sail, tack, or alter course in any way. He had ordered the crew throw out first one anchor, and then another, trying to slow the hurtling eastward fly of a ship out of control, a ship heading for a lee shore, and then had to cut them both free or watch the ship be pulled under at the bottom of the deepening swells. The crew did as they were told, but wary looks and pointed stares grew as their shock at his incompetence established certainty. Between him and their gods, they began to lose hope. He could see disaster reflected in their sideways looks, hear their morose sense of doom in each query, each reflexive bit of macabre joking. He ordered them to rig a counter sail but the foremast split with the tension and a terrible cracking as jagged pieces of oak shivered off the smaller mast and the crew below scattered beneath the deadly shower. Although the lessening sail power gave him a moment's hope, in the end he lost control of his vessel entirely and now called on the heavens to protect them, crossing himself with real and honest fervor. He felt the ship release and lurch, and grimly turned away from the wheel, leaving the mates there to wrestle her down.

The navigator went below to his cabin, collected his maps, compass, pistol, and his wife and went back on deck to accept his fate. The navigator gestured toward the lee shore, and though fog obscured his vision, in his mind he knew there were small islands of rock—sea stacks the charts call them—looming in the darkness. He could not imagine their fate as other than running up upon them, but he cannot bring himself to admit such a defeat before his wife. The *Sv. Nikolai*, saint though she might be, was in the hands of God now, God in the form of this terrible storm. He stood on the quarterdeck or what would have been the quarterdeck if there had been one—this being a sloop there was by habit an area forward of the mainmast, steps from the hatch access to his cabin, which was sacrosanct to the navigator and his officers—and it was here he stood, his wife next to him with her back against the mainmast, staring into the fog until his eyeballs began to ache. Horizontal rain from an impenetrable cloud whipped his cloak in sodden knots while the wind screaming in the rigging threw all spoken words east toward the land.

Every one of the twenty-two members of the crew was on deck regardless of his watch; no one wanted the dreaded fate of being trapped below when the ship went aground on rocks, sucked down and down into the depths of the hold by the rush of water through the hatches, and none of them swimmers; they would rather drown in the open water, though they knew, without doubt, that drown they would.

He heard the hiss of rain, the crash of waves on rocks

he could not see, he heard his wife's gasp now and then as she began to anticipate a terrible end, and he saw her fingers, white and strained holding tight to the heavy silver cross at her neck. He saw her begin to sink down, like a child on a grand staircase, lowering herself to peer through the rigging, but he put his hand under her elbow and guided her back up to stand next to him in some sort of posture that he felt was right, as befitting the wife of the Captain of this vessel; and when he did so he felt the fear in her body, and felt it slide snakelike through her arm and into his, and suddenly he had a memory of standing at the altar with her, his palm lightly cupping her elbow in just this way, knowing that now and forever he would hold her fate in the palm of his hand.

"My dear," he said, applying gentle but insistent pressure. But beyond that he found no other words to follow.

The ship did not run aground to a crashing and mortal end. Instead she lurched and parried with one and then another great wave before she came cleanly through the rocky stacks and wallowed slowly into a safe landing on a gentle slope of sandy shoreline where, like a slightly tipsy lady, she heeled over and stopped with an audible, sighing, gushing grind, her spine cracking as the weight of her hold settled along the fifty feet of bottom length, unbelievably, in sand. The crew cheered. The navigator heard Anna's sigh and felt her straighten, straining to see toward land as the full light of morning began to open before them. He was sweating under his great coat and he felt as though he had swallowed some great thing he could not digest. He covered his unbelieving relief with orders to belay, and hasten, and rouse. The crew were already throwing crates overboard, launching the skiff and taking orders from the company man, Tarakanov, for what to save of their cargo, what to jettison. They loaded the skiff with supplies and began the short distance through surf, timing their hardest pull to ride the crest of a dead-on wave to meet the narrow black sand shore. The men leapt free and heaved the boat to safety on the stony land, their feet slipping on grey, wet boulders, and made large, hurried, illogical piles of goods they deemed necessary to survival. The first thing off the skiff was the gunpowder, shot, and wads. Back and forth between ship and shore, throwing what they couldn't use into the sea in their haste to get to what they would need for survival, the momentum of panic the primal force in their heads.

They had not much food. After all, the necessity for this trip was that they had been starving in New Archangel, and many of the men suffered from scurvy, losing hair and teeth and sporting a liverish pallor that belied their many weeks exposed to sea air and light. The single cask of Russian birch beer now bobbed in the waves, floating away. Shot, powder, the two muskets they had in total on board, these were the essentials. Following these, they salvaged wooden crates full of badly made gaudy beaded necklaces, and pouches of loose beads and simple buttons. They had been told that if they met the *dikari,* the savages—though surely there could be none here, not in this solid landscape of forest as impenetrable as anything they had seen in the far north—they would value these beads and buttons in trade more highly than any other currency. The Russians had laughed at such a stupid people as that, while the Inuit and Hawaiians looked grim.

Now they hoped very much that that was true because they would need someone's goodwill in the form of trade for food or they would never survive this towering wilderness. For wild it was. One or two ships had sailed passed this place, one or two had stopped, Barkley for one in the ship Captain Cook some twenty years past, but his intent was mapping the sound to the north and name it for himself. He longed for the fame garnered by his ship's namesake only a few years before, and gave little care for these rocky shores. The people who lived here had rarely seen any other people but their own wild tribes who traded, fished and trapped this coastline, and as yet had not been enlisted to trap and trade fur seal pelts to those ships who did come. This was his job, his mandate as navigator from the Company, find the land they called the Oregon territory and make trading arrangements with the natives conducive to establishing trading dominance before the Americans or English trading concerns arrived to do the same. There was even talk of a colony that could be built in Spanish California, warm California where food could be grown year round for the northern outposts of New Archangel and her sisters far to the north. The company would be starved out before they became wealthy otherwise. Isolated during winter months, the Russians had thought the natives would keep them alive. They found instead a hostile reception from the most proximal villages, and enlisting food from the Alutiiqs farther afield left them malnourished. They simply could not exist on the same diet of raw seal and whale meat. They might keep warm enough, but they would starve. The *Sv. Nikolai* had been sent south as far as she could manage, her mandate contact, perhaps even contact the Spanish, but surely to make trading agreements with the varied tribes along the way. They were to make trade agreements for furs without getting killed, drowned, or starve in the process. The little schooner wasn't much against the open ocean of fall and winter storms, their time was limited, and they had to get down to California and back to Sitka before winter. A bleak thought now.

This immediate coastline looked untouched, uninhabited. No distant trails of smoke filtered the sky, no evidence of shore fishing, *no boats, no boats surely, not in this surf,* the navigator thought. He wasn't sure whether this was good news or bad, but he thought perhaps they would be alone here.

The only person waiting for his orders was Anna. Young Phillip Kotel'nikov, the supercargo's apprentice, had been called up to stand by, but the navigator knew full well whom he looked to for orders, for direction. Phillip was here at his side because Tarakanov had needed to take charge, there was no time to relay orders through an ineffectual captain when everyone down to the last most insignificant crewman knew what was what.

He felt Anna strengthen at his side. She was leaning out on the rail, watching, still hidden by his bulk and his dark coat flapped against her dress as she strained to see the shoreline.

"It's unbelievable. Beautiful," she said.

"Aye, what?" the navigator responded absently. It seemed to him that her comment was outstandingly inappropriate.

The shoreline was a landscape of large scattered volcanic rock formations skirted with a lip of sand to the west and reaching twenty or more yards in a slight incline to forest edge. The towering wall of cedar trees sheltered an undergrowth of fern bracken and damp soil here and there dotted with pools of standing water, iron red and stagnant. The shoreline was littered with broken tree limbs, long snakes of brown and bulbous kelp, and ribbons of wet leaf sprinkled with shells left by the tidal retreat. Giant smooth rocks, like eggs from some prehistoric monster, dotted a sea of smaller smoothed stones forming almost impenetrable areas of shingle that made walking difficult, landing a small boat nearly impossible. The navigator could see now the line of the tide. Nearly full. There was an urgent need to clear off the ship as the surf and receding tide would likely pull her apart within hours. The tide might even pull her, leaking hull and all, back out to sea to sink away.

Then no one would know.

The urgency rushed back through his body—the shock had mesmerized him into a reverie of speculation—but now he felt the harsh blood rush of life. He shouted but it was for form's sake only as his crew of nearly twenty men were frantic with their effort to empty the ship. Beside him stood the young apprentice to Tarakanov, Phillip, spyglass in hand, watching the tree line now with acute attention, anticipation.

"Phillip?" the navigator said, "What d'you see, boy?"

Phillip pointed to the north end of the beach, passed the growing stacks of off-loaded cargo.

Almost immediately two natives came out of the dense cover of cedar woods. They wore woven rush conical hats and mantles of fur and bark over bare bodies thick with tattoos.

"Spears and knives," the navigator said, with palpable relief.

Phillip looked at him and then back at the advancing men without comment.

The natives seemed unconcerned with the shipwreck itself or her chorus of twenty men yelling at them to "bugger off our stuff" and "belay there you scum, put that down!". They sauntered up to the piles of supplies, now unguarded as the little skiff was then retreating to the ship for another load. No one had thought to leave guard, no one had thought there could possibly be another living soul so near this place. But now, the foolishness of this notion made the navigator's bowels loosen. He clenched, and when he shouted his voice came high and wild like a frightened hog's, and he had to stop and clear his throat, his face reddening.

"You there! You there, on shore!"

"Blast you, put that down! Stop or I'll shoot!"

"Phillip, bloody hell, where is my musket?"

Phillip

Young Phillip wasn't sure what was more exciting, the potential for shipwreck or their subsequent salvation—or rather, quirk of Fate—swanning onto the sand bank without a single loss of life was impossible, incredible! But now that natives had appeared he had forgotten about the ship entirely and stood staring, excitement and some other emotion he could not name squirreling in his belly.

It had been three years since he'd seen his native Alutiiq mother. His life was attached to his father's people. He was now primarily Russian in language and learning, the missionary priest had seen to that, and yet Alutiiq in looks except for his startling green eyes and his tall lanky height, his black hair wrapped haphazardly in a leather thong was curlier than the dead straight hair of his mother's people, but Russian black or Alutiiq black, who could tell? His skin might have been paler at birth, but he had spent most of his seventeen years out in the open and so, like most people of the Kodiak, he was rough tanned and seasoned. He couldn't recall that he'd ever spent a whole day inside, except the last winter when the sickness came to the island and even the shamans died, and this made the people very frightened. Phillip too was very ill, raging with the fever they all knew and dreaded. His mother had kept him with her, wrapped in sealskin parkas in a room dark and close with burning sedge grass to sweat out the sickness. She sat by him and chanted the shaman's songs that she had learned from the others, chanting day and night in a low urgent voice that when Phillip recalled it, seemed like a man's, not his mother, and the rhythm had echoed in his brain like a drum. Now, far away from her care, when he was sick or worried, he could bring the sense and smell and sound of that time back and find comfort in it.

On Kodiak Island, school was only a few hours a day, children had chores, and the boys often missed classes for the joy and excitement and necessity of fishing with the men.

His mother, he couldn't be sure, but he hoped she was still on the island. When his father had taken him to New Archangel to apprentice to the big company, she had refused to leave. She was the only healer left, their curing woman, she would not leave her people, her island. Phillip could still see her standing on the shore, she would not even step on the wharf to see him off. She said bad things happen when people take their feet off the earth. She wouldn't go in a boat either, and that was very strange among his people, but because she was the healer, they accepted that many things she did would be strange indeed and it was impolite to ask questions. So there she'd stood, her hands at her sides, her eyes intent on Phillip's, and with the spyglass his father lent him he watched her there, unmoving, until his boat was out too far, and the waves made her image swarm up and down in his eyes. He'd been thirteen, a man, and the island Kodiak had become too small for him.

Somewhere deep within his unconscious mind lay a cache of knowledge he did not yet know he had, but there was a small spark of recognition that fluttered now as he watched the native men advance down the shingle with sure-footed grace and confidence. Phillip's toes twitched in his heavy boots. Before Phillip was able to give the scene more thought he was being shouted back into the urgency of the present moment.

"Sir..!"

Phillip fumbled for a split second for the powder flask at his belt. He slid the musket, butt down, on his boot toe and pulled the small cork from the flask with his teeth, tapped the measure of powder into the barrel of the gun and then rustled in his pouch for the ball and bit of muslin. He slid the ramrod from its catch on the barrel and shoved it hard down into the shaft, two good taps with the brass end and back out, pulled back on the action releasing the trigger, set the cap, and gently reset the hammer into place.

"Primed, sir."

Phillip offered the musket to the navigator with an unfortunate and dubious tone in his voice, regretting the effort, knowing how poorly the man shot; he would never even come close to hitting the marauders from this distance.

Waste of powder and shot. Phillip turned aside to avoid the long stretch of musket as the navigator swung it up to his shoulder and squinted over the barrel sight. But the navigator hesitated, canting his head toward Phillip, one eye still squeezed shut.

"Call to them. Surely, you can talk in their language?"

"What language would that be, sir?"

Phillip was genuinely perplexed for a moment, wondering if the navigator actually knew who these particular natives were.

"It's most same, ain't it, boy?"

It was a statement not a question. The navigator lifted his hand from the musket's action and waved, dismissing the issue.

"Try something. Something simple. Ask where their village lies. Tell 'em we'll be no trouble, just want to trade. That's it, trade. Ask about pelts, boy."

The navigator kept the musket at eye level, steadying the considerable weight of it under his elbow on the half rail.

Phillip called out in his own language. The other Alutiiq

crew members stared at him as if he'd lost his senses, and he shrugged at them, and they shrugged back in the smallest agreement of the ridiculousness of his actions.

He called out again. In Russian this time.

"You there! Greetings!"

The two natives on shore were unfazed, even casual, as they continued to move back and forth across the shoreline, carrying off the smaller crates and baskets of Russian goods into the forest. So far they had not tried to move the larger and heavier few barrels of gunpowder or the casks of salted horse and beef. Phillip thought they had made a few trips to test the men on the ship, and would sprint off to call back to some larger party in the forest for assistance. His speculation proved true, for soon there were half dozen naked men, cloaks discarded, moving about on shore, stealing everything they could in an easy way, so that their manner made it seem as if they had a perfect right to do so.

They're so brave. Phillip wished he had a glass through which to study the young men.

In fear, the Russian crew held to the ship, impotently calling out, and occasionally firing a shot, though it was clear from the start they were not in range to make headway with musket fire, most shots spitting short in the water at the edge of the beach. Phillip began to realize that they must make a stand, take hold of the situation or they would continue helplessly watching their means of survival disappear into the forest. Very soon the natives would find the gunpowder at the bottom of the pile. They simply could not allow that to happen.

Phillip had been watching; speechless and fascinated, he took in everything, their nerve, in particular.

How is it that these people show no fear? The small seed of something in his belly was growing. He absently rubbed his navel with his palm, and his fingers twitched.

Phillip was an "apprentice mathematician," on this ship apprenticed to an employee of the Russian fur trade company, Timofei Tarakanov, the supercargo, to learn the trade of the accountant. He could read and do his numbers well enough. The priest had taught him back on Kodiak. But he had also willingly applied himself to the art of the navigator, eager to learn maps and charts and celestial navigation. Keeping accounts was fine enough, but what he truly loved was the night sky, and the idea of finding one's way simply by the stars in a clear sky was near to magic in his mind.

Tarakanov was patient and young enough himself to understand Phillip's drive. Tarakanov was the formal representative of the Russian America Fur Trade Company. In effect, he was in charge of the cargo, in charge of the men on board whose job it was to hunt and haul the goods. He had the pompous titles as supernumerary, supercargo or plenipotentiary—a representative with the authority of the company behind him—but really, fat lot of good that did him out here, stranded with twenty men and these women. Once the cargo was stowed, he spent much of his time teaching Phillip. He was both extraneous to the sailing of the ship and yet its entire purpose, mandate, was in his hands. The Russian America Company had purchased this vessel, built in Hawaii for King Kamehameha I, from American private owners for one hundred fifty sea otter pelts. That had been a funny thing, hardly a trade, more like stealing. Those Hawaiians were mad for furs, not for themselves, not in their climate, but for trading partners in the Orient, the whole of the Pacific Ocean quickly transformed from uncharted waters to active trade routes, with Hawaii and the west coast of the continental Americas in perfect position for the main chance. Tarakanov's business was to know these things. They outfitted the schooner to make an expedition south from New Archangel in the north along the coast to the Columbia River searching for food, desperately needed food, in trade or otherwise in order for the small colony of Russians in New Archangel to survive the long cold northern winter. How much, and when and where, these were the issues for Tarakanov that Phillip must learn. Phillip's apprenticeship was an agreement between slave and master even though his titular master was some far distant personage deep in the hierarchy of the Russian American Fur Trade Company who more likely than not had completely forgotten about Phillip's very existence. Phillip was not free, and that, too, he could feel in his belly.

The ship, relieved of a small weight of ballast, suddenly settled herself into the sand with a groaning and shifting of sodden timbers, canting at an angle that threatened to pitch them all off, alerting them that time was running out. Phillip refused the pitch, adjusting his long legs against this last roll and looked up at his master for direction. Tarakanov stood on the quarterdeck talking to the navigator. *Arguing, more like.* Tarakanov was waving his arm, gesturing toward shore.

"They're called Hoh, do ye see, Bulygin? Hoh's the people

live in these parts north of that river there." And parenthetically, "'Tis on the charts as such."

Tarakanov waved his hand to the river inlet that lay just five hundred yards to the north of the sea stack that had foundered the ship.

They all looked, and saw for the first time, slightly upstream and down a short embankment carved out by the tidal flow, three long cedar canoes pulled up on the southern shore. Women were loading the canoes with all of the plundered goods. They had only taken the crates into the woods to distract the Russians.

The crew stood in small clutches on the crowded foredeck of the listing ship. As the ship settled and twisted they edged closer and closer to the low angled rail and the short drop to the choppy shallows below.

"We need to leave the ship and head south if we are to get away alive," Tarakanov said.

Phillip saw the navigator's shocked look, saw his eyes flash toward his wife in anguish.

"Abandon ship! Yes, yes. Tarakanov, I see, I see. By all the saints...Phillip! Take care to get my wife into the skiff. She's your responsibility, hear me Phillip? Do it now!"

Phillip felt the navigator grab at his collar and give him a shove.

"Aye, sir. I'll do it!"

Phillip did not need to be invited twice to quit the ship. Coming to Anna's side, he offered his hand and then pulled it back, wiping it on his tunic before holding it out again to the woman. He smiled at her with encouragement and jerked his head over the rail toward the skiff bobbing at the waterline below them, held fast by two Alutiiq men.

"Ma'am?" Phillip said with studied firmness.

He held his body rigid with excitement. He caught her eye and smiled at her again with forced courage, tamping down his impatience as he saw the utter terror in her face. He reached down and took her hand in his, engulfing her small, thin fingers with his large brown, ink-stained, and dirty hand.

"Come on! Come—please ma'am—hey, there! You, there in the skiff, mind your oars—give a heave on those lines now."

—and then in a gentler voice as if talking to a small child—

"Now then, just watch your skirts, ma'am."

He helped her navigate the descent into the boat, encumbered as she was by three layers of underskirts and white stuffs that snagged and caught at the planking of the ship's side as she was let down in a sailcloth chair. Phillip wondered at the notion of loading her with all these clothes when it had seemed they would drown, what was the navigator thinking to do such a thing? He shrugged and let himself easily over the rail and scrambled down the schooner's side in time to catch the canvas chair's main line and ease it to safety.

"Now, then, Ma'am, stay close and we'll see what's what."

Phillip handed Anna to a seat beside him. She was pale and almost seemed not to see him there, but he saw her hands clutched together and saw her knees tremble beneath her skirts. He took off his short dark coat and covered her shoulders with it, and looked away. The skiff ran off the bow of the *Sv. Nikolai* and turned into the surf catching the next swell for the fast ride to shore. The moment the prow touched sand, four men in the bow, jumped free and heaved the skiff into the shallows, and with a quick backward look at Phillip they ran down the beach to the piles of stores.

Phillip and two Alutiiq crew members helped Anna climb from the boat into the sandy shallows, the skiff backing and turning toward the ship again even as they stepped free. Her skirts wicked water and seaweed and the men had to help hold up her clothes to move her toward shore, each wave of surf pushing her, controlling her movement just the way they would have muscled a killed seal away from the tide at home in order to strip it of its flesh. At last, beached, she sank down onto the sand, but it was not in prayer at their salvation, only the unsteady unfamiliar lack of momentum of the earth.

Phillip looked down at the woman on the ground before him with equal parts impatience and sympathy. But he was not allowed to dwell upon her comforts. From the darkening cedar stand before them came two natives, *almost like ghosts*, he thought, as they stepped from the deep shadows of the huge trees into the glaring sunlight. Phillip felt a thrill of danger. The two men were young, strongly built. Their faces were covered in tattoos, dots and lines, that made their expressions fierce and unreadable. Strong black lines mapped across cheek and nose, and dark red dots spilled from their lips down the chin as if blood dripped out of their mouths. Phillip stared. These men were not simply here to steal. They held clubs in their hands, and Phillip saw their confidence, their complete sense of control as they moved toward them, their gait solid and sure. The other natives who were tasked with plundering were lining up behind these two. Suddenly stealing goods wasn't the goal. Something was going to happen. Phillip could feel it and he swallowed hard.

"Dear God," he said.

His hand tightened on Anna's shoulder.

"Stand up, ma'am! We will have to run."

"I cannot! I cannot!"

She was shaking her head, her small delicate chin trembled.

Anna's face turned up to Phillip and she splayed her hands as if it should be obvious to Phillip that she had lost the ability to walk from simple fear.

The two natives in the lead began to sprint through the sand toward them. Their legs were short and powerfully built and they nearly flew through the sand and over the rocks.

"Ma'am..."

Phillip looked to the ship and saw that the little skiff was now nearing shore behind them filled with the second load of crew. The crew were all shouting, everyone having different advice. Soon enough they would all be on shore. But how to keep these natives at their distance in the meantime? He did not know. If only he had a musket.

Tarakanov was in the bow of the skiff, his eyes fixed keenly on Phillip and the warriors behind him.

Phillip cupped his hands and hollered as Tarakanov jumped free of the skiff.

"The musket, sir, fire it! In the air, sir, do ye see?—Over us—in the air, so as they will run away. Fire, sir, fire it!"

Phillip stooped his lean body in a protective arc over Anna's, shoving her to the wet sand as his did, and he felt her breath leave her with a grunt, felt the painful strain of her whalebone corseting beneath his chest. Phillip's body tensed, waiting for the shock of a bullet or the blunt force of a stone club to strike his body. He hated not being able to see. He buried his head in Anna's streaming hair and held on.

Tarakanov stopped where he was, ankle deep in rising tide, swung the musket to his shoulder and fired over the crouched bodies of Anna and Phillip. Once. Reload, the butt on his knee to keep it dry. One, two, three precious minutes, and then fired again. The gunpowder rang out over the sound of surf.

"Keep down, boy!"

The natives stopped, crouched, exchanging words, and as one, turned and sprinted for the forest.

Tarakanov shouldered the musket and made his way through the surf to the mound that was Anna, crumpled on the sand, and held his hand out to her.

"Madam," he said. He tried to make his face less severe, less alarming.

"They will return, sir," Phillip said. He stood up brushing sand from his arms and legs, staring at the spot in the trees where the native men had disappeared.

"They will indeed, son, you can be sure of it."

The last boat load of crew, now twenty-two in all, came into the shore with the navigator, Bulygin, as was his right as Captain, being the last. As they crowded around their belongings the crew began to argue. Phillip stood at the edge of the group, watching the forest. Waiting. The tangle of nerves in his belly made him jumpy. He looked from the forest to the group of men and back again.

Tarakanov, Diary Entry
Hoh River, 1808

Having been at sea for four weeks, bound for New Albion of the Columbia region they call The Oregon, to deal with native traders for pelts and then to go on southing to Bodega Bay where we seek to establish a community of Russians in the Spanish land California, we were blown in a northwest gale, during which we lost our foreyard and all anchors. We are twenty-two stranded souls: navigator Bulygin and his wife, Anna Petrovna, eleven other Russians including my assistant, young Phillip Kotel'nikov, one Englishman, four Alutiiq crewmen, three Hawaiian Métis women, and myself, Timofei Tarakanov, representative of the Russian American Fur Trade Company.

We have come ashore through no fault of our own to a hostile place just south of the mouth of what the charts name the Hoh River, sheltered by many outcroppings and islands of rock so that we will be hard pressed to see another passing ship to which we might hail for our salvation. Some goods and stores of foodstuff marauded by hostile natives. No lives lost. The crew has determined they will not follow the navigator and have voted me in charge now we are on land, and since there is some small legitimacy for this action it will politely not be considered mutiny on

their part, and I think this navigator, Nikolai Bulygin, himself relieved and in truth, the company would consider it right.

We have determined to work our way inland along the river
and then make our way southing, to remove ourselves from obvious native interest, but I think these people wild and vicious in
their habits of war, and that we will face our survival without
their ready help.

Most of our goods must be left behind. We take what we can
carry along with two muskets, powder, and shot. We leave behind
in hands of the natives our small collection of pelts, mostly otter,
and what stores we could not easily destroy. We put ourselves in
the hands of God.

2

The Lie of the Trail

Anna

Even though she was cold, the first thing she did when she could even think and act for herself was to stop and relieve herself of the worst of her sopping ragged clothes. Between the sea legs she had grown accustomed to that now made her stagger as she walked, and the extra layers of clothing—three petticoats of rough linen alone—she could barely keep the men in sight. The navigator followed her as if herding a great prized old cow, clearly anxious to be with the men, and yet there was something touching in his occasional solicitude, as if now and then he remembered something sweet about her, something he treasured, and he would touch her arm as she tried to regain balance from a stumble. But when she looked at him, his eyes shifted away, away to the front of the line of people trailing away in front of them, to Tarakanov at point, and she could see a small fire of jealousy alight in his eyes.

Apart from Anna, each man carried a bundle that they threw over their backs with as much of the most precious gear as they could salvage. The bundles were fashioned from a large canvas square of cloth packed and tied in the manner they always used for carrying bundles of pelts and other goods on land. By nature the men were short and stoutly built, and they carried their bundles with steady ease, used to much greater weight in the norm. But it wasn't much, what food they had. It wasn't enough, Anna could see that, she could make calculations as well as anyone else here, she wasn't incapable. They had muskets and shot and could hunt, but for how long?

She looked around her as they gained a level patch of ground and the pace and footing allowed her to take her attention elsewhere beside the monotonous focus on placing each step carefully. They had left the roar of surf behind, amazing her at how quickly the sound died behind them. Then, beyond the first shoreline stand of cedars, they found a swamp of ferns, trillium, and lamb's ears steeped in nearly a foot of cool brown water. The broad green variegated leaves of the trillium were slick and treacherous. Anna's boots filled with water and cedar bark slash that pricked through her woolen stockings and jabbed her feet until she thought she must stop, must sit down.

But when she faltered she pictured the natives coming behind them. They would not be stopping, this she knew. She brought clearly to mind the face of the fiercest man, the one who had come closest to her. The one she could see clearly as she had cowered on the sand, her head on her arms, her knees tucked to her chest. His naked body had shocked her. She tried to see his face in detail, to catch the nuances of his eyes, his tattoos. She felt, suddenly, that in doing so, in thinking so closely about him only as a man, that he might become less frightening, and she might become more brave, but all she could bring forth was his brown fully naked form, and there was no comfort in that image.

Anna removed half of her clothes and abandoned them in a dark lumpy pile in spite of the protests of her husband, who declared she would regret this. She wanted to say, *Fine, then you carry them for me.* But she felt this was obvious and since he would not, that too was obvious.

"Leave me be," she said.

She looked at him closely as she said it. She knew he felt demeaned by losing his command of the men to Tarakanov. She wondered if this was what made her brave enough to add her own comment.

She took off her boots and cleaned them of cedar scraps and wrung out her stockings. Her feet were remarkably unscathed, small red scratches only. She sighed, rubbing her toes, knowing that this would not last, this being strong and unscarred.

The others were not waiting. Some had spread out into the forest in twos and threes following deer paths in hopes of discovering....what? She shook her head. *What was the use in this retreat? Where did they think they were going?* There was no civilization here. Their only hope was to stay alive, keep close to the shore and watch for ships, hoping the rare ship that might come by would stop at anchor just beyond the dangerous stacks and range ashore, tempted by the mouth of the river for fresh water, and prime otter feeding grounds. They had only to walk south, and eventually they would arrive at Gray's Harbor where they were to meet their sister ship, the *Kad'iak*.

By all the saints, let her come. She crossed herself.

Anna turned and looked out toward the west, toward ocean. She shook her head, the smallest gesture, part disbelief, part disgust.

The Navigator

"Phillip! Boy, come back down here and give us a hand now."

The navigator gestured toward Anna as he would have a sack of unruly potatoes splitting at the seams. He wanted, no, he needed, to be at the head of this line of men.

"Mind her progress, boy, and don't fall too far behind, ah, you know, if she…" he gestured toward the forest and grimaced, embarrassed "…has necessity."

He nodded at Anna, and his hand might have come out to touch her head, it looked so bright, brown and sleek in the sunlight as she sat on the ground, so like a pelt, but he saw she was sitting straight as a pole and he knew that posture. He turned and hurried up the line of men, jostling them here and there with his bulk, his breath coming strong by the time he reached the lead where Tarakanov was talking with two of the junior officers.

Just before them lay a large open meadow, certainly not the place to hide out and the navigator was about to say so when he realized what they had been talking about. At the far side of the meadow, four or five deer contented themselves within a patch of late wildflowers. The meadow was too exposed, and too wet, but they would never find a better place to kill a deer.

"But, we cannot shoot, surely? The noise will bring 'em down on us quick."

The navigator looked behind himself as if he expected the natives to round the bend at that moment.

"No, of course not. But later, perhaps so. We need to hide nearby, and then, when we can safely do so…" Tarakanov grinned and tapped the flintlock's butt on his boot toe. "We eat."

The navigator nodded in agreement. His stomach, encouraged, growled, reminding him that it had been a good while since he had eaten a full meal.

In the end, dreams of venison died with the waning afternoon sun and the sense that any notion of stopping was premature. They had for the most part been walking parallel to the shore embankment southward along an obvious and logical trail that they came back to once their ranging eastward proved futile. They stopped now and then for water from the iron red and brackish streams that flowed from the snow capped mountains of higher elevations to the east. Now and then they found major obstacles, rock outcroppings overhanging large pools or great downed cedars that caused them to scramble over and then realign their direction. Spread wider as the ground allowed, they broke into small parties following deer paths east through the dense forest only to find they often just looped and intersected with each other, but they persisted nevertheless in hopes that some perfect stopping point, sheltered and safe, would present itself. They felt pursued: a palpable sense of being occasionally watched, always followed.

It was usually necessary to walk in single file. The embankment track was worn with human use, not just deer, and cleverly placed just out of sight of the beach yet within sound of the thundering surf so that they were all of them by now jumpy, not being able to hear should an enemy approach. The navigator kept pace with Tarakanov, who was a young muscular man. Every so often he would put his hand on Tarakanov's arm, arresting his progress, to ask some question, to delay the push of pace while he regained his breath, his belly heaving and catching over the wide leather belt of his breeches.

"What…"

Tarakanov interrupted him by pointing.

Following his direction, the navigator saw that the land took a sharp gain in elevation, the top of which culminated in a group of huge rocks.

"If we stop here, we can post a sentry there. We have fresh water at least near enough. Tarakanov gestured back down toward the meadow full of deer left a good hour's walk behind by now and shrugged. They will find us in any event;

we are not clever enough to hide in their own country." He looked keenly into the navigator's face. "You know this, aye?"

The navigator thought about arguing for the sake of establishing his position, but he knew he could not. Nothing more could be said. He glanced back through the line of men, looking for Anna. For a moment, all he saw was Phillip, standing off the path quite a way behind, but then a movement to Phillip's left revealed Anna, her dark green shawl printed over with roses had for a moment allowed her to blend entirely into the fern leaf behind her. She straightened and he saw her smooth her dark blue woolen jacket and shake out her skirts. He turned back to Tarakanov, satisfied.

Phillip

Phillip would give anything for a musket in his hands. He felt excited, vulnerable, skittish as a fine bred horse. And he loved being the last man in line. He watched Anna, of course, watched her carefully with a mixture of duty and curiosity, but something had changed within himself and he wanted to give it free rein. Perhaps it was just the simple fact of being back on dry land, but no, he'd spent a few years now on and off ship and this didn't feel like that. He watched the forest, watched the shadows expand and contract, listened to the sough of cedar bough. What was it he anticipated?

Silence. That was it, silence. He was waiting for the birds to stop. He wanted to be far enough away from the ocean that the rumble of surf faded and once again every branch that buckled, every tree that swayed into its neighbor would tell him a new story of this place. He remembered something from his childhood with his mother's people, a kind of listening that was wary and controlled and yet accepting, integrating. He reached deep into his memory for the way of it, his face set with concentration. His mother's people, the Alutiiq, hunted otter and seal without the benefit of cover. They knew the depth of silence, how to glide along an ice floe toward an open water gap, how to creep up slowly on a basking sea beast. Phillip had a sudden, sharp longing for clear cold air, for his island home far away to the north.

He worked out what he was after. He felt his heartbeat, steady and strong. He allowed that heartbeat to fill him down to his boots and draw him into the earth the way his mother's father taught him before the hunt. He felt his linen and woolen clothes tighten and wished he could take them off, exchange them for simple coverings, coverings slick like seal skins, rain proof and warm, clothes that would let him move like the deer they had seen in the meadow.

Phillip fell farther behind. It was not his intent to lose the group, or to lose Anna. He would protect her. Instinctively he knew that to protect her properly he needed to know who or what was coming up behind them. To do that he needed to recognize the silence when it came. He felt for his gutting knife and tugged it forward just a bit, his fingers fluttering over the hilt. He was better at skinning something dead, he had done that a lot training with the fur trappers, he could skin an otter or a seal as fast as any man. *Well, not as fast as grandfather.* His mouth twitched in a small, brief smile. But no one was as fast as grandfather—grandfather could stalk, kill, gut, and strip down a seal so fast the blood was still hot and gushing from the heap of inner parts when he was done, the tart metal smell of it strong in the air. Still, Phillip thought he could handle his knife well enough if he had to, or wanted to. He'd protect Anna, sure. But would he kill natives? He looked at his hands, dark tawny brown and nearly hairless at his wrists. His Russian father had been fair skinned but black haired. Phillip's hair was thick and black, tied back in a tail at his neck and slicked with oil to keep it in check and free from lice.

Who would I look like, were we set out naked as seals in a row?

Phillip had studied the charts in the navigator's cabin. He had the map in his memory, all of the rivers down to the Columbia, passed Gray's Harbor where they were to meet up with the other ship. It wouldn't be hard to find. Along the coastline, the map named a number of native tribes. Strange exotic names, threats in themselves, in the speaking of it aloud. Hoh. These people were not his people. They were the people to the south nearest this river they followed. To the north, behind them, were the Makah, the people of the Cape known as Alava; and farther south the Quinault, and the Quileute. Did they war with each other, or would they band together to rid themselves of invaders? Which people had discovered them as they wrecked, and had they sent word to others? Was it the Hoh as Tarakanov had said? Slave catchers, all of them. He knew that. They warred with each other over beings, over people they could trade and enslave. These tribes were fierce. Phillip had heard stories. Of slaves traded like pelts. Of people caught and adopted into a family to replace a dead soul. Phillip shivered, but out of this recollection, he also saw one thing: they would not kill them readily, not as long as they were healthy, not as long as they were useful.

Anna had stopped ahead of him. Phillip saw she was adjusting her boots again. He stopped too, turning away from the sound of surf to the west, keeping his distance from her. He wanted the time to hear the quiet without seeking it beyond the swish of skirts, the crush of grasses beneath their boots. He became instantly still, letting his eyes scan the forest methodically, learning how to read the shadows. He had no fear of losing the company ahead. Were it not for Anna, he might have deliberately fallen off and disappeared, taken his chances. The idea appealed to him, took root. It gave him something else to do, to think about, how he could survive on his own, and what might happen then.

They walked for two hours, Phillip discreetly and gently chasing Anna along the path. Sometimes, the deer trail disappeared, or abruptly ended in a huge rock formation and Anna needed his help. She kilted up her skirt, tucking it into her waistband. Phillip looked away, but she didn't seem to be embarrassed. He clambered up the side with the least sheer face, set his feet and crouched down reaching for her hands. This way they worked around several obstacles, falling behind the rest, but always catching up eventually. Phillip would watch the path behind them when he could, and it seemed to him that they were not being followed. He hoped that was true.

The fog came in, swirling and caressing the massive cedars until it might have been rain falling. Phillip shook his arms, casting a shower of droplets, and brushed the damp from his coat. After two hours of steady walking he felt his land legs coming back; his feet hitting the ground no longer felt like the ground was jumping up to meet him. He noticed that Anna stumbled less often as well.

After conquering a particularly sharp and sheer rock stack, the only alternative to trying its face having been a massive prickly berry patch, now seasonally died off but more tangled than if there had been ripe fruit about, Anna held onto Phillip's hands as he lifted her down. She squeezed his hands.

"Thank you," she said.

He shrugged. He was beginning to think of them as a pair of survivors independent of the body of their ship's company. He was enjoying himself. He wouldn't go so far as to say he almost felt free, but he felt challenged in a way that he had never felt before, and it lifted something in his heart. He tried not to laugh, and covered the urge with the most pleasant smile he could give her.

They weren't making fast progress. He knew this from the charts, studied over and over until he could see them in his mind, every curve of landfall, every inlet and river. The rocky ledges that separated the beach from the forest forced them to walk up and down over and over again as they tried to keep hidden from natives who, he thought, would surely stick to the shoreline as a much easier pathway and being unconcerned with keeping hidden. They had covered several miles, he and Anna losing sight of the men and women in front of them more often than not. But Phillip could hear them, and didn't worry.

A thrashing ahead made Phillip hurl himself toward Anna, pulling her to the ground in a quick roll into the giant ferns that grew at the base of the cedars. She let out a whump of surprise but instantly stilled in his grasp. Phillip strained to hear what was happening ahead. Shouts from the crewmen, and a curious series of whistles came in reply from below at the shoreline. Phillip pulled Anna to her feet and holding her arm ran as fast as she would bear into the cover of the forest. They were under attack. He hoped to circle wide and get abreast of the others without attracting the attention of the natives. He could tell they were slinging rocks from the shelter of the natural bank. Now and then one would hit one of their party and there would be oaths and curses in reproach, but the natives didn't take the attack further, seeming content merely to harass. Phillip and Anna found a spot on a small ridge where they could watch, protected, lying flat in the ferns. They were still behind the rest, off to the east, but within safe distance should this skirmish turn into a real battle. Phillip didn't want to be cut off from the rest. At least not here, not now. He would do what would be best for Anna.

The noise of the skirmish subsided quickly. Phillip sat on his haunches, completely rigid, intently listening. He heard the others excitedly talking as they regrouped. Two of the crew edged toward the bank to see if they could spot the natives.

"They're gone," he said. He stood fully upright and gave Anna his hand. She seemed dazed.

"You're well?"

"Yes," she nodded as she shook out her skirts. Her hands were scratched, bleeding slightly from tumbling beneath Phillip's body.

"Thank you," she said.

"Ay, well, if ye keep thankin' me ever time I give ye a hand, I'll have a right full basket of thanks," he looked at her with a grin, "no need, Madame Bulygin."

He used her formal name as a mark of respect to make up for how he had been physically handling her body.

It might be that this was the longest sentence he'd uttered in a year.

Anna

Her hands were scratched, her feet hurt and she dreaded taking off her shoes, for she was sure her toes were bleeding by now. She could feel the cold slickness of blood. She stopped at a stagnant pool. The water was red and dark, but she didn't care. She cupped her hands and scooped water, splashing her face, and drinking some. It wasn't awful. She dribbled water on her neck, pulling her hair up. She untangled the braid that had nearly collapsed, combed out the three long snakes of rich brown and mechanically rebraided it, twirling the braid into a knot at the base of her neck and then covering her head with her scarf. She sat back with a sigh.

Phillip was scanning, listening; it seemed to her as if he were hearing things she could not. She couldn't hear a thing, she almost felt deaf, though she was not, but the wind seemed to rob her of any other sounds. She watched Phillip with interest. It suddenly came to her that she was watching him become a man before her very eyes.

Anna and Phillip caught up with the rest of their party within minutes. Her husband took her arms, shaking in himself, seeming to check her body for all limbs and parts in fair order, and pronounced he was glad she was well.

"Yes, well," she said.

He let go of her as Tarakanov began to give orders.

"We'll camp here the night," he said.

"Bulygin, and you, ma'am, you shall have the tent with the Aleutys." He nodded toward the three Alutiiq women who were part of the crew. And then, as if to explain the sudden gesture of propriety toward the native women he shrugged. "We'll be standing watch and watch."

"You are wounded?" Anna gestured toward Tarakanov's torn and bloodied sleeve.

"Aye, 'tis nothing." He backed away as Anna moved toward him her hand raised.

She looked at him with raised eyebrows but did not comment. As she looked around she noticed a few of the other crew had cuts and bruises, but no one was badly injured. Their blood was for the most part dried. These wounds must have happened in the initial encounter. Anna had heard shots, but the bullets fired were all from their own side. *These natives do not own guns.* The thought struck her with a rush of relief. The skirmishes with flying rocks suddenly made sense. She dusted her hands on her skirts and made for the tent where the three Alutiiq *kaiury* women were busy settling in, doing what little could be done to provide a safe resting place and a little food before darkness folded them in. These women were not her servants, they were workers and wives of other workers with tasks far more important than catering to any of Anna's small needs. She nodded to them with respect.

Tarakanov began speaking to the men. Anna listened from the modesty of the tent.

"Those savages were Hoh. That river back there,"—he jerked his thumb northward toward where they had been—"that's named the Hoh river."

Some of the men laughed at the name, but their laughter withered under Tarakanov's intense gaze.

"Make no mistake, even without muskets, they can and will kill you, though they'd rather take you alive, make you a slave." He made a sort of grimace pursing his mouth.

The laughing stopped, and Anna froze.

"That's right, a slave. These natives trade slaves like tobacco and rum. So stick together, and don't take chances. We'll stay in camp tonight, I want pairs of eyes on watch from all sides now."

Anna was perfectly able to imagine what slavery to a native of one of these tribes would be like. She'd seen enough in the north of the way the natives there were used, and used each other. How fierce the Tlingit warriors were, vital and hard. Serfs, slaves, apprentices. In a tent, a shack, a log lodge. It was a killing state barely better than Russia.

Reunited with her husband for the night, they hardly talked, exhaustion taking over the moment they allowed themselves to sit down. As night fell and darkness gave them an eerie sort of protection, they collapsed next to one another on the damp ground under the shelter of the tent. The navigator, as was his way, fell instantly asleep, and Anna lay on her side next to him, her knees curled toward her breasts, listening to his regular breathing grow deeper and deeper. It was such a relief to lie down. Lying quietly she took inventory of her body. Her feet were on fire with fatigue and when she rolled onto her side she felt the pinch of bruises on her knees. It seemed as though her small frame ached everywhere. She hugged her arms to her breasts, said her prayers to her own particular saint, Saint Anna of Kashin, her namesake, the heavy silver cross held tight between her palms. She thanked Saint Anna for bringing Phillip to her aid, closed her eyes, and slept lightly, somehow aware that she was the only one in the tent who would remain alert, even in sleep. Her last thought was of Phillip; she hoped he slept well.

Tarakanov, Diary Entry
Day One – South of the Hoh River

Our ship Sv. Nikolai having wrecked near the mouth of the Hoh river at 48° North latitude is lost. Our crew intact and only lightly injured in several skirmishes with Hoh natives, made our way south through the cedar forest, following the edge of the land. We have killed three Hoh natives, and this fact has probably brought them to follow us as we flee.

By unanimous agreement, I have taken command of this adventure and decided that we will walk to Gray's Harbor, which I reckon some ten to fifteen miles as the crow flies, there to rendezvous with the ship Kad'iak. May god provide her to us.

We have no food, but a dry night before us. We have set watches, but fog has enveloped our camp, and I am unable to get a sure sense of our position or progress toward our goal.

3

Southing

The Navigator

A rebellious stomach woke him before dawn and kept him awake until the cold wet ground beneath him crept into his joints and he sat up with an oath. Anna and the Alutiiq women slept, curled in heaps of clothing around the tent. Somehow this irritated him. He scrubbed his hands over his face and rubbed his belly where the thick buckle of his black leather uniform belt had laid a welt during the night.

Outside, the light came slowly creeping through the fog, battling with the trees and the elevation to the east, making sun, were there to be any, a long time off. He stretched and ambled to the cedar grove grabbing a few fern leaves as he went, and not a long way off, he crouched and loudly evacuated his bowels. It was cold on his bare flesh, and he rapidly dressed, buttoning his thick trousers with numb fingers, cursing softly.

He was a young man and not unattractive in his sturdy way, but his family tended to fat, and it didn't seem that even the shortage of food at New Archangel had made much difference to his belly.

I can still dance. He huffed his breath, visible in the morning air. As he turned he noticed movement in camp, and to his astonishment, saw a deer, a young doe, wandering unconcerned between the sleeping figures of the crewmen, nibbling grasses here and there. The navigator watched her, unbelieving, but helpless. He did not possess either one of the two muskets. They could not risk either the noise of a shot or the smoke of a fire. He watched food walk away into the forest.

The crew began to stir, ten Russian countrymen, in addition to Tarakanov, one Englishman—a wild adventurer, or so he liked to think—along with eight Alutiiq native men and three women made up the total of twenty-two passengers and crew. The promyshlenniks were hard worn men, used to sleeping rough, accustomed to carrying heavy loads for long distances. They wasted little time in grumbling, knowing how useless it was. To amuse them, and perhaps bring them closer, in an unusual moment of volubility, the navigator told them about the doe that walked over them in their sleep. The navigator had not earned their respect, but they listened to his story nevertheless, as any story, however trivial, might find its way to being useful at some point in the future. They marshaled their energy and worked with an economy of motion that the navigator could only admire. And they looked only to Tarakanov for direction.

The navigator retreated into the tent and spoke softly to Anna, momentarily afraid what she might say as she came awake not yet fully cognizant of where she was, but she opened her eyes at once, and he knew she had been awake for a while.

"Did ye hear me say about the doe?" he said.

"I did, aye. Was she alone, then?"

He shrugged.

"Don't know. Are you well, my dear?"

The navigator's need for intimacy found solace in the banal breakfast table repartee even without either the breakfast or the table. He gave her a hand to help her stand, then watched her as she shook out her clothes. She straightened her shift and rehooked the short camlet of her stays, then reached for her jacket, exposing her breasts for a moment before they disappeared behind a wall of wool and buttons. He felt a hint of protective interest stirring. It had been some days since they had been intimate with each other. Seemed like an age and more to him, but perhaps it was only a week. He wondered if she missed their joining, and at once that protective stirring made a singularly pronounced shift.

"Anna," he said, touching her sleeve, "take care today." He hoped she saw in his eyes that he meant that, and more. She stopped her brushing and tidying and looked at him with her soft, grey eyes for a moment, then a gave a quick nod.

Anna and the *kaiury* women hurriedly cleared the tent, leaving the navigator no choice but to seek other companions.

He joined Tarakanov who was perched on the rock above, watching up and down the beach beneath his vantage point with his spyglass.

He was grateful for the acknowledgment to his position when Tarakanov lent him the glass.

"Nothing. For now," he said.

"Aye." The navigator peered intently up and down the beach and then swung the glass due west where in the clear morning he could see a small island.

"And that there," he said, "might be the one Barkley called Destruction Island?"

"Aye. Might be. We won't make Gray's Harbor for a while yet, not at this rate." Tarakanov stood and scratched vigorously at his hair, wiped his eyes with the heels of his hands and nodded when the navigator offered the glass back. "Keep it by for a bit."

There was no food, and no one asked. Winter was nearly upon them and there was as a consequence very little on the ground. No berries, and no trees that would produce nuts. Tarakanov sent a few men down to the shore where volcanic rock made it likely they could find mussels, as they did. Each of them consumed ten or so of the small rough shelled salty creatures, and so their fast was broken. The navigator grimaced as he ate, he suspected the fish diet they had been forced to eat had been the means of his unruly digestion.

They each had their burdens to carry, the promyshlenniks carried the heavy tent pieces and pouches of gunpowder and such. Tarakanov had his journal and glass, musket and shot pouch. The navigator carried the charts as if they were sacred texts, and his log book, though he had given over tracking their daily progress to Tarakanov whom he knew wrote each evening, optimistically detailing the events of the day, as if he had a certainty that there would be a time to look back and read about this disaster from a point of safety. The navigator nervously fingered the strap of his satchel as he watched Tarakanov gather the group with an ease that mystified him.

Tarakanov passed the second flintlock musket, shot pouch and horn to the Englishman, shouldered his own, and set the pace, circling the rocks and finding once again the forest deer path. With Tarakanov and the navigator in the lead the Englishman fell in towards the rear, with Anna and Phillip deliberately, it seemed to the navigator, coming last. He shouted to her to catch up, but if she heard, he saw no indication of it, and he did not want to lose pace with Tarakanov. Phillip would mind Anna.

Phillip

Phillip had already been up when the navigator came out of his tent in the morning, he'd watched him from the cover of the cedar forest as he squatted to relieve himself, unoffended, his own sense of modesty was peculiar to his people, he supposed. But he didn't see bodily functions as being anything other than one more thing animals did. At home on Kodiak, before the Russians came, his mother's people just went outside and found a place that was clean, often down near shore where the ocean would wash the sand clean again. When the Russians came and made their little fort, they showed the Alutiiq to build little houses, but the frozen earth made this a bit of a puzzle. Slop buckets worked. The natives in return showed the Russians to use ferns and other soft fiber plants to wipe their arses. They'd been rather shocked that the Russians didn't already know these things. The Russians knew nothing of wild herbs and medicines. Though they could cut off limbs and pull out teeth, they could do nothing for fever, or rashes, thus the medicine keepers were valued by the Russians once they saw how powerful they were at curing people. Phillip knew some of these things from watching his mother work her healing on the island people. As a little boy he had loved to help her gather the plants that she used, sometimes the roots, sometimes the leaves or flowers, or sometimes the whole plant. His mother told him which plant to collect at which time of its growing season, and now, sitting quietly in the dawn serving his watch, he amused himself by looking around the forest to discover which plants he could recognize and how well he could recall what they would be used for. Ferns of all kinds packed the forest floor shading mosses, those being so useful for wound healing. Ferns could be eaten as well. Phillip collected a pocketful of the giant fern leaves, rolling them tightly, to share with Anna later. He wondered if she knew ferns were food.

Phillip wasn't tired. He served the last watch shift, sitting in complete darkness after moonset in the early hours and then watching with something like joy in his heart as the light crept upon the forest. It almost seemed to him as though one moment it was dark, and then he blinked, and the light had come. He watched as shadows formed and dispersed making the giant trees into all sorts of wild shapes. Studying them he saw how one could use the shapes as shelter, hide within the light and dark of it, disappear if need be. In fact, some of the massive cedar trees were so big they had small cave spaces at their root base that you could simply walk into and disappear. At one point he lay flat amongst the ferns, letting them pop back up around him, completely enshroud him in leafy green, the orange-red bark of the duff beneath him soft and quietly comfortable. He experimented with invisibility, and so, when the navigator came out to relieve himself, Phillip kept quiet, testing his methods. And while the navigator did look around—Phillip thought he looked a bit frightened, in fact—his eyes passed right over where Phillip sat, still as a hunter sitting over an ice hole, spear in the air.

Phillip laughed at his analogy and then had a pang of homesickness. Ice hunting, it was a task of dangerous importance. It took patience, strength and skill. Wisdom. Phillip went with his grandfather often as a boy. His grandfather would say almost nothing. He would find his spot, where ice parted and the sea made room for the seals to come up, and he would arrange himself facing the sun so as to cast no shadow, downwind of the hole, and nod to the boy to do the same, and sitting thigh to thigh, they would wait. Phillip remembered how hard it was to sit still, how much he struggled at first to keep from talking or wriggling as his knees ached and his feet tingled. But his grandfather knew how to teach him and he would always spend time with Phillip the day before a hunt, telling him a long story about their people and how they were hunters in this world and the other. So much of a story, that all the next day Phillip had plenty to do, sitting still by the ice, going over and over the story in his head, making sure that he remembered every detail. That was how Phillip could sit his watch, and now be awake and ready for the new day. He knew how to occupy his mind to keep it from talking to his body about how tired he was.

Anna found him as they started out from camp. Her face told him she had not slept well. She looked so young to him. She had rebraided her hair into two braids that tumbled out of her kerchief and down her back nearly to her waist and bounced back and forth as she walked. He noticed she walked a little gingerly. Her feet must hurt. He started scanning the trees and downed wood for a limb from which he could make her a walking stick.

They didn't speak, she only nodded to him, and smiled. *A bit of a brave smile*, he thought. But his mood was contagious, and he soon saw her step ease and the tension in her spine relax just a little as she walked. He knew she would feel better at the end of the day if she walked more easily, so he concentrated on finding her a walking stick. Within an hour, he had a decent tree limb, and took the opportunity of a flat stretch where the whole group walked fairly close together to pull out his knife and strip the bark from the thicker end, cutting off the knobs of branches that shot off at the same time. He was done in minutes and caught up to Anna, handing her the staff.

"I'll peel the rest of the bark tonight."

"You're very kind," she said.

"Ah…" Phillip looked reproachful, wrinkling his lips.

"I didn't say thank you," she said smiling, and her eyes lit for a moment with humor.

"No, ma'am. You didn't." Phillip nodded abruptly and waved her forward with a gallant sweep of his arm, a little half version of what he had seen Russian officers do for Russian women. Anna broke out laughing and the last of the crew before them turned to look, curious about the joke.

Like conspirators, they managed the rest of the day, entertaining each other in small ways, pointing out interesting bugs, plants, and the small animals that scurried across their path in such a constant way it seemed there must surely be an enormous population scattered across the forest floor. They kept the rest of the group in sight for the most part, and while Phillip was enjoying himself, he also paid careful attention, honing his listening skills to recognize the soughing of the trees, the hum of waves cycling onshore. He watched the sky for birds, knowing that the great flesh eating ones could point them to a new enough kill that they might have meat to eat, some partially eaten deer, recently downed by one of the terrifying mountain lions who often merely gutted their kill in the initial feeding, leaving meat for later. And he listened for what wasn't there. This was the hardest part. His grandfather had taught him about the place between the noise, that what wasn't there was just as, or more important, than what was. He heard the rush of wind come down on them from the north, blowing the trees audibly before the trees immediately around him moved even an inch. It would be completely still, and then the noise would come, and then the breeze would blow Anna's hair and her skirts would collapse around her knees, pushing her along down the path.

Phillip realized he had separated Anna from the navigator in his consideration of her the moment she left the ship and climbed down into his skiff, and he hadn't given the navigator a second thought subsequently. He looked to Tarakanov for direction, he was still his master, though Tarakanov made it clear that bond was very lightly tethered. Unlike some bondsmen, Tarakanov was more a teacher. He was a young man as well, in his twenties, sure, but handling a servant, an apprentice, for him it was more like Phillip was just his student. Tarakanov didn't give him many orders, and perhaps because of this, when he did do so, Phillip responded immediately. Phillip felt that Tarakanov trusted him, and certainly for his part, he trusted Tarakanov. He noticed that periodically as they traveled down the coast, Tarakanov would turn and seek him out, and Phillip would always be ready for the man's gaze, and he would raise his hand in a kind of salute. They were the head and tail of the pack and had almost from the start created a means of understanding, one that didn't include the navigator. Not that Phillip didn't feel sorry for the man. No captain, true, but he was an officer in the Russian navy, trained and kitted out. He might not be a fighting man, but he had his qualities even if he was a little bit out of his depth just at the moment. Phillip smiled.

While they were in the forest working their way south, Phillip felt secure. He walked and worked out strategies in his head for escape, diversion, and defense should the natives attack them again. He decided he would ask Tarakanov to trust him with the musket next time. They were vulnerable at the back, Anna was vulnerable. And while the Englishman was only just ahead of them, every so often Phillip had the distinct sensation that they were being followed.

It wasn't until afternoon, when they were forced out of the trees and onto the shingle because of a large area of marsh, that Phillip's sensation was proved correct. Once again the Hoh came at them, slinging stones down on them from an outcropping the Russians were attempting to skirt on the seaward side. Their group split in half, the front half ran for it, trying to gain enough ground to outdistance the stones. The back half retreated, scrambling up the embankment and tumbling into the muck of the marsh grass. Tarakanov had shouted orders, but Phillip couldn't hear him in the fray. He reached for Anna, took her arm and they ran together, she holding her skirts as best she could, stumbling now and then, but with each trip, Phillip held her up and kept running, giving no thought at all to the others, only to himself and Anna. He took her walking staff and carried it across his belt at his back like the natives did, and they ran. When they reached the marsh he steered her toward a large group of trees on the far side of the marsh. By the time they got there, sloshing noisily through a foot of water all the way, they were soaked and panting. He pulled Anna behind the tree cover and hitching her up at her waist he placed her abruptly in the crevice of a tree, and then hooked himself up nearby in a spot where he could watch across the marsh to where they had been. The others had scattered, everyone working in a southerly direction, but again, as before, the Hoh didn't follow. It was as if they were intent on harassing them, making it impossible to stop, to relax enough to search for food and to rest, wear them down.

Eventually, they will win, he thought.

"Are you hurt?"

Anna shook her heard. "No. Only wet," she shivered, "and scared."

He nodded. He was looking at her feet. Her boots were dark with water. He was sure they would hurt more now that ever before, and worse as they began to dry and tighten as the leather shrunk. She lifted her feet and frowned.

"We'll go again soon," he said, "they're not coming after us. We'll need to be catching up the others as soon as you're able, aye?"

"Yes." She put her hand to her chest, which was still heaving, struggling for a calm breath. "Yes."

Phillip ran his shirtsleeve over his face, surprised that he was sweating. His own boots were sodden and he could feel them beginning to tighten as they sat there. After a few minutes, when Anna's breathing was steady, he put his attention to the noises around them. Every so often he'd hear one of their own men call out, but not in panic. No sound at all from the natives. He thought the danger was passed for now.

Anna slipped off the tree limb and into Phillip's sure hands. He led her carefully across the remaining marsh, avoiding what looked like the deeper pools, though the dark red of the water made it difficult to be sure, and impossible to spot submerged logs or tangled roots. They walked close together, Phillip's hand on her arm so that she wouldn't fall.

He was completely certain that she had put her life in his hands, and she would respond to his direction. He no longer felt the difference of her station as he had on board nor allowed that distance to structure their ability to communicate. He was amazed at how easily that veil had fallen. He watched her when he could, when she walked in front of him, watched the sway of her hips, her braids, the way she held her hands in such a determined fashion, almost fisted, ready to fight for herself.

"We'd better catch up to the others. Are you able to pick up the pace, uh, ma'am?"

She laughed at him then. A full, throaty, womanly laugh.

"Ma'am?!" She guffawed, gulped, and then sank down to the ground, laughing and laughing while tears streamed down her face and she ended up with the hiccups, still laughing.

Phillip had no idea why. Helplessly, he just stood and watched her fall apart in laughter.

At last she wiped her nose on her sleeve, wiped her eyes with the backs of her hands, and put her hand up for Phillip to give her a lift up.

"Anna, Phillip, my name is Anna Petrovna Bulygina. Anna to you. Or Anna Petrovna if you must be formal. From now on. Yes?"

"Yes. Sure, yes." Phillip studied his boots, but a small smile came across his face.

Tarakanov, Diary Entry
Day Two – The Hoh Trail

Rose to clear skies, and resumed our pace southward toward Gray's Harbor. Midday assaulted by Hoh natives on the beach. Our party was split in half for a time but were reunited and not bothered again by natives. Half the group being very wet, we stopped early and made camp, and with some disregard for our safety, we made a fire so as to dry our boots and avail some comforts for Mr. Bulygin's lady who was obliged to clear the mud from her skirts. We are a day or two from Gray's Harbor at this pace. I fear we may miss our rendezvous with the ship Kad'iak.

And in the margin, he couldn't resist writing, Young Phillip asked for the loan of my shaving edge.

4

Fever Dreams

Anna

Anna sat close to the fire, yet shivering from cold. She had been obliged to remove her skirt, the mud from the marshes caked the hemline and then dried in the afternoon until it was like walking with lead fishing weights attached to the edges. They camped on the beach this time, up against the shoulder of erosion where a ledge of four feet or so thick with roots defined the forest edge, and were thus sheltered from wind by a large rock formation to the north. While the Alutiiq men collected driftwood for the fire and the others settled in, setting watch and erecting the tent, Anna moved toward the water's edge. Phillip, like a puppy, watched her and eventually pulled his lanky frame up, stuck his knife back in his belt and followed her at a discreet distance. She turned once, noticing Phillip, and beyond him, noticing her husband also watching blandly.

At the water's edge, she slipped out of her heavy wool skirt, took the skirt and beat it against the tall rocks at the water's edge, knocking loose the clumps of mud. She held the skirt pleated in both hands and swung hard against the rocks, chips of mud and a cloud of dirt and crumbled leaves showering her. It was the only way, for the wool was wet enough as it was and salt water would not improve its condition. She lay the skirt against the rock and moved back to the water's edge where she kilted up her petticoat, and squatted, relieving herself in the water and washing even though the water chilled her almost immediately. Intent on her bathing she forgot about her husband watching, forgot about Phillip who stood a little way off, giving her no real privacy, only the sense of his respect for her situation. She untied her braids and used her fingers to comb out her hair. Standing at the very edge of the water, she felt her feet grow numb and was grateful for it.

"Anna!"

She heard Bulygin's voice and jumped. She'd been lost in the small actions of bathing and nurturing her tired feet, could almost have been somewhere else entirely. But when she turned toward his voice, she saw he was just calling her back to the fire that was by now burning nicely. She waved, acknowledging his call, and looked to poor Phillip who looked worn and exhausted, standing sentinel for her.

I'm being selfish. And yet, while Phillip's presence comforted her, she felt constrained by this party of men, and took this moment at the water's edge as near as she could expect to get to some sense of privacy.

She rebraided her hair, thinking about hot tea laced with lumps of sugar and sweet cream which made her stomach growl. Even hot water would be welcome. She looked back to the fire and suddenly motivated herself out of her odd mood, realizing her feet were freezing, numb. She tripped and nearly fell full into the water with her first step. The rocky shore was even more difficult to navigate, holding her boots and stockings, and recovering her wool skirt, she cast her modesty aside completely and walked to the fire in her shift.

Now she sat shivering in her jacket, her skirt laid over her knees so that she could turn it, occasionally rotating the warmth toward her legs and feet, and drying its full circumference.

My boots will never dry, not in this damp. She looked up at the darkness, the overcast sky rather bleak. She could see the fog in the firelight, tiny droplets settling on her upturned face, her hair. Soon she would be completely soaked again, but her only refuge was the cold tent, and she couldn't face so many hours there, dark and shivering.

Anna put on her stockings and boots, because to leave them off would mean that in the morning her boots would be stiff and unwelcoming to her scabbed feet. She would stay by the fire until forced inside.

The men began to relax as Anna watched them around the fire, taking turns tending it with driftwood, sometimes a long log that they periodically had to drag into the coals, burning it gradually along its shaft. Four men were posted sentry, two to the north, and two to the south. The risk of a fire seemed necessary, and a consensus of opinion was forming among the men as they talked around the fire, that the natives we not after killing them, but seemed to be herding them in some way. Knowing what they did about slaving, they couldn't understand why the Hoh hadn't just pursued them with violence from the start, after all, three of their kind had been shot and probably killed in the first encounter. They speculated that perhaps the Hoh had not been killed, perhaps the party had been on the move and it was more important to return to their lodges, thus they couldn't afford to risk their small numbers against the Russians armed defense. Guns. That's what it was, they concluded. They don't have any, they're not like the Tlingit up north, who got hold of guns early on and used them to advantage, to brutal advantage, destroying the first fort at New Archangel. The Russians began their stories, heatedly describing what had transpired. The Russian settlers had not anticipated such a virulent and violent resistance. But the Tlingit were a strong and well developed tribe, fierce and wealthy enough that the cheap baubles and trinkets that the Russians thought would subdue them were derided with laughter, and then with gunfire.

"That was a war, there, that was!" one of the promyshlenniks said. Anna thought he sounded almost proud of the Tlingit.

Ah, yes, he has a wife of that clan. She remembered seeing the woman in New Archangel. At the time, she was curious about this habit of taking "country wives" and wondered how the Russian wives at home in Okhotsk and Kamchatka felt about being replaced, not just left behind. *Where was the loyalty in that?* Anna began studying Bulygin's face. *Would he have been better off leaving me behind? Adopting the fur company tradition of a wife/slave, a woman more suited to this harsh environment?* Anna wanted to think of herself, had always thought of herself, as strong and opinionated. But she would admit she had never been tested, nothing she had experienced thus far on board the ship during their passage from Kamchatka to New Archangel, nor at the fort outpost itself, no nothing had tested her. And while she had pledged her faith and fealty to this man, her husband, she didn't really know him. Married only a short while, they had not met the trial of childbirth together, they had not created that illusive intimacy that she felt surely must exist, perhaps only existed after years of exchange side by side. She didn't know.

What she did know, now, just today, was that she was being tested, and rather than fear, what she felt was some small tender spark of survival, of power in herself, an instinct for living, that if she would listen to it, she might pass the test.

She observed Bulygin with a sense of kindness that she felt she owed him, but she knew that she did not see love in her heart when she thought of him, and she suspected he did not see love either, though he surely felt his duty toward her and his privilege. To him, perhaps, that was all there was. *No fairy tale.* He would do his best, of that she was sure.

The Navigator

Bulygin watched Anna at the shoreline, shocked when he realized he was watching her squat and relieve herself right there with the men around the fire watching or not, as if she didn't care. He looked quickly at Phillip and saw Phillip turn his face respectfully away. But watching Anna kirtle up her skirts, baring her white legs, knowing that she was then open and naked, brought Bulygin to life, he wanted her. Frustrated with no avenue through which to achieve that sort of communion with his wife, he sat by the fire and thought about the other times, the times when he had come down to their cabin, for in truth they had been at sea for most of their short married life and when he thought of her he thought of her in scenes aboard one ship or another. He thought about coming down to their cabin, throwing off his greatcoat, and with a pinch of his fingers dousing the ship's light, going toward her, knowing she was never prepared, never knew when he would want to take her, or when he would simply head to his cot, and he was excited by this power. He pictured how she looked as he pulled out the pins that harnessed her beautiful hair. How her breasts looked when he removed her jacket, moving his fingers inside her shift as his hands worked down the row of cloth covered buttons, and how she almost expanded out of the tight fitting jacket into his waiting hands. He watched her in the pale darkness, and sometimes saw her close her eyes. He liked that.

"Bulygin!"

The navigator was startled and flushed, his attention to his comrades had completely vanished for a moment, he had been staring intently at Anna.

"I did not attend. What is it you said?"

It had been Tarakanov who spoke directly to him.

"Do you not agree, tomorrow we should make the last river ford before Gray's Harbor? What is it called on your charts, sir?"

Tarakanov's politeness soothed some of Bulygin's sense of dignity lost. Maintaining these simple pleasantries, these customs between men of honor, this was important to him.

"Aye, we should do. Queets, is the name of the river, it's not said to be as wide as the Hoh there." Bulygin jerked his thumb toward the north. "We might make it. I hope you are right that the savages have better things to do than chase us down the entire coast, I can't see it myself." He shook his head, his youth and inexperience showing brightly as fear, as dread.

"Well, God grant it be easy to ford," Tarakanov said, prompting the men to cross themselves.

They had had other difficult crossings after abandoning their skiff that had taken them across the Hoh. They spent hours along the river bank walking inland until they found the river forked and the resulting streams easy enough to wade across, though slick and tricky. Sometimes fallen trees provided a bridge. With the season of rain just beginning, they had fared better, the waterline was generally lower, but they could see by the immense banks rutted with erosion that the spring flow must be frighteningly high and they were grateful at least for the season of their travail.

Anna joined them at the fire. The men shifted to make room for her and she sat next to Bulygin, modestly covering her legs with her skirt as she set it out to dry. She was chilled through, he could see that.

"My dear, he said, shall I fetch your shawl?"

He jumped up to reach for it, and brought it round her shoulders, keeping his hands on her arms a moment protectively.

"You're terribly cold, warm by the fire a bit before we sleep."

He felt magnanimous. They sat with the others by the fire until the wood was gone and the fire beginning to die down to coals. The watch changed. Bulygin was glad he wouldn't stand watch. He rubbed his hands together warming them and then stood.

"My dear?" he said in his most gallant voice. He offered her his hand and helped her to her feet, taking her skirt from her. It looked simply like a gesture of assistance to the others.

After he had finished and pulled away from Anna's warm body, he lay the wool skirt over her, covered them both with his great coat spooning close to her back, and fell instantly asleep, his breath blowing evenly in her ear.

Phillip

Phillip leaned back against a rock, sheltered from the wind, hitched his coat up around his neck, and pulled his otter fur hat down over his ears as far as he could. Tarakanov had given him the musket to clean, prime, and watch over during the night. Phillip hoped that meant he would keep it the next day. The men had settled down after drifting away from the fire for a last piss, they curled themselves against their bundles and fell asleep. Four of the promyshlenniks replaced the four Alutiiqs who had been standing watch, and they were the only ones awake now, sitting silently at the waning fire.

Phillip was too close to the tent. He heard Bulygin huffing and knew what he was about. From his earliest memory he knew those sounds, his mother and father made them, his older sister and her husband had giggled and huffed and sighed under their blankets in the small open log house on the island. He wanted to move away from the tent, now, but knew he couldn't, and besides, he had claimed the best spot, with Tarakanov right next to him, they provided warmth for each other. Phillip wondered if Tarakanov was awake and could hear Bulygin. He tried not to, but he couldn't help strain to see if he could hear Anna. *Was she just lying there?* He shook himself and tried to think of other things. Of home on the island. Of seal fishing, of his family. But when he heard Bulygin groan his belly clenched. Embarrassed and angry, embarrassed for Anna, angry that the navigator couldn't control his urges. *Anna must be exhausted, surely, we all are. What brute would add to that? Is that what marriage is?*

Phillip fell asleep wondering what it was going to be like, almost never talking out loud. He realized that he had barely spoken more than a dozen words the day before. In his head, there was a complicated conversation raging, but he did not speak unless spoken to, and rarely did anyone address him directly. He resolved to try to speak to Anna.

As dawn arrived, Phillip woke with a start realizing he had been dreaming deeply, one of those important dreams his mother told him about, dreams that could foretell the future. In his dream he had been carried ashore by the great winged sea-mermaid, the guardian of the dead; she had spit him onto the shore, and spoken to him in a language he could not make out. The dream was so real that Phillip thought he felt wet, which he soon discovered he was. A thick fog had enveloped them overnight, the fire was doused, and all of the men were dripping wet. Phillip's woolens were steaming from the warmth of his body, but he knew that the moment he stood up and met the north wind, he would become very cold. He wanted to creep back to his dream, find out what happened next. Instead of forgetting the scene as so often happened with dreams, it somehow became more vivid as he woke. He wished his mother were there. He would share his dream with her and she, as a healer, would know what it meant. He felt a strong connection to her still, and it tugged at him now.

He stepped away from the group quietly, cherishing the silence and the presence of his dream as he straightened his clothes and pissed against a tree, the hot stream emptying him of urgency.

As he had done the day before, he picked ferns, choosing the youngest of the leaves though it was springtime when they were at their sweetest, old and bitter now with winter coming fast, and yesterday when Phillip had offered one to Anna, eating one himself to show her he wasn't having a joke at her expense, she had puckered her mouth at the bitterness, but he noticed she ate all of it. He found a few soft lamb's ears in some moist ground and added them to his pouch, rolled carefully to protect them. He found a small pool of standing water and sat on his haunches concentrating on his image in the stillness, and taking the thin blade that Tarakanov had lent him, (and not without a grin and a poke in the ribs for it was the first time Phillip had thought to shave and Tarakanov had said it seemed like a damned funny time to decide to do that!), Phillip splashed water on his face, and using some of the greasy mixture he used to keep the insects at bay, he shaved a clean precise line down his cheek, left and then right, and then his chin, leaving only a ridge of black hair across his lip as was the custom of his mother's people. It hadn't seemed as though there was much to shave, but now it was done, the contrast was significant. He doused his face in the pool and waited for the lens of it to settle again, peering seriously at his new visage.

Once done, he was faintly embarrassed as he walked back to camp, returning the blade to Tarakanov who was packing his bundle. Tarakanov smiled at Phillip and patted his check.

"Well done, boy! Not a scratch!" Tarakanov winked. Phillip blushed. Tarakanov was not the winking sort, and Phillip felt sure he would be in for much joking that day.

Anna came from the tent, saw Phillip, and looked at him carefully for a minute or two. She didn't say a word, just nodded her head, and went back to the work of preparing to leave.

Bulygin emerged from the tent behind Anna, coughing violently. He didn't look well this morning at all. His face was a waxy white, shiny with fever, it seemed to Phillip. Phillip had been trying to recall all the medicines his mother had used when he was a boy and what they were for, just as a way to amuse himself, challenge himself as they walked, but now he began to look at the plants and trees around him with serious calculation. He vowed to start collecting the plants he knew would heal sicknesses and wounds, and figured he might as well start with the navigator's cough. He watched the navigator wander into the meadow grass, still coughing and spitting gobs of mucous. He saw that Anna watched as well, but she looked resigned and helpless rather than thoughtful.

The Alutiiqs had taken mussels and a few crabs the night before, enough for their supper as well as cold bits for this morning. Phillip had offered to make a tea for the navigator; cedar was a cure for cough, but Tarakanov had insisted they get on. He was growing more concerned that they would miss the *Kad'iak* which should have made Gray's Harbor by now. They filed out, Tarakanov in his usual lead post, Bulygin somewhat farther behind, laboring, stopping frequently as a coughing fit overtook him.

They had been on the path only a short while when Tarakanov spotted a scat pile and stopped to inspect it. Bear. The scat was fresh, dark and full of green vegetable matter. Although bear were common, and some bear were the huge and fearful sort who would stalk and kill men, this was the first sign they had seen of bear in their two days of travel. Phillip caught up with Tarakanov and listened as he gave instructions to keep together, watch for bear, but otherwise, there was nothing to be done. The disturbing thing was that along with the bear scat were tracks. Native tracks. It looked as though they were being followed by one group of natives and following another. Perhaps the southward group followed the bear, known to be a prized kill. Whether the band south of them knew they were there or not was anyone's guess. What was sure was that they could come upon them without warning and must watch with more care.

As they walked, Phillip showed Anna some of the plants he recognized. They quickly collected small quantities of several things and Phillip explained them to her.

"This cedar will make a tea for the navigator's cough," he said. He collected several fans of newer growth. "Along with our ferns, this one here," he said, showing Anna the frothy soft fern that looked like hair, "with the cedar together will be a fine tea for his cough."

They also found food—almost by accident. Phillip was searching out the last of the sweet little red berries that peak during the fall when his boot kicked the forest floor revealing a bright yellow mushroom.

Anna clapped her hands in joy, recognizing a familiar food at last. Fungi and wild onions were a common meal in her homeland, a singular treat. Together they found five large mushrooms, some wild onions and ginger. Anna tied up one end of her petticoat and made a makeshift apron of it to carry their bounty as they hurried to catch up to the others. Anna chattered excitedly about making soup, if only they could find a little meat. Phillip added squirrel and rabbit to the list of things to watch out for.

"Look alive there, Phillip!" Tarakanov's shout startled them both, and Phillip felt instantly chastened. He had forgotten his duty: they were making much too much noise talking.

"Shhhh," Anna said, putting her finger to her lips like a child, but behind the finger was a grin that showed her white teeth brilliantly. She turned and stepped briskly onto the path, her two braids swinging against her wool skirt. Today she had tied her green shawl loosely around her head against the morning dew, wrapping it under her braids in a big knot whose ends trailed down her back. As the morning wore on, she took her shawl and folded it into a carrying bundle for more plants. With his help, she seemed determined to find enough food for all of them to eat well. Her kerchief tied around her neck and her shawl wrapped as a bundle over her shoulder, she looked like a child from a fairy tale, bareheaded and fresh faced.

"Catch up to Mr. Bulygin," Phillip said, "I'll look for meat."

He pulled his knife from his belt. He didn't have the rifle today, he'd decided it would only get in his way if he were going to be foraging. Somehow, he didn't think they were in danger from the rear in any case, it was just an instinct, but that's what he thought and it guided his actions, allowing him to push Anna toward the main group and their general protection while he disappeared into the forest.

Without the opportunity to set snares, he wasn't sure how he would catch a single thing, but he was going to try.

He spent an hour scaring up the small furry beasts that hide along the path, but he was helpless to catch them. He finally had to concede he would be better served to cast in a line when they stopped for the night and hope for a few fish for Anna's soup; he was fooling himself if he thought he could catch these little beasties without snares. And unless they stopped for more than a night, there was no time for trapping.

He jogged up to the main group. Anna was walking steadily behind Bulygin and didn't look around. Phillip had made a quick reconnaissance before rejoining the group, confirming his feeling of safely. He squinted, looking for Tarakanov at the lead. He wondered if he should run up and let Tarakanov know.

Phillip shrugged, no news was not worth jostling the others along the narrow path. It would just jar their pace. The promyshlenniks wouldn't be happy either. He'd noticed how they established a cadence, they were all of a size, short-legged and powerful men who carried their burdens easily and stepped along the path with sure footed economical strength. Phillip settled back in to his own easy step and resumed his search for food. He noticed that he saw about him the same six or seven plants growing in the cover of the cedar forest, no great variety. And then when they came out to the rocky edge where the embankment led down to the beach, the plants changed entirely. And so as well, the wet meadow gave another set of six or so primary plants. Phillip wondered if this was why his mother always said only four or five plants were needed at a time.

He did his best to collect anything edible, not worrying so much about medicine except for things that would aid in easing the navigator's cough. He found most of these in the cedar landscape, adding to that some marsh grass he knew aided in expelling cough. The plants nearest the ocean seemed less edible, at least as far as he was aware. Many of the plants he saw were new, some seemed familiar yet not exactly what he recalled from the far north or his island. He often took a leaf from a plant and nibbled a bite, checking the taste and what his mouth and tongue said about it. Some plants were minty and sweet, but most were rather bitter and one or two made his mouth fill with saliva so that he had to stop and spit copiously, and rinse his mouth from the nearest pond.

The fog overnight cleared by late morning, and the welcome sun cheered everyone. The dogged march eased, not so much that they lost time, but there was at least a little conversation along the path, now and then a burst of laughter as one of the men told a joke in Russian and they passed it back down along the line so that the laughter rippled back toward Phillip.

Anna stepped out of line with a gesture to her husband. Phillip stopped. She smiled demurely at him and he nodded, then made a pretense of adjusting his pack and realigning his knife while she stepped off the trail and squatted down. Phillip thought she was humming.

When she finished, she turned and started back down the trail, Phillip caught up to her quickly, but they didn't speak. Realigned, they felt secure and easy with each other. *Perhaps like a sister*, Phillip thought, and he missed his own family severely then.

The Navigator

He knew the signs too well. Overnight his chest had tightened and his fever risen until waking brought him upright with a terrifying, choking cough that strangled his vocal chords. It felt as though his chest was held in some great unrelenting grasp. By midmorning he felt sick to his stomach from coughing, and he alternated between chilling cold and sweating.

Holy mother of God, not now, please, not now.

He'd started having these episodes just before he married Anna. All the doctor in Okhotsk had said was that the sea air would cure him. It was what all young men needed in any case. So he'd purchased his commission, done his training with a kindly Captain between Okhotsk and Hawaii, had shown he had a knack for the charts, and charting unknown waters quickly became his passion. It was during one sojourn in port at a military ball, that he had met Anna Petrovna. Thinking of her now made his chest relax just a little. She was lovely: small, but firm and strong, her long brown hair lustrous with brushing and smelling of roses. She had received his attentions carefully and with grace. Now he could recall that he hadn't noticed anyone else vying for her time and favors, but it didn't matter. He wanted a wife, wanted one before he left for New Archangel and his post with the Russian

Fur Company. He wanted a wife who would stand at his side, share his adventure as well as his work. He didn't want one of those simpering women from the East who wanted to stay home with their family while their husband did his best to provide her with vast sums, or furs and jewels, or silks, or whatever. No, he wanted someone, well, someone just like Anna seemed to be.

"Nikolai," his mother scolded, "Nikolai, find yourself a Russian wife." His mother was terrified of the new world, terrified her son would never return, and she made a habit of creating a dramatic stage play of every arrival and departure.

Anna's family accepted his suit with pleasure. They had no pretensions about their own place, nor Anna's, and Bulygin received their good wishes assuming Anna was equally enthusiastic. Anna's father worked the docks, managing shipping for the fur company. Anna's mother came from Kamchatka and had the look of the people from there, dark eyes and hair. Anna favored her mother's people.

At first, he was certain she was happy and suitable. She was shy, yes, but she sat with him often enough, their heads together, while he explained the reading of charts, and drew pictures of the various ships he had sailed. He told her about furs and their tremendous value, and about the savages that dwell in those distant lands, and he was sure she was as excited by it as he was.

They married in a quiet way, an Orthodox father presiding over the small but nevertheless military style gathering, Anna beautiful in a lace head scarf and silk dress. At the end of the day, Bulygin took her to their rooms in a boarding house by the wharf. She had never visited him there before,

Bulygin had always gone to her at her parent's small house. He put his sword, his belt, and the fur capped hat of his very best uniform on the upright chair inside the door.

"Anna."

She turned toward him, carefully lifted the lace veil, folded it, and put it on top of his sword. They stood close together, Bulygin could feel her breath as he leaned toward her. He had kissed her hand many times, kissed her lips now and then in the three months of courtship. This was different, he knew. He wondered if Anna knew.

The navigator was having difficulty keeping pace with the rest, his breathing rough and sharp, and sometimes he bent double in coughing fits. By midday, he seemed to bridge his discomfort into a sort of fevered daze where his thoughts gave him the balm of memory. He was startled to run into the man in front of him as the line stopped.

"Ho, there, sir." The Englishman caught his elbow and prevented him from falling to the ground.

"Are ye well, man?"

The man was smacking Bulygin on the back, it wasn't helpful. Bulygin waved his hand, trying to move away from the man's good intentions.

Tarakanov had jumped to the top of some rocks and was checking up and down the line in both directions, scanning for natives, but also scanning for physical features of the landscape that might tell them more accurately where they were. How many miles had they done today? Yesterday's sighting of Destruction Island had encouraged the navigator and he'd assured Tarakanov he knew where they were. But their progress was slow, always stopping, wary of ambush, often detouring deeper into the forest off the path in order to avoid a particularly open area or one with obvious vulnerability. These stops and shifts in direction meant their southward journey was more of a zigzag than an eagle's path. And they were hungry. Late season salal berries and a few mussels were not enough to feed a promyshlennik carrying a burden weighing three stone or more.

Bulygin cleared his throat and spat.

"What is it? What do ye see? Tarakanov, are ye seein' anything yet like a river?"

Tarakanov turned and looked down at him from his perch.

"Just so. Aye, just so. Maybe two three mile more. The ocean's brown, that must be our river."

Tarakanov jumped down.

"Push on. We'll not stop 'til we reach the river."

The Englishman slapped the navigator on the back again.

"Hear that, Bulygin? Be ye well, now, we'll get fish for supper sure!" He laughed heartily and started off behind the others.

The navigator didn't like the Englishman's familiarity. He felt they were not equals and was aware that somehow the Englishman didn't realize that fact. The Englishman was an odd one, the navigator chalked it up to his having simply been adventuring in this godforsaken wilderness for too long. He'd forgotten his place. The man just didn't realize they weren't comrades. Bulygin had never given him reason to think otherwise, even in such a small ship's company as theirs, the social hierarchy was imperative. It was bad enough that Tarakanov had undermined him from the start. By now, in his own mind the reality that the company had given Tarakanov general control, and therefore by more than just implication, Bulygin worked for Tarakanov, not the other way around had sunk home. And yet, the *Sv. Nikolai* had been his ship to command, his alone. Tarakanov wasn't a ship's captain, wasn't even a good sailor though he was stoic enough. The navigator's mind ran on with this line of thinking, alternating between anger at Tarakanov, at the Englishman who walked in front of him, and at himself for being less than he expected to be. Where had this Englishman come from? Bulygin decided to try and figure out the man by observing him more closely. He couldn't ask him direct questions, surely that would invite further breaches of social process. No, he'd study the man, that would distract him from other things, keep him on the path, calmer, keep his thoughts off of Anna, off of Tarakanov, who seemed to Bulygin at this point to be almost sprightly as he led the group at a brisk pace down the deer track.

Bulygin started with the man's boots. *Land boots, not a sea going man.* Like the Russian promyshlenniks, his boots were an amalgam of a European leather knee boot made with New World hides. The fur traders, by custom, used hide scraps, animal skins not saleable, sewn together, lined with fur, fringed and always knee high so that the boots protected the men from water, from snakes—the frightening great rattlers that lived in the tall timber upland—and kept the leg warm and stable in rocky terrain. If the man had a country wife… *ah, here was a clue*, beading and quillwork, fringes with small decorations. Bulygin picked up his pace enough to take a look. *Yes!* The Englishman's boots were moose hide, he thought. *From the north then.* And across the toes there were neat geometric rows of beads in blue and white. *No sailor.* Bulygin's own boots were black military leather, not looking the spit and polish regulation of naval life just at the moment, and in fact, sadly, he thought his boots would soon fall apart, a flap had opened on the side of one sole the last time they had been doused with water; the small nails around the edges holding one part to the last had rusted through from the salt air. As he walked, the water spurted out with a regular cadence like the pumps on a three decker ship. Bulygin would have to find someone to make him boots like the veteran trappers had. If only he had a country wife of his own. This musing left off on a tangent that he took to its fullest, satisfying climax before returning to his profile of the Englishman—how she would cook venison stew for him and sew buckskin clothes and come to his bed each night with dark and eager delight. He noticed the Englishman's pantaloons were wool, dark blue and thinning, patched in places, sometimes with a nicely turned needle and other times crudely with oddments of garish cloth. The pants were belted with a woven sash knotted at the side. Nothing unusual, the Russians did the same. He moved on to the coat. Now here was something. Hide, not wool, fringed and modestly decorated like the boots. Simple in construction but made with care, it fitted the man perfectly. The navigator was beginning to want to ask the man questions. Was he a trapper from the Canadas? Had he worked in the great inland lakes, and if so, how came he to the far north and the Russian company? Had he met the Indians from the Great Slave Lake? Or farther east than that even, had he been on Hudson's Bay? These places were still a part of Bulygin's imagination of his potential world, yet nowhere he had been himself. He had a picture in his mind of vast clear water lakes full of fish and surrounded by timber, by fierce bears, roaming packs of wolves, and elk in the hundreds. Of freedom, the kind of freedom one can only gain on land, virgin land. Nothing of the constraining values of the sea life, men packed in together in a false and peculiarly distinct society. If it hadn't been for his cough, he would have avoided the sea, the navy. He would have loved the adventure of moving from place to place, having a country wife here and there...

*A nice fat arse, willing and...*He pictured her, reframing the image, refining the details, his native wife sitting in a lodge, sewing boots for him. He continued his previous musings, but then he recollected himself, this was unfair to Anna. Everyone understood that women weren't expected to like being bedded. He was who he was, he owed it to himself and to Anna to hold himself to a higher standard than those around him portrayed, he had a right to hold Anna to that standard as well. It was a part of their marriage contract. Perhaps getting her with child would bind her to him, open avenues of access that he perceived must surely exist in married life. There was so little between them, but he felt strongly about her. *Get her with child!* How could he even think such thoughts here in this god forsaken wilderness. Shame washed over him.

They walked on, the pace hypnotic in the afternoon sun. Long shadows from the fall light made him uneasy on his feet, stumbling where he thought there was a dip in the land or a tree root when there was nothing but shadow; and then the western sun bursting through blinding him. He was beginning to feel his fever rising. This business of walking single file, enforced quiet so as to hear approaching dangers broken only occasionally by a comment, usually either received with a brusque barking reply or laughter among those closest to the speaker, Bulygin was feeling isolated, and with fevered isolation came insecurity. He began to chuff under his breath, *Where was Anna, now...why had they fallen back again.*

And yet, there Anna was, no more than a meter behind him. *What was I thinking?* He wiped his brow with his coat sleeve. Anna came up alongside, Phillip close behind her.

"You are fevered, Nikolai." She put her hand to his brow and he leaned into it, closing his eyes.

Phillip put his hand to his pouch and patted it. "I have medicines for tea. As soon as we can build a fire, I'll brew you a remedy. It will do you some good, sir, I'm certain of it."

"Aye, boy, thanks for your concern." The navigator nodded and winced, his head hurt. The welcome sun was drying their damp clothes but it bothered him, pierced into his skull and made him squint.

"Aye," he said again.

Anna gave him her walking stick, and took his pouch of charts, though he objected, she insisted, pushing him back toward the others.

"We'd best go, husband. Sooner we go, sooner we can make you feel better again. You know how these spells are with you, you need rest. We have picked cedar, and plants for tea Phillip knows of from his mother. She's a healing woman. It will comfort you, I'm sure of it."

Bulygin thought this was the longest conversation he had had with Anna, or heard from Anna, since they boarded the *Sv. Nikolai*, and it warmed his heart. He saw Phillip watching the interchange, his face intently curious, an extraordinary change from the youthful indifference the boy usually portrayed. *Why did he look so...so grown?*

With a fire built and the navigator installed with what comfort could be produced—his great coat and a pack to lean against—he sat staring into the flames, feeling the fire redden his cheeks and dry his aching eyes.

Phillip was busying himself creating the tea of healing herbs. Bulygin watched as he shredded cedar needles, discarding the brown or old bits and shaving only newer shoots into a tin cup. Then he used his knife to strip open the thick rubbery stems of the marshmallow—for that was what Phillip told him it was—and scraped the insides into the cup as well. Other plants he selected for the root, now chopped fine, or the leaves which he pressed with his knife handle until a green mush was produced. All of this he covered with water and set in the fork of a burning piece of driftwood. Phillip watched the water carefully, timing how long the boil, and then how long for it to steep by some inner sense. At last he nodded, satisfied, and brought the cup to Bulygin and without a word, watched as the navigator drank it off like the medicine it was, for it tasted bitter.

"Now you'll sleep," Phillip said. And within minutes the navigator felt himself slipping gratefully away, the warm fug of the fire filling him.

Tarakanov, Diary Entry
Day Six – North of the Queets River

We awoke to dense fog, clearing as the sun rose. Our navigator, Nikolai Bulygin, is taken sick with fever and cough thus obliging us to reduce our pace. We were alternately followed and set upon by Hoh natives, though they seem not intent on killing us, they are perhaps only working their way southward as well, and we are only in their way, for surely we are not an appealing band for slavery, scurvied and hungry as we are. I fear we have missed the good ship Kad'iak. Our purpose now should be to survive as best we may.

5

Swift Water

Phillip

As was his habit, Phillip rose with the dawn, not waiting for the sun to find him in his sheltered place, this time merely a downed tree against which he had spent a restless night in any event. He collected his things, and cleaned the flintlock musket, tearing off a scrap of his shirt to jam down into the barrel over and over until it came out clean, or clean enough. He checked the powder, it seemed dry, though one could never tell, not until the striker hit the pan and either you were dead out of luck or the spark exploded with a puff of smoke and a moment of surreal delay as the ball gained momentum spiraling down the barrel, this nice clean barrel, and out into the air, smoking with intent. He loved shooting. He loved that moment, just after the trigger was pulled, the snap and click, the pause, while you stared at your prey, man or game, and hoped they wouldn't move, hoped the powder was dry, the ball true. Had he put enough powder in, had he made the ball carefully enough, holding the heating mold over the fire as hot as he ever could get it, watching the lead scraps melt into the shape. Then later, smoothing them round with a stone, the rounder the ball, the truer the shot.

He used the remainder of his shirt scrap to make the wadding, the small square patches that snugged down in the barrel ahead of the ball. Shot, patches, and powder, one load already in the musket, he set his things upon a rock and leaned back to wait. No one but the watch was awake, and from the look of him, the watchman to the south of camp wasn't awake either. Phillip had been watching the man for a while now, and watching for him. No need to wake the bastard up. Phillip scratched his head and reset his cap.

The mountain lion walked slowly, her gravid belly swaying side to side. Phillip hadn't heard her, not a sound; she seemed completely unconcerned with his presence, just like the deer from the navigator's story that first morning. Only this was a predator, and Phillip knew how strongly he and the others smelled, she must know of their presence. Phillip shivered, she had probably been watching them for days. Perhaps her pregnancy, nearing to term as she must surely be by the look of her, kept her from daring a catch. He crouched down on his haunches and watched the lion. He had never seen one before. He had seen bear taller than three men, but never seen this.

She padded down to the shoreline, stepped delicately into the water. Phillip thought he saw hesitation, as though she didn't like the cold water. And then she lay down in it and rolled, rolled and rolled in the salt water and black sand, scratching her back, easing her belly, rubbing her head back and forth. At last she stood on all fours again and shook hard, from head to her long tail. She turned and it seemed to Phillip that she looked right at him, right into his eyes, her cool glittering look daring him. And then she was gone.

Phillip found he had gripped the musket and was holding it clenched tight in his hand, he could have swung it up to his shoulder at any time and taken a shot at the vulnerable lion, anyone here would have done had they had the chance. Why hadn't he? Phillip shrugged. *Surely no good luck.* And he admired her confidence. *No known enemies in this world or the next.* He heard his mother's voice in the thought.

He didn't know why, but he didn't mention the lion when the others woke, not even when one of them came across the tracks in the sand. He just shrugged and said he'd seen nothing. The others were fearful, suddenly aware of what had been the case all along, they were watched by many creatures and perhaps not the least of the dangers came from far beyond the known perils of the natives who chased them with stones and clubs. They were becoming both more desperate and more certain all at the same time. Desperately hungry, terrified of missing what might be their only chance at rescue, but also aware over time that the Hoh natives who followed them were without guns. In fact, this was surely why they continued to follow. Even two muskets were a distinct advantage against a handful of men with slings and rocks.

Phillip checked on the navigator and found him improved. He gave him the rest of the tea, held overnight in his only tin cup, rinsed the cup and hung it from his pouch by a leather thong.

"I thank 'y," said Bulygin, his voice raspy in the chill of the morning.

Tarakanov had decided to seek higher ground for two reasons, first to find game, they needed food, and second to find a spot where they could have the advantage of a southward panorama from which they might see the coastline—down to the river Queets of course—but also beyond that to Gray's Harbor, and out to sea, where they might see and perhaps signal to the *Kad'iak* as she passed. If they built a fire and burned it wet they could produce smoke, and if they were lucky enough, the captain of the *Kad'iak* wouldn't just assume it was fire from native lodges. Or, if he did take the smoke for native fires, that he might take the convenience of the shoreline location to stop for some trading, check the area for otter colonies, see if the natives were hospitable, open to forming a hunting agreement.

It had been a mistake. Walking inland took them off the coastal path and into rough brush, berry bushes with sharp thorns, boggy marsh ground that sometimes gave way entirely swallowing a man up to his knees in muck. Deer paths roamed aimlessly crossing and crisscrossing each other with a maddening randomness and yet always tempting the party to try one and yet another. Often they spent an hour thinking they were gaining elevation in some permanent fashion only to find the hillock deep in forest and of no use whatever. By the end of the day, Tarakanov turned them around again and they headed back to the coast.

For six days they zigzagged in a generally southward direction, sometimes spending hours in a defensive clutch for fear of attack, sometimes wandering inland in search of fresh water. As they approached the Queets River the path along the shoreline became more clearly defined, clear evidence of a fair degree of traffic, animal and human.

The Englishman had gone ahead as scout. Presently he returned, out of breath but looking happy.

"The river's just ahead," he said, "the trees go right up to the edge, no cliff-side, and there's smoke, maybe from the other shore."

Tarakanov and the others followed the Englishman as he retraced his steps and led them to the edge of forest cover where they huddled down in silence, watching the river.

They saw with a mixture of absolute relief and absolute fear that two things were true. The river was full of migrating salmon fairly leaping out to be eaten, and on the opposite shore sat five native fishing lodges, smoke billowing from drying fires where strips of salmon were layered onto wooden branches, and a dozen or so natives, men and women, stood clearly occupied with the busy work of harvesting fish.

Had they come all this way to be turned around? Who were these new natives? Were they Hoh? Their little group suddenly huddled together, hunkered down, did they dare simply show themselves?

The desperation of hunger that clenched their bellies at the smell of smoking fish wafting across the river and up the bank overwhelmed their fear in short order.

"I'll give them a go," said Phillip.

Tarakanov looked at him sharply for a moment, but Phillip could see in his eyes that Tarakanov was just as happy to let him test the temperament of these new natives, his features being more nearly native and thus perhaps not immediately responsible for a hostile reception. He sighed.

"Aye, all right, lad. You leave the musket here." Tarakanov reached for the weapon and Phillip unstrapped the shot pouch from his belt.

He moved his long knife into position, it had been out of the way on his hip, its sheath slanting across his back in the way that allowed him to run with ease, but Phillip wanted it prominently in sight now. Tarakanov was looking through his glass at the cluster of temporary lodges on shore.

"You know," he said, "I don't think they're Hoh. Can't just say why, I just have a feeling. Maybe we'll fare better with them, eh?" He passed the glass to Phillip who peered closely at the scene across the way, counting buildings, and men.

Phillip closed the glass and handed it back. Without a word he left the cover of forest and sprinted down the gentle embankment, gaining the river's edge in a few strides. It was deep, swift, and tidal. Phillip's heart fell. Without boats they would not get across, at least not here. He looked across to the natives' lodges and saw men and women on the shoreline. They had seen him. Phillip raised his arm and waved a salute he hoped seemed friendly, but even more importantly, that indicated he wanted them to come for him. He could tell they were talking about his sudden appearance, there was much chatter among the natives and pointing across the river. Finally, two natives hauled a small canoe out from the rough shelter they had built. They launched it easily into the river flow and paddled expertly across using the river's outward current flow to advantage so that they made a diagonal course and landed nearly exactly at Phillip's feet with a minimum of effort.

He stepped back unconsciously as they jumped clear of the canoe and hauled it dry with precise practiced motions. Before him stood a young woman and a young man. Both were dressed in short cloaks of skins and cedar strips, attached at the shoulder with a straight bone pin. Both of them were tattooed with black and red dots on their faces. The woman smiled at Phillip shyly. The young man looked wary.

Phillip had pulled his knife from its sheath and held it in a casual, but meaningful way. First he spoke in his own native Alutiiq. For some reason, he thought the native sounds would assure them that he wasn't a threat, though he was certain they wouldn't understand a single word. He tried Russian. He tried one of the sentences the Englishman had taught him. The Englishman claimed to have more native tongues at hand than anyone along the Pacific Ocean but Phillip judged he probably knew very little except how to barter for a whore. He hoped what he was saying now was innocuous.

"Do you have food?" He asked the obvious.

Recognition. They smiled, and rubbed their bellies.

He smiled and nodded and rubbed his own stomach and it growled for him in reply. They all laughed. The girl covered her mouth with her hand when she laughed, but not before Phillip saw that her two incisors were sharpened into points. He looked away. In some cultures it was rude to stare. His stomach growled again.

The woman pulled something from a small pouch at her waist and handed it to Phillip. It was dried fish. He ate, smiling all the while.

Phillip decided to risk exposing the rest of the group. He turned and whistled, his own particular whistle that the group knew was Phillip's imitation of an osprey. He pointed up the embankment as the members of his party showed themselves.

The two natives jumped back in their canoe and shoved off. Phillip followed them, trying to talk them into waiting. The paddlers maneuvered, eddying in the shallows, talking rapidly to each other. They must have concluded it was too risky for they spun about and shot across the river toward their camp.

While Phillip watched across the water, Tarakanov and the others lined up along the shore exclaiming over the sheer abundance of salmon shimmering through the current. They all watched expectantly across the way to the animated conversation that was happening between the fishermen. Phillip saw now that the crude lodges he had seen were cut from massive cedar trees cut into logs stacked and roofed with green boughs to provide just enough shelter for the fishing party to escape the rain and wind when need be. Five huge ocean canoes, for surely that was what they must be, their keel depth being too much for them to get very far upriver even at high tide, sat in a row high above tide line on the ocean side of the river entry. Two fires burned between the canoes and the water, one producing so much smoke that Phillip knew it must be for curing the fish, while the other provided warmth and daily cooking needs. Phillip kept track of the young woman. She and the boy were being interrogated by the others, there was a flurry of waving arms and discussion. It seemed that the young woman held some sway with the group. Phillip alternated between the demands of his desperate belly and some resident anxiety about these people. While the promyshlenniks were tough, hard men, and they did have the advantage of two muskets, for Phillip had scanned the group on the far shore carefully and not seen a sign of weapons other than knives and fishing spears, the natives clearly had the advantage of food, canoes, and knowledge.

The excitement on the other shore seemed to die down and the natives returned to their work gutting and slicing up fish. The guts they threw back into the river caused a commotion of competitive begging between seagulls and the great whiskered seals, the sea lions, who seemed to also be fishing the salmon run.

There must surely be bear as well. Phillip scanned up and down the forest cover behind him and was not comforted.

Feeling puzzled and let down, the group organized themselves to camp on shore, Tarakanov said it would give the impression of friendliness to camp in the open, though they'd mount their usual watch. Dark was coming on. They gathered driftwood and Phillip used some of the moss he had collected, now dried, to kindle the fire. With his back to the wind, crouched over the little pile of moss and dried leaves and twigs he struck his flint once, twice, and with a third click a spark hit the moss and a small glow appeared. Sheltering the spark with his hands he blew gently, knowing that to rush the process would put the spark out. Four, five gentle breaths and the spark became a tiny flame, and then the twigs caught, the leaves smoked and burst into little flares of flame as well, and the deed was done for another night. Phillip carefully put his striker and flint back in his pouch and sat back to enjoy the warmth, feeding pieces of driftwood into the fire until a good blaze burned, the darkness coming down around them as the firelight took hold.

"We've got comp'ny, sir!" The watchman's voice was low and gruff, laying down the warning in a pause in the low conversation around the fire, and as they all held for a moment they could hear the rhythmic cadence of paddles approaching. Anna and the Alutiiq women huddled near the fire started and made as if to rise, but Tarakanov held them in place with a quick flap of his hand. Anna pulled her shawl over her head and watched the flames.

The young woman and three companions, all men, approached the fire accompanied by the watch who looked at Tarakanov hoping for approval at the friendly welcome.

"Aye, right," Tarakanov said. And then under his breath, "Phillip, mind the firearms, boy," though he didn't look in Phillip's direction.

Phillip realized Tarakanov had stepped away from the other musket, that was why he'd said "arms" he thought. He moved slowly and easily, like creeping up on a basking seal, just sideways enough to reach for the musket and tuck it along with the one in his own charge. He stepped behind the women, disappearing from sight in the darkness, both muskets at his side.

The tension in the camp eased when the women and her friends squatted at the fire and smiled at them, pulling out handfuls of dried fish and offering it up to each of them. As they spoke, the Englishman and Tarakanov both responded together.

"Ah, Makah!" Each of them could speak some little bit of this language, mostly trading talk, and each began talking to the nearest man sitting with them while the woman just smiled and handed out fish strips.

With theatrical exclamations of disapproval the Makah men made it clear that the Hoh who had been pursuing the Russians were very bad, and would never stop chasing them. There was much shaking of heads and expletives that neither the Englishman nor Tarakanov could translate, but seemed to have something to do with the Hoh's eating habits. The Makah seemed genuinely at ease. Perhaps that also meant they were genuine in their offer of friendship and help.

It didn't really matter. They had no choice but to accept the offer of friendship from the Makah as far as it might go. The Makah said they would bring the canoes right away while the tide was high. The navigator and Tarakanov both objected to immediately attempting to cross with the current swift and full dark coming down. Initially the Makah insisted, and made it seem to do with the tide. Perhaps that was true. The canoes were two of the large ocean going boats, and while the water was swift and full at high tide, it might easily be silted with sand in places at other times in the flow. The Makah were pressuring them. Phillip had no say, he just listened intently and tried to grasp what he could of the language.

Tarakanov resisted the pressure with an adamant stance of his own and refused to budge. The young Makah woman at last stood up and with a bit of an exasperated grunt seemed to tell them that in the morning they would send the big canoes to fetch the whole party. The Hoh would not follow across the water, she shrugged as if to say for the night, they were on their own.

They spent an uneasy night doubly fearful now that the Hoh would be upon them at any moment, leaping out of the darkness of the forest. With a double watch set, including Tarakanov and Phillip, no one really slept, each sat near the fire conjuring in their own imagination the changes that would come with the morning.

The Navigator

Bulygin spent the night in silence sitting on the wet ground next to his wife. Tarakanov had taken control of the party and recovered his musket, and the Englishman had pretty much taken over possession of the second musket, though now and then he would hand one off to Phillip if they stood different night watches. Since running point as they approached the river, the musket had remained in the Englishman's charge. Phillip was sitting behind Bulygin with his back to the fire, facing the water, and periodically got up and walked the shoreline a good distance. This constant rustling began to undo Bulygin's composure, and he found himself restless yet always drawn back to Anna, suddenly keenly aware of his responsibility to her, of her vulnerability. *Now surely, but to-morrow?* The thought of the increased threat to his wife's virtue filled him with dread. He couldn't command, he couldn't protect himself, how could he protect his wife?

How will we ever survive this? Surely Anna must be thinking the same thing. Somehow this shamed him. How could he have been so naïve as to bring a woman into this madness, this vulnerability. The only place he wanted his woman vulnerable was in bed, and they hadn't seen one of those in some months. Not that the quick, not so private, takings hadn't had their moments of thrill. That too shamed him, but only a little. Making forays through the volumes of clothing to reach her body, never seeing her in the light, and rarely touching except to enter her—might have been with anyone. She never spoke. Bulygin wondered if it was usual for a woman to speak during the act of sex. He wouldn't know himself. Whores did, sure, but even he knew it was only to make it end faster. Finish them off and get on with the next customer! It was humiliating, so easily done. Did Anna wish she could talk him through it faster as well?

He shifted uncomfortably, the log that they leaned against poked his back. The damp sand had seeped moisture into his wool trousers and his legs were chilled. Anna was asleep, or at least she looked to be asleep. Bulygin couldn't imagine how she could sleep in these circumstances, on this night. He wanted her to wake up. He wanted to talk to her in some close, quiet way. God help him, he wanted her, even here. He needed her to see him in a way he was afraid she did not—to distinguish the man who was her husband from what seemed to him as he looked around at his fellow travelers to be a random collection of lost souls. *We are lost.* He shifted again, hoping his accidental rustlings would make Anna wake up, or open her eyes. He knew that sometimes she feigned sleep. Not that that kept him from his desires, and surely, she didn't really mind that. He had the sudden knowledge, the awful brilliant awareness of truth, that what she minded was talking.

Anna

Anna watched silently as the big cedar canoe launched from the opposite shore just after dawn, caught the tidal current and curved across the river, two Makah men deftly steering the craft ashore. She held back, behind the group of Russian men, standing behind the fire with the Alutiiqs. Tarakanov was talking to the natives, shaking his head and gesturing.

"What is it?" Anna said, as Phillip came up from standing watch to the north.

"Tarakanov wants another canoe, he don't trust 'em fully. Why would he?"

"Ah," she said.

Tarakanov seemed to succeed in his request, for one of the powerful Makah men waved his arm and whistled, signaling the shore. Immediately a small canoe launched. Anna was surprised to see when it drew near that it was paddled by two women, one from the encounter the night before, and another, slightly older woman.

Even so, both canoes could not take the entire party. Nine of the Russian promyshlenniks volunteered to go first, and with that advance muscle, Tarakanov thought it best to send only two women, with Phillip and an Alutiiq hunter to look after them, in the smaller canoe.

Anna hesitated, but Phillip caught her eye and nodded, promising in his brief look that she would at least not face this alone. They gathered their small bundles quickly, the Makah were becoming increasingly restless. If they hesitated much longer, it would look as if they did not trust them and the negotiations might break down entirely.

And well right they'd be. Anna wrapped her shawl against the wind, shouldered her pack and stepped down the embankment. The Alutiiq were in the small canoe already. Phillip took her pack and helped her through the shallow water, lifting her easily into the canoe. He and the Makah point paddler pushed the small craft off the sand and jumped in. With a quick rush of her paddle the stern paddler acted as a rudder as soon as they cleared the beach, swinging the canoe around. Anna clenched her hands around the gunnels and leaned forward against the sudden rush of cold wind shocked at how quickly they shot out into the river.

The larger canoe launched with nine Russians on board and took a wider path out into the center of the river's outgoing current. Anna watched the shoreline where the rest of the Makah were lined up waiting for them. The woman paddling in front of her paced steadily, her brown arms rising and falling with ease. Just as they were reaching the landing point of the opposite shore, they heard shouting from the other canoe. Phillip looked back and saw several of the Russian men standing in the boat. The two paddlers were in the water holding on to their paddles and swimming for shore.

Anna, Phillip and their two Alutiiq companions were dragged from their canoe as soon as it met the beach. They watched in horror as the Makah shoreline erupted in a shower of stones, arrows, and spears aimed at the Russians who were being carried at the whim of the river tide helplessly right along the Makah shoreline. On the far shore, Anna could just see her husband. He was shouting, but she couldn't hear him. She could only see his arms waving, the wind had taken all his voice. Tarakanov, was firing the musket wide of the foundering canoe, trying to scare the Makah into retreat from their attack, but they seemed to know his shot would not reach them.

Anna was grabbed by the arm, and led away from the beach and into the shelter of one of the lodges. Pushed roughly to the ground, the Makah woman then patted Anna briefly on the head, as if she were a child. Phillip had been taken away, his hands bound, and the other two had disappeared, Anna had no idea where they were. It had all happened too quickly. She closed her eyes, all she could see was the pantomime that was the navigator, small and wild on the far shore.

Tarakanov, Diary Entry
Day Seven – Queets River

Duped by Makah villagers, our party has been split. Four of our group are now in the hands of the Makah, Mrs. Bulygin, poor soul, Phillip, and two Alutiiq who are husband and wife. Nine of our brave Russian men suffered serious wounds as they were nearly drowned by the duplicitous trickery of the Makah, who once their canoe was in deep and swift water, pulled plugs in the canoe bottom and jumped overboard, swimming to shore. To think they would sacrifice their boat in that way!

Mr. Bulygin is understandably distraught at the loss of his wife. We will endeavor to retrieve her by bargaining, but we must first find a defensive position from which to work. I think we should no longer assume our swift rescue and proceed with the idea that we may have to winter here.

Part II

Hostages

6

Raven

Phillip

Phillip sat against a tree, his hands bound with cedar lashing, furious and frightened, cold and wet. Light rain had begun falling, and the lowering sky to the west gave the clear message that they were in for nasty weather. Fog obscured the far bank of the river now, but Phillip had clearly seen earlier that the remaining Russians had gathered themselves together and left their beachside camp, disappearing into the tree line. Phillip figured they would head up river, certainly not stray too far from either this bounteous source of food, or from access to the hostages should they figure out some strategy for rescue.

And what might that be? Phillip was young and strong. He knew the Makah were slave traders—all these tribes warred and traded incessantly—he knew his own value as a hunter, but what of Anna? He didn't like to think.

It was at least a blessing that Phillip, in a last minute assessment of the danger by Tarakanov, had left the musket in his charge with the Englishman. He observed right away that the Makah didn't have firearms. He knew they'd prize having the muskets, perhaps above all other things, and he wondered if Tarakanov would use them for trade. Dangerous business. Tarakanov had discussed the muskets the night before. Who should take them in the crossing. He'd been wise, Phillip knew, to hold them back from the first group, even without suspecting that the Makah would try to drown them the way they did.

From his position, Phillip could see across the river should the fog lift, and see the lodge next to him, but he was prevented from seeing the bulk of the activity going on in the little village. He could hear fires burning, the crackling of fresh green boughs and the great plumes of ensuing smoke; and he could hear the general banter of people going on about their day as the excitement died down. He saw two Makah men head inland along the river, and he thought they would follow the Russians' progress from the safety of the southern shore, and report back. Phillip could understand some of what was said. As he sat in the rain, his mind became calm as his stomach began to object. The smoking salmon, great racks of long strips of pink flesh, were just feet away, and his stomach produced a loud growl just as a young woman came to load a new row of salmon pieces. She turned and laughed.

He must have looked miserable because while she didn't stop laughing, she did take pity on him, crouching down by his side to feed him salmon jerky in small bites that he ate gratefully, smiling at her in his most friendly way considering his mouthful of food. She left his side for a bit and he was disappointed, still ravenous, but she soon returned with a cedar bowl of water which she held to his lips to drink. She seemed to sit back then and consider him. Phillip felt a little bit like a prime heifer on display. Any minute he expected her to pinch him, or grab his vitals to see how much of a man he was. The thought made him choke and fidget.

The young woman took her bowl and walked away. Phillip was disappointed, but at least he would sit here in the rain on a belly satisfied by salmon, that was some comfort.

His arms were prickly with their bindings tightening in the dampness, his clothes were soaked, and his sense of loss and misery had mounted over the last few hours. Why had they left him here, out in the rain? There had clearly been some discussion, some movement, perhaps related to Anna. Phillip wondered what would happen to the Alutiiq hunter and his wife. They were not so different in looks from the Makah, would this help them or make their fate more dire? He couldn't know. They were hard working, and could earn their living, unlike Anna.

Phillip must have fallen asleep, for he was startled to find the young Makah woman unlacing his bindings and pulling him to his feet, chattering to him too fast for him to gain any of her intent. He was grateful to be doing anything beyond sitting against the tree. He struggled to stand, his legs were numb and wobbly and for a moment it seemed he might not be able to walk as he staggered and pitched forward grabbing the nearest rack pole to support his weight while he reformed his long lean frame.

He noticed that the girl had his knife. This was new; she hadn't had it before. It had been wrenched from its sheath at his belt the moment he reached shore in the canoe, the woman paddling behind him giving him a wide grin as she snatched it before he had a chance to react. He'd thought it lost as spoils of war, now he wondered, was it a mark of his captor? He hoped he would be in this woman's hands, at least he thought she would have the basic kindnesses. He knew of fierce and terrifying things happening to slaves, starvation the least of it.

The young woman led him into the lodge and motioned that he sit by the fire. She pantomimed that he remove his coat and shirt, and she gave him a rough blanket woven of some coarse fiber. While he stripped off his shirt, droplets of water casting an arc around him she laughed and wiped water from her face, and he saw she was assessing his strength. His arms, and his chest were not broad or muscular and she frowned, clearly disappointed. Wrapped in the blanket, his boots and pants sending steam up from the warmth of the fire, Phillip longed to close his eyes, rest just for a while before anything else happened. He feared for Anna more than for himself. He felt she was in his care now, and yet the moment danger had come he had failed her.

Sad protector I am, when I don't even know where they've taken her.

He rubbed his chaffed wrists and tried to pay attention to the talk around him. Other Makah had entered the lodge. Dark was coming on and the rain had increased. The

members of this lodge were clearly a family of women, perhaps because the work of smoking fish was women's work and
this was a temporary lodge. One of the women was the bow
paddler from his canoe. The other was the younger woman
who'd fed and released his bonds, and who'd taken his knife.
They both, he noticed, watched him carefully. He didn't de-
ceive himself that he could easily escape, or that should he
act in any way other than as a captive, as a slave, he would
end up outside again, tied to the tree. Two older women sat at
the lodge fire with him, working constantly, but quite clearly
also guarding him. One tended the cooking, the other was
braiding rope from long cedar bark strips. Every few minutes
she would take the braid and stretch it with a snap, giving
Phillip a raw look.

The women gave him food and drink and then tied him
to the lodge pole. It was clear this was how he would spend
the night. Phillip gave himself up to the tremendous weight
of fatigue that the food and warm fire had brought on, knowing there was little to be done. He let his eyes relax watching
the younger woman settle down to sleep herself, he glimpsed
for just a moment the glow of her body as she wrapped
herself in furs, and curled by the fire exchanging a last few
words with the old women. She reminded him of a story his
grandfather told about a fish that turned into a beautiful girl
with long dark hair who would lure men into the sea to their
deaths. The Makah girl's hair was long and straight and black
as night. It had been twisted in a braid and held out of the
way with pins made of bone, but before she bedded down,
she undid it and sat with the old woman who combed it carefully with a wooden comb and twisted it loosely with a strap

before releasing the girl to her bed. This intimacy fascinated Phillip, but he saw that she took no notice at all that she had performed so feminine and private a ritual before his eyes.

In fact, the girl ignored him entirely. Phillip was struck as he fell off to sleep by the realization that he was nothing in their eyes, that was why she ignored him, he wasn't her equal, he didn't matter. It sent a chill to his heart, and yet, he slept, his body simply and ferociously giving up to his dreams.

The Navigator

Bulygin's distress consumed him. He had lost his composure the instant the canoe hit the opposite shore and he saw Anna being led away, and he could not, would not get it back. There was nothing he could do but rage.

"We must find a way to attack, find a way across this river, come down on them at night! Attack and get them back! It's my wife!" Bulygin was pulling on Tarakanov's sleeve and gesticulating with his other hand.

"Dear God, man, it's my wife!" he said again, despair coming over his face, and he sank to the sand his head in his hands.

He felt Tarakanov pull him up, felt him settle a pack on his shoulders, and felt his firm shove as they formed a line and started inland along the river. Bulygin stumbled along as he was directed, periodically turning to look back across the river for as long as was possible, back to the lodges and the thin trails of smoke the wind carried up to them.

Dear God, she's lost. How did I let this happen?

Inside he cringed. He had never considered the possibility before, but suddenly he felt he might be a coward. He had let Tarakanov take complete control, and here he was letting Tarakanov lead them away from his wife, leave her to some unknown savage threat. All he could do was follow.

They walked east in the rain, following the shoreline but hidden in the trees. Tarakanov and the Englishman talked, forming a plan. Bulygin couldn't tamp down his panic enough to contribute more than the occasional terrified oath. The nine Russians who had been in the sinking canoe were suffering, some with serious wounds, some from exposure to the cold river water. Bulygin had helped them as he could and found it distracted him from the terrifying images his mind created of Anna subjected to torture or, dear god, some private abuse. He had bound wounds and made splints and taken over the packs of the worst injured, sharing out the contents with the others. But he had nothing to say as to a plan; fear controlled his mind. He felt hot, and wondered if his fever had returned with the shock of events.

They walked several miles to a bend in the river. Shallows which low tide exposed enough that they would have good fishing advantage from here; and a good vantage point back down the river made the place a good spot for a camp. Tarakanov set parties to cutting crude cedar branch shelters, and others to build a fire.

"The Makah will know where we are. We can at least have a fire, cook our food."

The Alutiiq hunters caught salmon with ease, gutted them and skewered them with branches set over the fire. Relieved to have food coming, and beginning to revive from their collective panic, the men began to talk amongst themselves, recollecting the events of the morning, and speculating on their future.

The navigator set his pouch with its precious charts near to his spot by the fire and sat there shivering under the shelter, coughing from the smoke the rushes caught within the space. Anna was the only thing he could think about. He had not the least idea how to save her, but he knew he must try or die in the process.

Anna

Anna sat by the warm fire in the lodge, waiting. Surely, something monumental was going to happen to her here. Though her female captor had been brusque with her, she hadn't been abused or used cruelly. In fact, she was never bound, though she had seen them bind Phillip and it pained her, struck her heart to see it as he was led away beyond the lodge where she sat.

Poor Phillip. Anna chewed at her lip.

She tried to occupy her time in drying off without undressing. She'd been given a blanket, the fire had been stoked, and she'd been left alone, though it had been made quite clear that someone stood just outside the lodge's entrance. She didn't know who, nor did she think she would find out by calling out. Somehow she had the impression that they were, as a group, almost too busy to deal with captives and hostages, that the appearance of the Russians simply created work for a group of people already working hard at the fish harvest. They needed to get back to work, to do so, they expected her to behave as if that were the logical thing to do.

Well, and right they are, she thought, *since I wouldn't try to run.*

She had a small bowl of water and a flat rough board with a pile of cooked fish on it. She ate slowly and as she ate, she held one part of her clothing after another before the fire so that at one point she sat facing the fire with her skirt in the air in front of her, and this would have made her giggle if she'd been in any other time or place than this. The warm wet wool smelled of wood smoke and her particular smell. She thought of what that was. It used to be lavender, at home she would rinse her hair in lavender water. Someone once told her that Empress Catherine of Russia used lavender water, and so she had adopted the same scent. She blew out her breath, *not now, now I smell like a cedar tree and dirt. And fish.* She added this, wiping the fish oils from her hands onto her skirt. Her clothes were becoming warmer, if not dry, and she sat at different angles, chewing fish and occasionally drinking water, rotating her body to stay warm all around. She thought about tea and wondered if she would ever drink a cup of tea, real tea from China, again. Her beloved samovar was at the bottom of the sea, or perhaps natives had paddled out after they left and stripped the ship bare carrying the great pear-shaped object away with glee. Her brass samovar might turn up as earrings or some other decoration. She spent some time analyzing the whole ship for precious commodities like her brass samovar, and then imagining what the natives might make from them. She realized that she had really not left anything behind that mattered, and this was a revelation to her, and a comfort. Now, there was nothing to be done but wait. She heard the rain coming hard on the roof, she tended the fire herself from the pile of wood nearby keeping it hot, so hot that her cheeks grew bright with warmth. It grew dark—she could see from a slice of outdoors between the flap of the door covering and the lodge frame, that night came down black outside. With no notion of what was to come, she wrapped herself in a blanket, laid down by the fire, and waited; it was sleep that came first.

Anna woke to the sound of wood being thrown on the fire, sparks showered across her blanket and warmth flared. She sat up quickly aware she had barely slept but had been just in the beginning of that sinking pleasure of deep sleep coming on.

A young man sat across from her, cross-legged, wrapped in an elaborately patterned and fringed blanket very different from her own rough one. She pulled her clothing into place, looked intently at him and nodded.

"Oh," she said.

"Oh," he said.

She knit her brow. "Oh?" she said again, changing the inflection.

"Umph," he said, and he nodded.

"Umph," she repeated after a moment's consideration. And they stared at each other.

"Anna," she said and pointed at herself, "Ah-nah."

"Yutra-mak-i," he said and did the same.

"Oh! Yu-tra mak-i?" She repeated the long word and had almost lost the last syllable swallowing it in her nerves, but he had supplied it for her so that they said "ee" together and he smiled a big smile.

"Oh." Anna tried to smile back and was only weakly successful.

"Yu-tra-ma-ki," she said again, practicing.

He stood and adjusted his blanket. It was beautifully woven of a soft pale colored fur. She wondered if it could be dog hair or goat, but she had seen neither. It carried in it a pattern of geometric images, it looked like one might be a bear, another a whale. She had not seen anything so fine on any other natives, Hoh or Makah. Was he a chief? Did she belong to him now? Was she his?

Yutramaki was smiling. He started talking, a series of short harsh sounding phrases that sounded oddly familiar to Anna. Familiar and yet, not. She look confused and he read the look on her face and started again slowly as if talking to a peculiarly stupid child. It was almost comical. Yutramaki seemed happy to be talking to her, and she not understanding what he was saying, so far, wasn't annoying him in the least. He seemed almost to be practicing certain phrases and words. Anna hadn't heard much Makah, only what the envoys had said the night before around the fire, but these words didn't sound the same as those had been. The phrases, or sentences, whichever they were, had a more flat sound to them, while the Makah sounds had been more musical in cadence. He repeated his phrases again and then laughed, pointing at her.

Anna caught the last word. Egleesh. "English?" she said. "English?!"

Yutramaki nodded, grinning, he came around the fire toward her, and squatted down. He poked a finger at her chest and said again, "Egleesh."

Anna started to laugh, she suddenly realized that the phrases he had been saying really were English, or sort of English. He had obviously learned them by rote from someone, but did he know what he was saying? She knew a very little English, but she tried to bring all of it into her consciousness now. Surely being able to communicate directly with this man would make her life easier.

"Russian," she said, pointing to herself. "Anna. Russian." She repeated words and accompanying gestures, and then shook her head, no, and said, "English, no."

"Oh," he said, looking crestfallen. And that made her laugh, and laughing seemed so completely inappropriate that she clapped a hand across her mouth and stopped, her eyes wide.

He stood up and taking her hands, brought her standing in front of him. He looked closely at her in the pale firelight, scrutinizing her clothing, walking around her as she stood awkwardly smoothing her clothes with nervous hands. He fingered the fabric of her jacket and then his hand went to the silver cross at her breast. He held it, balancing its weight in his palm. She stepped back an involuntary pace but he held on.

"Nice," he said.

Her eyes widened. *Nice!* She got it, she knew that word! She nodded affirmatively.

"Nice," she said.

"Jesus," he said. And she looked shocked, for the tone of his voice made the word sound like an oath. "Jesus!" he said again. And she crossed herself.

Full dark also brought attendants with food. For surely that's what they were, it was obvious from the deferential treatment in their demeanor as they came and went without a word, the elaborately carved wooden serving boards heaped with food. Yutramaki ignored their presence for the most part, but she noticed it wasn't in a particularly authoritarian way. The women who served him didn't seem to also fear him. Their servitude seemed more familial. Perhaps they were his sisters, or his aunts, for he must have been near to Anna's own age, in his twenties. She wondered how she could ask him how old he was. She took comfort in the problem at hand, how to learn to communicate with this man who held all power over her, and do so quickly. Somehow, she knew her life depended upon it.

The women brought the food to him, but at his quick and easy gesture they gave some portions to Anna adding them to the bits of fish on her board, and so she sat with Yutramaki and ate from her platter, and still waited on her fate.

Yutramaki for his part didn't seem to have anything else to do but stare at Anna and talk to her in the funny phrases that she worked out must be English of a sort, though the accent wasn't like the Englishman they traveled with, or the accents of the other English fur trade people she had met in New Archangel. And while much of her attention was needed parsing out the phrases, most of them remained unintelligible, so she set herself to watching the man carefully, taking in his looks and demeanor as if his countenance would elaborate on the foreign assemblage of strange words. She noticed that compared to the other Makah men, this chief Yutramaki looked very different. While they were short, stout, muscular men with dark skin and slanting dark eyes, Yutramaki had more height, standing a head taller than her husband Bulygin she guessed, and a slimness of body, and most incredibly, he had blue eyes. His face was decorated with the same frightening tattoos that she had seen before on the men on the beach; dark lines ran from his lips down his chin, and dots scattered across his cheekbones and the bridge of his nose. He wore a ring through his nostrils, and another through one earlobe. And yet his nose was long and straight, not as flat or wide as the other Makah. Anna wondered if he knew he had blue eyes, and what it meant to his people that he looked so dissimilar.

With a start, she realized he was scrutinizing her with the same curious intensity that she was examining him.

Rather like a young boy looking at a tea cake in a shop window, she thought.

He set aside his food. He walked around her several times, and she noticed he pulled himself up to his full height, enjoying the sense of how much taller and more dominant he was, as if inhaling the power of his stature. She stood still while he inspected her clothing. He picked at the layers of her skirts, lifting one after the other until he came to her legs, and then being satisfied with finding two much like his own, he dropped her skirts with their interesting button fastenings—he had mastered them by repeating the opening and closing system a dozen times before satisfying himself that he understood the notion—and moved on to her blue jacket. He had her take it off, helping her as if she were at a fancy ball being assisted by a groom, and once off, he dropped his blanket aside and shrugged on the jacket. He couldn't manage the buttons—being far too broad for the jacket to close— but he flipped at them with his index finger and smiled. He smoothed his hands down the flat wool, fingering the braided edges. With a short nod, he handed Anna his blanket, satisfied with his trade, and returned to his plate of food.

While they ate, and grew to know each other in this superficial way, Anna noticed him looking at her fingers. Her ring. Her wedding ring. The only mark of her marriage that she owned. Anna cautiously folded her hand in her lap, trying to eat with only one hand exposed. Perhaps he noticed, she wasn't sure. But the moment brought her back to the uneasy sense of waiting as never before. After all, she was his captive. She pulled his blanket around her and inhaled his smell. She began to feel her stomach buckle. Surely she knew where this was heading, she would be his concubine, isn't that what they called it? If her fate were to be anything else, she wouldn't be here having this private education with him. He seemed thrilled to be there, not so much to be there with her, but to be in her jacket, speaking phrases to her that she was slowly working out as bits of English such as *How are you? I am hungry*, and some words she was sure were very, very crude oaths, the likes of which she had only heard on the deck of a ship, and then only when the men didn't realize she was there.

To distract herself from the growing possibility that she would vomit she tried to work out a sentence she could say to him using the words he used in order to see if he understood them, or was merely repeating them. But when he repeated the phrase that contained the word *bugger* in it and accompanied the words with an unmistakable thrust of his hips, her stomach won and everything she had eaten that day came up onto the ground. Yutramaki leapt to his feet and put her onto all fours where she retched until tears and snot and vomit ran down her chin onto the dirt in front of the fire. He stood back and watched until the turmoil of her stomach died away and she sat back, snuffling and wiping away the accumulated mess from her face with her sleeve.

Yutramaki pulled her to her feet.

"Come," he said, with absolute certainly in his word. And taking her hand, he led her from the lodge and down to the water's edge away from the smoking fires. They walked only a little way from the village, the moonless night enveloping them in darkness immediately, the river's edge a sand beach with areas of shallow calm water where he led her into the water, sloshing through reed beds that Anna, in a curious daze, recognized as the basket materials she had seen stacked and drying inside the lodge. Yutramaki gestured to her to wash.

She held up her skirts with one hand, squatted and cupping her other hand, splashed her face with water that was a mix of river and salty sea, but Yutramaki didn't seem to think that was adequate. He pulled her up and yanked at her shirt. She staggered backward away from his grasp, striking out at his hands instinctively, lost her footing and fell into the water. For an instant he just stared at her, and then he began to laugh.

He was strong and deliberate as he stripped her down to her shift pulling at the buttons of her skirt until they popped. Then he lifted her and walked into the freezing water with her in his arms. She shrieked at the cold, but he just laughed, the icy water didn't seem to bother him at all. He grabbed sand and scrubbed until her arms were red, and her teeth chattered and he finally led her to shore where he rubbed her body with fresh boughs of prickly cedar before wrapping the blanket around her and carrying her back to his lodge.

The vomit had been covered with dirt and cedar chips while they were away. Sedge grass had been placed in the fire, and the smoke was strongly aromatic. Anna sat coughing by the fire, trying to comb out her long wet hair with her fingers.

Yutramaki said something to an older woman who sat by the lodge entrance. Immediately she produced a wooden comb with thickly spaced teeth and a handle carved with a whale. Anna reached for it, but wasn't allowed to comb her own hair. The old woman sat behind her, unbraiding and combing her long wavy hair, clucking under her breath. Yutramaki watched with benign curiosity and something like approval. The old woman pulled a handful of tiny brass bells from her pouch and carefully braided the bells into Anna's hair so that the ends of her braids tinkled whenever she moved. The old woman sat back, finished and satisfied, lifting Anna's hair and letting it fall so that Yutramaki could hear the bells. He nodded and said something, dismissing the woman.

Anna felt for the bells at the end of her hair. They chimed against each other with even the smallest movement. Yutramaki had arranged his sleeping pallet across from her and was lying down, ignoring her. But his knife was out of its sheath and at his side.

She knew if she tried to move in the night he would hear her. She curled up as close to the fire as she dared, and once again, willed herself to sleep.

At first light, she was awakened by the old woman. Yutramaki was gone. The woman gave Anna her clothes, and Anna struggled to dress, compensating for the ripped buttons with strips of cedar sash. Her jacket was still missing. She wondered if Yutramaki would keep wearing it. What would her husband say if he saw it? Would he think she was dead? She shook her head, she had a conviction that she couldn't think about anything except the present moment or she would die of fright. She wrapped her shawl around her waist, in the style of the country folk at home, knotted it, and looked expectantly at the old woman.

Anna spent the day cutting strips of freshly caught fish. No one spoke directly to her except to urge her at her work, cut faster, cut thinner, cut more precisely: all these things were imparted to her by showing her with brusque efficiency. Whichever woman was nearby might stop what she was doing, take the half moon shaped scraping blade from her hand, and with careful, deliberate gestures, teach Anna how to prepare fish for smoking. Anna sat before the wooden slab bench and concentrated. *Do this well, and think of nothing else.* Her belly was satisfied, she was clean, tired, and frightened. The only thing she allowed herself to worry about was Phillip's whereabouts. She had seen the Alutiiqs, the other two hostages from the ship. They were working with the fishermen, they seemed all right, though clearly they had been made to sleep outside, and looked the worse for it. But Phillip...

Whenever Anna slowed down, or paused to push a strand of hair back from her face, one of the other women would give her a gentle nudge. There was no question that she was there to work, and if she failed to please in that, then what? She refused to think.

Sometimes one of the young women would walk by and playfully tug at Anna's braids making the brass bells tinkle, and they would all laugh and wink at Anna knowingly.

It wasn't until evening that Anna saw Yutramaki again. And with him, Phillip.

"Phillip! I am so relieved to see you," she said. She had been allowed back in the lodge and was warming her stiff and tired hands at the fire when they entered, Phillip behind Yutramaki looking urgently for her, his eyes lighting as he saw her there.

"Are you well, then, have they treated you fairly?" She wanted to reach for his hand, but didn't dare move from her spot, thinking suddenly that if she showed fondness for the boy it might reflect badly in their treatment of him.

"I'm well enough," Phillip said, shaking out his long

frame in a gesture that was so familiar to her that she felt a sudden sense of her real affection for him. "And you, ma'am? Are you all right? Have they mistreated you?"

"I'm well, aye. Phillip, did ye know he can speak English?" Anna said.

Yutramaki heard the word, and repeated it, grinning. "Egleesh! Jesus!"

Anna and Phillip smiled at the same time.

"Yes," Phillip said, "we've been talking a bit, a bit of Makah, a bit of English. It works out. He's not a bad sort." Phillip looked at Yutramaki and gave a half smile. "It may be our luck."

Phillip

It became clear that Phillip was there because Yutramaki wanted him to translate. Phillip's guards, the two young canoe paddling women, stood just inside the lodge door, and there was no doubt they were prepared to kill both Anna and Phillip should any attempt be made to harm their chief, or to escape. Phillip sat next to Yutramaki, across the fire from Anna's small form huddled in the blanket. Yutramaki spoke, first in Makah, and as Phillip caught his meaning, his heart sank.

He looked at Anna sadly.

"He wanted me to say to you that you and I belong to the Makah now. You to him, and myself, well, to those two there for now. Not to try to leave because they, the Makah are better than what's out there." Phillip gestured to the door, just as Yutramaki had so that the chief would know he was translating fairly. Yutramaki nodded.

"Is there no way to get help? Is there no hope of rescue? What of the others?" Anna's words tumbled over each other.

Phillip shrugged. "They're camped up river. Yutramaki took me along the shoreline today with the other men to see." Phillip looked hard at Anna as he said, "Yutramaki laughed at them."

Yutramaki interrupted with a long speech. Phillip sat quietly until the chief finished, staring at the fire. Without looking up, Phillip translated.

"You're his wife now."

Phillip's face felt hot with embarrassment and anger. Yutramaki gave the two women a look and they immediately pulled Phillip to his feet and marched him to the door.

"I'm sorry, Anna." He choked on the words.

Phillip's lodge was full of people. The women from the night before were joined by their men who had been hunting and fishing along the shoreline. Phillip was given food and shown where to sit; his captors made it clear he would be beaten if he moved, killed if he tried to escape. *Some things translate easily. This is one of them.* All day Phillip felt as if he were being assessed for his skills, his value. If he failed to provide them with a reason to feed him, to keep him alive, he would be traded away, left to starve, or killed outright. For now,

Phillip thought he had reasonable value as a trading negotiator with the Russians. Yutramaki wouldn't have taken him to check out their camp otherwise. It was in that three mile hike that Phillip realized they weren't alone here. It was obvious there were other bands of natives fishing and hunting along the Queets River. While Yutramaki seemed alert, he also was unmistakably confident about his superiority, about the superiority of the Makah as a people against the other tribes of this isolated world. He also make clear his certainty that he, Yutramaki, was benevolent in a way not usual among his people. The man genuinely wanted Phillip to think well of him, if not befriend him outright.

Periodically during the day, the chief had stopped and spoken to Phillip, giving the boy a chance to watch the man. Yutramaki became talkative, combining his English phrases with lengthy descriptive Makah images. Phillip began to piece together a history for the man and his little band of followers.

They were out on a seasonal fishing camp. This wasn't their home. They lived farther north, back the way the Russians had come, and then that far again at least. Yutramaki was chief. His mother was the daughter of a great Makah chief and his father was a man he called Mak-ee. Phillip thought the man surely must be European, English maybe. Phillip asked him where his father was now, and Yutramaki had let him know that he had sailed away on a great ship. While they walked, he had shown Phillip a carving in a stone of a single masted sailing ship. Yutramaki waved, and said, Mak-ee! And slapped Phillip on the back. Yutramaki's mother, it seemed, was the old woman who watched over Phillip when he was in company with the two young girls. He thought they also were the woman's daughters but clearly they were full blood Makah and not métis like their brother the chief.

Phillip sat behind the gathering of family members at the fire and listened, trying to learn and translate their words. The men and women ate quickly and well, sharing a plank of food with him as well as a cup of something that tasted like wild ginger. The fire smoked when new wood was thrown on it, sparks shooting up to the hole in the ceiling where the fan of lodge poles met and supported the cedar boughs. As they finished eating, they seemed to quiet their individual conversations. A sense of anticipation and excitement warmed the room. One at a time, they began to tell stories. Phillip's captor, the young woman from the canoe, took her turn last. It seemed they had asked her for a story, and she shied, giggling, trying to decline the honor, but eventually her brothers seemed to insist, and so she stood and stepped closer to the fire so that all those present could see her well.

She no longer wore her conical hat; her hair was straight and long, hanging loose down to her waist. She had a blanket wrapped around her body against the cold, under one arm and then pinned at the other shoulder with a long bone stick so that when she moved her arms the merest hint of her bare breast gleamed in the firelight. She began to speak in a quiet hypnotic voice, and as she spoke she raised her hands and using her hands and arms and fingers in long fluid motions she pantomimed the action while she talked, and the story she told was of Phillip and Anna's capture. Phillip watched as she made the river flow ripple with her fingers, exactly as rough and eddying as it had been. Her fingers danced the pattern of the current and then she flipped one palm over, and cupped it into a boat. She signaled that two of them paddled the smaller canoe, two women, she added gently, and she showed them that four Europeans came into her boat like flies to a spider's web, and she mimicked Anna sitting rigid in the canoe like a scared rabbit. The storyteller's body reflected in the firelight and cast its image against the lodge wall, making the girl seem sometimes dark and terrible. The audience around the fire murmured their approval, and when the girl showed them how the men had sunk the big canoe they all laughed uproariously, and then quieted again as she lifted her arms to throw imaginary spears, and fling imaginary rocks in the way that the people on shore shot at the Russians, nine of them she counted, with stones as their only weapons and yet still they made them bleed. Her hands fluttered and fisted and counted out for them, and she made the rain come down, and showed how she and her sister had paddled their little canoe hard and harder, and how she had taken Phillip's long knife from him and they all turned and looked at Phillip sympathetically to have been so duped by a woman.

She spun her story out with all the details she could think of, and sometimes, when she had forgotten something, someone sitting nearby would quietly add the detail, and she would incorporate that too into her tale, her hands always telling the best part of the story, showing where the boats were in relation to each other, and how the water had behaved, and how strong the current was that pulled the Russians along right next to shore.

And then her tale was done, and they all nodded their

approval at her storytelling skill, and it seemed to Phillip that she had won him as well with her story so finely told.

He slept well, deeply, dreaming dreams from his childhood, dreams inspired by firelight and the heavy warmth of blankets and the fug of warm bodies around him. When he woke he realized he was no longer tied to the lodge pole, and his captor was sleeping soundly nearby. He scrubbed his face with his hands, and looking around, knew that this was his life now. Better not to think about escape. *Escape to what?* Back to his apprenticeship, where would that take him? For now, best to learn this life. To help Anna learn it as well.

Tarakanov, Diary Entry
Queets River – 3 mile ford

Captain Bulygin insists we stop at the river fork and will not be moved unless we effect the recovering of Mrs. Bulygin. And I have sympathy for his plight. We have undertaken to build us some sort of fortress from which we may shelter from weather as well as native assault. It will take days to complete and store with drying fish, but as we have clearly lost any opportunity to make our rendezvous to the south, we will prepare ourselves for this siege as best we can. We remarked a party of native men at mid-day on the far shore but did not engage them in either conversation or battle. We are better served to reserve our shot and powder for hunting game than instigating war with the people of these woodlands. We are determined to prepare ourselves for the advent of winter, as surely there will be few ships traveling south from New Archangel over winter, and it may be months before anyone there has any notion of our travails.

7

How the Days Were Passed

The Navigator

He was alternately volubly furious and mute with rage, expending energy he couldn't afford to lose pacing up and down the embankment of the river, first out to the rocky point of the ford, where the water was shallow and thus swift and noisy, his footing unsure, but a place where he could see farthest down river, back toward the Makah fishing camp. He would peer intently, his fists clenched, willing something, anything to change. And then he would spin on his heels and head back to the tree line where the other men were hard at work building a fortification with whatever random lengths of drift logs they could find. They studiously avoided his gaze, his swaggering bustle, knowing that any opportunity for conversation would instigate a torrent of fear, weeping, and despair the likes of which he had not known himself capable of, and in fact, his fellowship had never been sought by any of the others, either intentionally out of respect for his position or accidentally as must surely happen when a party of men endure forced intimacy, be it onboard ship or surrounded by trees several hundred feet high. It was all a prison of one sort or another and Bulygin, newly discovering this certainty, became unbearable.

He allowed himself to be directed marginally by Tarakanov, to whom he completely abdicated all sense of power. And yet, his distress over Anna's capture made him seek out Tarakanov at every turn, insisting on one bad idea or another through which to effect her release. If he let his mind wander to imagining what Anna was doing, or having done to her, he would feel as though his heart were torn away entirely.

And so he paced, out to the point and back to the fort that, due to the amazing straight growth of the cedars and the abundance of trees downed simply from storm or the notoriously shallow rooted nature of the tree itself, was taking shape rather nicely. A barrier chest high in a decent sized square angled out of the tree line as far as they might dare, knowing that the rains were yet to come and judging by the ravaged bank would come swift and deadly by spring. And while from the forest cover they could not see as far west down the river swale as they could from mid river at the moment, they would be safe nestled against the dense packed forest with some advantage of cover. The Russians and the Englishman worked steadily building the fort, while the Alutiiqs hauled in the dazed and exhausted fish, knocked them sharply on a rock to complete the sacrifice, and had them gutted, stripped and hanging to dry on green wood branches over a smoking fire with the ease that accompanies tasks that they had been accustomed to doing for as long as they could remember.

Three miles in was far enough that the water was no longer affected by the salty ocean tide, drinkable if noticeably tannic. For now, fish and late berries would keep them alive. Later, they would need to search for game. The gulls had followed the scent of fish and now swarmed about the Alutiiq fishermen, becoming more and more daring. The Alutiiq threw the guts back in the water causing an explosion of wings and screeching. Bulygin wanted quiet. He wanted silence, a silence from which he could take apart his shattered emotions and put them back again in some semblance of repair that would befit a man of his rank. This screeching and chatter, calling about of the men, was fraying his nerves. It angered him that they could be talking amongst themselves about anything other than how to save his wife. For him, time had stopped. He thought briefly about making a leap for the musket, that he could load it and thrust it under Tarakanov's chin and demand action! He looked, and saw with a small twinge of... what, relief perhaps, that the Englishman wore one musket across his back at the ready, Tarakanov, the other.

"Nikolai! Nikolai, come come, man, we need your back!" Tarakanov yelled at him just as he made another completion of his circuit.

Bulygin sighed, but responded heaving his weight against the press of log as they lifted it into place.

Tarakanov slapped him on the back. "Keep busy, man. Keep busy, and you'll do."

Nikolai Bulygin looked at him as if he were mad, as if

they had suddenly traded places. Tarakanov was speaking to him as if they were walking along the harbor in New Archangel discussing tides and charts, just as they had done three months ago on an August morning of rare warm sunshine, excited to be heading off on an exploratory adventure.

Anna

He removed himself from behind her and Anna reflected that it wasn't any worse than any other time or way. There was no comparison to some lover, mythical or actual, by which to judge, and he had not been cruel. She had held still and watched the fire, and wondered what odd shape their coupling created against the darkness and shadow of the wall.

Yutramaki left her then. She straightened her clothes and lay quietly, knowing any moment the other part of her new life would come demanding. Whatever else happened, she wanted no extremes. She would do what she must do to survive without trial, and hopefully without pain. Somehow she knew that this was her single advantage, that she was good at making do and within the bit of space that not resisting would create, she could then have something for herself. It might not be a brass samovar, or a sweet cup of amber tea, but she knew how to remain intact and civilized in the small space allowed in her brain for emotion.

He isn't so bad, Yutramaki. His scent stayed on her throughout the day, and now and then, as she lifted an arm or turned she would smell him distinctly, as if she had been deliberately marked. Something more than the sweet grass and cedar of the fire, more than the drying fish that permeated the village, more than the smell of damp wool that was on them both. It gave her a means to occupy her mind, trying to piece out what smells surrounded her, what new smell attached itself now to her own, and would no doubt remain there, making its singular claim on her body.

She wasn't hurt, nor even sore. She had slept well and deeply, dreaming of water, and only wakened as he moved behind her and pulled at her shift. He was speaking to her, speaking quietly and yet firmly in his own language all the while. Without knowing what he said, his voice alone had a quieting effect, so that she didn't feel the need to fight or resist him. He managed her the way she had seen men manage skittish horses, how they gentled them before leading them into the traces of a carriage. He didn't touch her breasts or snuffle at her nipples the way Bulygin did. He fulfilled his need with a tensing grunt, and then left, leaving her shift hiked up and her thick belled hair pushed aside, her flanks exposed to the cool morning air. And now she wasn't hurt, or sore, and now she knew what he would be like, and she knew that she could bear that and so it was one less fear dancing darkly in her mind. And while Anna didn't know a thing about love, now she did know that this man was not a savage any more than Bulygin. To stay alive, she must be useful, and if being a vessel for this man's need made her useful, she thought she could manage. She said a prayer to St. Anne that she would not become pregnant, knowing that she would not, could not survive should that be her fate. Bulygin had accused her of barrenness, as he had certainly attended to his duty to get her with child. Now she prayed he was right.

She did not see Phillip all day while she sat at her chopping block and sliced fish. She was glad of that, *God keep him safe*, since she knew what had transpired would be clear for him to see on her face and she wasn't ready for that humiliation before him, not yet. What were her feelings about Phillip? Perhaps he was the only person other than herself that she had feelings for at all. She didn't want to think about how to look Phillip straight on and know that he would understand now what her life was going to be because it would be written clear for all to see who cared to look. It might be, she thought, that Phillip was the only one who would care to look. Perhaps Phillip wouldn't particularly mind: he was, after all, a young man. Surely he's had plenty of experience, even if only tangentially, being cooped up in small quarters with other men who spared not a moment's thought to modesty while slaking their need. Or would Phillip react like a brother should? She shivered. He would be hurt if he did so. She desperately did not want him to be hurt. *Where was he?* Suddenly she needed to see him, to get beyond this moment, move on to the present whose circumstances of safety she had so carefully prepared in her mind.

She applied herself fiercely to her work, developing a rhythm with her knife. Gut the fish, splay it open, revealing its long pink fleshed body, remove the bones. Then with her hand flat, fingers curved upward away from the knife edge, she cut thin strips as long as possible in quick single slices. Then she stood, stretching her back, and carefully placed each slice over a rail of the cedar drying rack. The smoke from the wet fire beneath the rack made her eyes sting and overwhelmed the scents of her body with the salmon's own smell.

Anna was also spared seeing Yutramaki. She supposed they had hiked upriver watching the Russians. She wondered briefly what her husband was doing now, but these thoughts brought with them an idleness that soon got her a nudge in the back from her neighbor. *Concentrate on the work at hand.*

The women around her chattered while they worked. The younger children, those who were still needing the breast, played contentedly with little carved bits of cedar wood, rolling around on their blankets at their mothers' side or held captive against their backs in cradleboards. The older children scavenged for firewood and kept the smoking fires properly burning with just enough dry wood to keep them going and enough grasses to fill the drying racks with smoke. The Alutiiq prisoners worked alongside her but made no attempt to speak. Anna thought they had been forbidden to do so and she did not test the premise, wanting only for there to be peace in the little space of isolation that she occupied.

Her fingers grew sore and tired faster, tiny cuts from the fish scales stung, and her back ached, but she worked as consistently as she could until she was allowed to leave her station. She was given a cup of water and a handful of a sticky mash of berries, nuts, and dried meat. She noticed they gave her these things as if she were a stranger, not a prisoner. She sat against the lodge wall and was happy the food wasn't fish.

Even the many questions she had about what would happen next took a step back into the shadows of her mind and gave her some respite from anxiety. Today there was less to fear than yesterday. That was all she knew.

Phillip

His hands came around two warm full breasts, covering them with his long fingers, and he felt his body fill and tense with excitement, his mouth moving over her body, his face tangled in a web of her black hair.

He woke with a start, had he called out? Been moaning in his sleep? *Jesus, God, I hope not.* He opened his eyes, it was barely dawn. In the near, spare light he saw that everyone was still sleeping. Everyone, that is, except his captor. He started, groaned, and blushed to the very roots of his hair, fixing his eyes tightly shut, hoping just to fade back to sleep.

But she wasn't having any of it. He felt his blanket slip, felt the warmth of a young body slide down beside him, and shut his eyes even tighter. He had, absolutely, no notion how to proceed.

With all the will in the world, he held still as the girl curled herself around him and began to run her hands over his body, laughing quietly now and then, as when she came to the hair in his armpits and tugged it and he squeaked in surprise. But the laughing and chuckling stopped abruptly as she rose on top of him and with eyes wide open showed him what would be.

"Jesus, God," he said, again, feeling that his mother's gods might not be quite up to the task.

Yutramaki

Holding several different conversations with himself at once was not new; it was, in fact, the lot of a chief to spend much of his time talking to himself, and he was growing used to it. When he was small, very small, he remembered his father teaching him to speak his language so that they could have secrets from the others, particularly from his mother whom his father loved to tease and who was never able to learn anything of his father's strange language. He would sit with his father, sometimes fishing or performing some other chore suitable to men, and his father would school him in the sound and inflection of English. At some point, he was able to listen to his father tell stories about his own boyhood and understand most of what he said, but that was long ago. Yutramaki had had no reason to speak English for twenty years now, and he was scolding himself for losing the words. At the same time, he was thinking how satisfied he was with the woman. He would like her to bathe again, perhaps, but otherwise, she did seem to have accepted her station. For a full month now she had slept at his fire, worked with his mother and sisters and aunts making the fish ready for storage. He found very little fault with her, and had even grown so used to her that sometimes he forgot she was a captive who might try to escape given the opportunity. Just now was one of those moments when he remembered who and what she was beyond being his property. And this was because he and the men were making their routine observations of the Russians in their fort, as they did every few days. He had sentries posted to watch all the time, of course, but he felt he should make a forceful appearance now and then, to keep pressure on the Russians. He longed to own their muskets. To get them, he would either have to kill the Russians or bargain with them. First, he needed them to be more hungry and more desperate than they were. Only time would make this so. Thus today, instead of leaving Anna by the fire, he had made her dress, called to have her hair combed and re-plaited (it wouldn't do to have her not look worth bargaining for) and now, dressed in her shift and skirts and wrapped in his blanket, she walked in front of him as they followed his men on the path up river until they reached the place just across from the Russian camp.

Yutramaki whistled a sound that resembled the warning cry of the raven. The Russian sentry looked up from his dozing and started to his feet, calling out to Tarakanov and the others who sheltered inside. The Russians tumbled out of the fort and rushed to the water's edge.

Yutramaki made a noise of satisfaction and taking Anna's arm he pushed her forward, stripping the blanket away as he did so. Anna gave a little cry. He hadn't meant to scare her, but she was taken completely unaware and had stumbled on the rocks, falling to her knees, so that it looked as though he had been cruel to her. He shrugged and pulled himself up to his full height, arms crossed.

On the far side of the river, the Russians were yelling at them, Bulygin chief among them. Yutramaki raised his hand in a neutral gesture, pointedly picked Anna up from the beach and set her on the path with a nudge indicating she should start walking. He could tell Anna was angry and upset. He was thinking about guns. He offered her the blanket, but she refused. He shrugged again.

The Navigator

Bulygin was livid with rage. He could feel the anger crashing at his chest.

"My Anna! My wife! Tarakanov, we must do something!"

"You would do well to take comfort that she appeared … unhurt," Tarakanov said, hesitating on the choice of words.

"Unhurt! That monster…that…savage! He, he, he was wearing her jacket! Give me your musket and I'll see to this right now!"

"Stand down, Bulygin!" Tarakanov put his hand out and two of the Russians stepped forward.

"You dare to touch me? I am...I was your captain! Back away." He pulled his sleeve out of the nearest man's grasp and backed up himself, breathing heavily. Suddenly his face paled and crumpled, and he sank to the ground with his head in his hands.

"Oh God, oh God, oh God."

He felt Tarakanov step over him and rest his hand gently on his shoulder.

"Take care, man."

But he had no plan to share, no other words of comfort. Bulygin was beginning to suspect that Tarakanov had written Anna and Phillip and the others off as lost. Even now, with this taunting, he seemed only to be biding his time. And Tarakanov steadfastly refused time and again over the past month of agony to even consider bargaining with the muskets. He was afraid to confront Tarakanov further for fear of alienating him into resolute abandonment of the captives.

He began refusing. He refused to eat with the others, taking his meager rations of fish off into the trees just out of sight. There he would wolf down his food with avidity and then sit in silence under the giant cedars, his eyes pressed shut, listening to the wind and the trees make their plans. He refused to stand his watch. At first he showed up at the correct moment, but he began to turn his back on the westward river direction, and would stare fixedly into the sky, or over the tops of the trees above their fort. Sometimes he would fish from the rock site, not with any intent of helping with the gathering of food, but because he identified fishing with idleness in the extreme. And when he actually caught a long silver trout he had been tempted to throw it back, and he might have if Tarakanov had been watching.

He refused to wake with the others at sunrise, refused to take pains with his person; his hair became matted and wild and his uniform coat had significant tears in the seams. It was of no concern to him. Bulygin, the man who took pride in how well he danced, how he sat a horse with distinction even though he was a naval officer. Bah! That was only so that he could be an adventurer—someone everyone at home in Russia would admire, would look to for enchanting stories of the wilderness that is the open ocean.

How could, he wondered, *anyone as young as I feel so wretchedly old all of a sudden?*

He would gladly have given up, crawled behind a tree, covered himself over with the duff of the cedar forest and turned his face to the earth to become the red of cedar clay. *I am not a coward.* He, Bulygin, would stop at nothing to regain his wife.

When he was with the other men he dogged Tarakanov. He begged, threatened, and even attempted to bribe the man to bargain with the Makah and bring his wife to safety. The others in their party gave him a wide berth, nodding at the exchange of watches, or the passing of a cup of hot fish stew, sometimes with a small comment such as "Ay, and watch ye don't burn yer mouth," that several of the men repeated often enough that Bulygin began to suspect them of a hidden meaning and so he would stare at them with narrowed eyes as if to say, "I'm not the dunce you take me for."

One evening, after their second full moon in the little makeshift fort, he lost his temper and his mind all at the same time, screaming at Tarakanov in a voice that could surely have been heard at the Makah village as it echoed down the river valley on the wind. He screamed until his voice deserted him, and then subsided with a whispered apology.

"I will not speak of it again, sir. You must bear the consequences now," he said, and since that evening, Bulygin had not exchanged a single word with any of his companions.

Tarakanov, Diary Entry
Queets River

We have been here for a full month now, and camp order is reasonably returned with duty watches set, foodstuff, mostly fish, being stocked. And while our position is surely temporary, more so with every day that passes, the things that keep us alive are well in hand.

Our poor navigator, Bulygin, seems quite unwell, in part due to his ongoing fevered state, but more, I believe, to do with his extreme anxiety over his wife. I do not see that we as a group have much choice but to bargain with one group of natives or another, and since the Makah who have Mrs. Bulygin and young Phillip have not as far as we can tell mistreated them, and since we know that the Hoh would be happy to dispatch us the instant they could, I confide here that I will take the next opportunity to speak with the chief of the Makah and see what may be done to reunite us.

I would wish my countrymen many happy returns on the new year, but I think they have not kept an account, and the knowledge would be too hard to bear.

8

A Blood Offering

Phillip

Phillip walked with amiable concentration behind the girl he was beginning to think of as "his woman" though he would never have admitted to those words. They were headed down the beach toward the canoes. Phillip walked beside a young Makah man, he didn't know his name, but the man seemed friendly enough and was always at the lodge fire in the evening, sometimes telling stories, often sitting carving things from cedar. Phillip admired him. He saw him as someone completely comfortable in his skin. Thinking about that made Phillip remember a tale told by an old Irish seaman on the island. The story went that the seals were actually beautiful women if only one could get them to come onto dry land and take off their skins. If you found a seal skin and hid it, the creature would live with you and love you as a woman.

Phillip liked the story except that it made him terribly sad after that to kill so many fur seals. That was one aspect of being a captive of the Makah for which he was grateful. The wholesale killing was at a pause at least. But when the girl came into his bed that first morning, it was the story of the seal woman that came instantly into his mind flooding him with a sense of wonder and truth.

Raven, for that was the name Phillip gave to the girl, walked with easy grace, a canoe paddle balanced in either hand. Phillip had gleaned from the conversation around him that her name did indeed have something to do with raven, but he couldn't quite translate what it was, and so he had taken to just calling her that, "Raven", and it seemed to amuse her. She had laughed outright the first time he called her by this name. They had been lovemaking. He had never before said a single word, not in the month of their coming together almost every night. With the full moon, she had left his side for a few days, which made him wonder if he'd done something wrong, but then she came back and they took up as they had been, snuggling under the blankets in the late firelight, or early in the morning. He thought she liked to wake him, it made her laugh that he was ready for her even in sleep, and sometimes he would wake and find her already on him, and he participating as if in a dream. It was at one of these times, only the week before, that he had opened his eyes to find her over him.

"Raven." It was all he could say, but the word made her eyes smile.

Now Raven turned her head and flashed a quick smile. The boy walking with them caught the smile and jabbed

Phillip in the ribs, laughing, and chiding him with a tumble of words. Phillip didn't need a translator to understand, and he took the ribbing good naturedly and with not a small amount of pride.

He was not one of them, but they no longer watched him as though he might attack them, or pick up and run. He saw that they treated Anna this way as well. Both of them had been folded confidently into the daily life of the fishing village without fuss. Belonging might never happen. But there was little to complain about, and when Phillip and Anna were allowed to speak to each other, for they did not live in the same lodge nor work at the same tasks, he could not complain and saw that Anna did not either, and he admired her for that.

Anna

Yutramaki pulled away from her and his hand came up shiny with blood.

"Jesus!" he said, horror clear in his voice, and he pushed her. He jumped to his feet and strode purposefully out the lodge, throwing the door flap up so that light, air, and the outside world cast inward over Anna's naked body.

She had taken to sleeping without clothes in order to wash what she could, alternating which item she washed so that if it did not dry, which often happened in the damp climate, she would not be forced to sit working wrapped only in Yutramaki's blanket.

"Oh, oh no," she said. She recognized the small twinge in her abdomen and flushed scarlet with shame. "Oh."

She dressed in haste, searching for a discarded scrap of cloth, but there was nothing discarded here, no garbage, no waste, everything had a purpose and was used long past its durability. Reluctantly she tore a strip from her petticoat and wadded it up between her legs, lapping the ends over the waste band of her skirt. She needed to wash. Maybe she needed to run, far and fast. Her heart was racing.

Just as she was leaving the lodge to seek the privacy of the marsh, Yutramaki's mother and sister came in. Taking her by the arms, they led her away.

Anna resisted them with a terrified cry and pulled back, but they were firm.

"Oh, St. Anne, oh God, I'll be killed! Oh, God," Anna said, hysteria mounting in her voice. She tried to explain. Talking faster and faster to replace any semblance of intelligible language, but the women ignored her. They were talking to her as well, Anna thought it sounded like they were scolding her, but it didn't sound like death threats. She wasn't sure. She was too frightened to understand.

The two women walked her quickly out of sight of the lodges. With relief Anna realized they were taking her to the same place she wanted to go, the marshes. Once there, completely out of sight of the village, they stripped Anna's clothes off, and in a near exact reproduction of Yutramaki's first unceremonious bath they plunged her into the chill of the river washing her with sticky soap root. The old woman took the stems from seed pods and made a sort of sponge with which she scrubbed between Anna's legs. Then the women sanded Anna's body with handfuls of beach grass until it was red with cold and scouring but somehow she felt warm and fully alive inside.

Humiliated but clean, and possibly not about to die, Anna sat shuddering with cold and shame wrapped in her blanket on the beach while the two women collected her clothing. Anna waited for them to bring it to her, but instead they again took her by the arms and force marched her along a deer path that wound into the cedar forest behind the village and down into a dell. It was a startling place. One moment they were within hailing and sight of the lodges, and the next they were completely alone in a quiet gentle swale. Here the women had built a crude round hut: lashing young cedar branches into arcs, and covering that with fresh green boughs. Inside, captured within a small encircling of stones, a clean fire burned hot and sweet. A small fresh stream ran down the center of the dell providing an easy source to replenish the sole cedar bucket that stood near the door, a small carved drinking cup at its side.

The women stopped at the door to the hut. They took Anna's blanket from her and gave her a gentle shove accompanied by a rapid whispering of what must have been last minute advice, but which Anna didn't understand at all.

She was beginning to understand this though. She was banished for the period of her moon. The initial chill and shock of being left here alone and naked took a while to wear off. There was nothing to do. Nothing to investigate. The hut was empty except for the water, the cup, and the fire. The floor of the hut was still sweet with grass, it had clearly just been erected, and hastily so. The rocks kept the hearth of the fire defined, and a supply of dry wood sat near the doorway. With the flap of the door down, the light in the hut was dim, and yet comforting, and the space soon became so warm that she felt no need for clothing except within the habitual urge to cover her nakedness. She sat huddled near the fire, her arms clasped around her knees and rocked back and forth. She tried not to think about Yutramaki and what he might do to her for what happened. She clearly understood one thing: he had been shocked, appalled, and even frightened by discovering her woman's blood on his own body. Would he punish her or simply abandon her? *Perhaps he'll give me back?* This thought came to her accompanied by the odd sensation of fear. *And then what?* Bulygin would kill her rather than have her back after Yutramaki. *Or would he?*

Anna felt the blood accumulating between her legs. She tried to figure out what the women had been trying to tell her. The hut had one other thing in it. A small basket of sphagnum moss and the pods of tall marsh grass seeds. She'd thought it was for starting fires. But no, obviously not. She couldn't afford to let this fire die out, there would be no need to start one, and moss was surely too green and wet to use as fire starter. For the duration of her time here the fire must stay full and strong. She took one of the seed pods, it was brown and round and as long as her palm, and surprisingly soft. *Do I split it open? Or use it like this?*

The first one she tried without opening it to expose the white silky fibers inside. She slide it between her legs, wiping slowly, gently absorbing the clotting blood. When it was saturated, she placed it in the fire. The fire hissed and smoked, and the smell was something new.

Anna washed with the water from the carved bucket. She sat looking at the bucket for a long while, noticing that the carving was of a whale, and that out of the whale's mouth came a raven, a frog, and a bear. She traced the carving with her finger, letting it slide along the creases wondering at the beauty and care given to such an ordinary object as a water bucket. She lay her palm across the surface of the water creating small ripples and then sat still watching the water as it calmed, looking for some reflection of herself, but in the dim light none was there.

Her body was warm and she felt so removed, so isolated—she couldn't hear the ocean, or voices from the fishing village—she had the calming idea that somehow time had stepped aside and taken her along. She lay down by the fire, pressing a handful of moss between her legs, and slept, her last thoughts being of food.

When Anna awoke, the fire was low and needed immediate attention. She realized she had come awake because she was beginning to chill. She rose from her place by the fire, the grass matted in the shape of her body, and hastily put three logs on the fire. She opened the flap of the hut and peeked outside. There was no one around, but at her feet was a small deerskin pouch.

Anna moved away from the hut a little way down stream and crouched in the bushes, careful to avoid the small plants that caused the itching sickness, and the others that pricked and stung. She returned to the hut quickly, the chill air making her skin pebble.

Back by the fire, cleansed and warm, she opened the little pouch. Inside she found a small twist of soft cedar bark filled with a variety of crumbled leaves. Phillip came instantly to mind. *Ah! This must be medicine.* Along with the pouch of herbs was a small bag of dried berries and bits of dried fish gummed together with some sort of fish paste, the usual lunch. So they didn't plan to starve her. In fact, it decidedly looked as though they were caring for her as they would any other of their women.

Anna ate carefully, taking her time. She mixed a pinch of the herbs into her cup of water and sipped it as she ate. She was warm, safe, and cared for, and here, in this place, no one, not even Yutramaki, would bother her. It was as if a spell had been cast, a circle drawn around the dell, enclosing herself and the hut and the little stream of clear water in a warm, dry embrace. She sighed and closed her eyes, seeing the firelight make its magic on the inside of her lids. Without care, there were so many things she could allow her mind to seek out, so many things to consider. She reached for the silver cross that hung between her breasts and cradled it in her palms, and there, naked and at peace, she said her prayers.

For five days, Anna saw no one. Somehow, her visitors always came while she slept, leaving her fresh seed pods and moss, fire wood, refreshing her water and her supply of herbs and food. She grew to love the quiet. And while she did not leave the hut itself except of necessity, she grew to love the expansiveness of space that being alone provided. The herbs brought a gentle sense of relief to the aches and pains she felt as well as a desire to sleep, and to dream. In her dreaming, she experienced a different kind of intimacy with Yutramaki, one in which she turned to face him, and tried to open her eyes. Each time she slept, at some point in her dreaming, she would be with him, naked, their bodies aligned, and she would roll out of his grasp, turning, beginning to break free, to change the manner of their joining, but she would awake during the struggle in which she tried to open her eyes so that she could see him. She should have come awake disconcerted. Instead she would wake wet with a thin warm dew, curled on her side with her hands clasped tight between her knees.

As her blood flow waned, the herbs the women left for her changed, and she felt less like sleeping. She would wake and stretch, and take an accounting of her body. Nothing hurt, nothing was bruised. She was clean, and she was healthy.

On the last day of her confinement, the women brought her a small second pouch with a comb and dyed cedar ties for her hair. This time, she was awake when they came, and they did not leave. Yutramaki's mother had a small cedar pot of scented salve. As Anna lay before the fire, the clan mother rubbed her all over with the salve until Anna's skin glowed with a red-gold sheen. Then they wrapped her in a light blanket, wrapped under one arm, and pinned over the other just as Anna had seen the women wear in the evenings when they were not working with the fish. The pin was a long whale tooth with carvings of ridges on it. The clan mother was explaining something about it to Anna, counting the thirteen ridges over and over, but Anna wasn't sure what she meant and only smiled at her.

There was a rustling at the doorway, and soon the hut was filled with the other women from the lodges, speaking quietly yet with the occasional giggle, so that Anna knew whatever was going to happen would not be bad.

Anna sat in her place by the fire as the women gathered in around her. The hut grew warm rapidly. Raven had stoked the fire with sweet grasses that burned hot and thick with smoke, and when the women would enter the hut, each one would gather the smoke in her arms and pull it over her body in a cleansing veil.

When all the women had settled, the clan mother rose to her feet and spoke to the women in her storytelling voice. She gestured to the group, including each of them in a long pass of her hands to right and to left. She lifted her hands to the sky and chanted a short song, and she placed her palms on the ground and recited more words. Her eyes seemed to fill with tears, and her voice grew strong and firm. The women joined in the chant, a simple yet mesmerizing harmony of voices that began softly and grew in power.

The clan mother pulled Anna to her feet and dropped the blanket off her shoulders to the ground. Anna didn't flinch. She was amazed to find that she felt no shyness in her naked exposure, she realized that perhaps no one had seen her naked before, completely naked, in her entire adult life. The clan mother filled her lungs with smoke from a pipe and blew the smoke over Anna's body. Anna inhaled deeply following the mother's lead.

Anna closed her eyes for a moment, counting up the smells and sounds of the moment. She was moved to tears by this ceremony, she felt their welcoming even if she could not understand their words. Without thinking why, she raised her hands and unclasped the silver chain around her neck. She took her wedding ring off her finger and slipped it onto the chain next to the cross. She closed the clasp and dropped the chain into the little comb pouch at her feet. She stood again.

"I'm ready," she said, and she stepped across the low fire, the glowing coals warming her body through and through, into the arms of the women of the clan.

Other things happened that last evening. They seemed to flow, one event into another, from food and drink, to sharing small jokes and intimacies of grooming. One of the elder women that Anna worked alongside gave Anna a tattoo, and with it, the knowledge of her clan, the frog.

"Daughter, daughter," the woman said the word over and over as she worked with the fine bone needle and the shell of dark inky dye. Anna lay still, her head cradled in the woman's lap, her eyes closed, her brain half dreaming. The woman's fingers tapped on her face as the needle pricked. The pain became something to count by, a distant drum calling in time to the chanting of the women gathered around her.

Before the evening ended, they had made clear to Anna that she must keep track of her blood cycle and retire to the privacy of the dell and build her own hut the next time, and that the women would still come with food such things as she would need, but she must never again contaminate their chief with her blood, or he would indeed kill her.

They filed out of the hut and stood in a circle as Raven and the clan mother put torches to the framing and burned the hut to the ground. Anna looked back as they walked up out of the dell, she saw no sign of her little comb pouch.

Phillip

Raven told him that they would be leaving the fishing ground in two weeks time to return north to their permanent village at a place they called Ozette. She described it as a big village built of cedar log houses on the beach, the central village of the clan of the whale. She watched him as she said this and was rewarded with the startled look and expansive smile that swept across Phillip's face as understanding came to him. She laughed, and nodded.

"Indeed," she said. "Whale. Just like your people."

She told him that they would portage the small skin *baidarkas*, but the large canoes would paddle north, and she showed him in the sand the route they would have to take to avoid the treacherous rocks, surf, and the Hoh—their sworn enemy—onshore. Phillip, in order primarily to avoid being cast as a crew member for the big canoes—he was done with the sea as much as possible, devoted as he was to not letting Raven out of his sight—volunteered to carry one of the smaller kayaks. Raven smiled, and shrugged. It wasn't going to be up to her, but Phillip had the impression she didn't want him out of her sight either, any more than he wanted to be out at sea and away from her.

"We return to the village before the next moon so that we may begin preparing for the whale hunt. There is much to do," Raven said.

He was excited to see the village, meet the big chief—he had only recently learned from Raven that Yutramaki was the grandson of a great chief who was very powerful but very old—and other clans also, all of whom lived together in the permanent village under his protection and guidance when they weren't hunting or fishing or defending their territories against their neighbors. Behind his excitement, the moment Raven had told him the news of their departure, was fear for the Russians upriver. He wanted to let them know that the Makah were leaving. He also wanted them to know that he and Anna would be well, were well, and...

Phillip fiddled the knife in his hands tripping it between his fingers, back and forth in a distracted way. *And what? What exactly did Phillip want to have happen? Did he want the life he had quickly adapted to disrupted by the others coming down and surrendering? Would they even do that? And if they did, would I be obliged to mount an attack on these people?* Did he want to run, should that be their consensus, try to make an escape and set his lot with hopes of a ship rescue some time in the future, while they tried not to starve or get killed by natives or beasts? If he could, would he leave Raven? If he stayed, could he protect her?

With no means of comparison, and the meager supply of words, he wasn't sure what Raven thought of him. What was she to him? What was he to her? Sometimes he felt entirely indentured, forsaken; though not really ill used, he did receive the occasional cuff on the head for his slowness or inattention. But he forgot all that when Raven touched him. Was it love that he would do anything she asked of him? He couldn't know. He had thought he was just a boy, and he told Raven so, and she had laughed and taken him in her hands and said, "Is this a boy?"

What he did know was that he wanted her to keep touching him. He wanted to see more of her world; and he felt a pull when he watched her and her people around the fire that touched something deep inside. When he heard the sound of a canoe slide along the sand and into the water, it reminded him of a time he couldn't quite bring back into images, but the sound, the sound was tinder for the spark of a memory, something that made him want to stand at the fire and tell them his own story. He thought if he could do this, then Raven, and not only Raven but each one of them would see him, really see him. See the man and the ancestors who backed him with the strength of their own stories.

He threw the knife down, a clean shot snug into a chunk of cedar, and stood up. That was it, tonight at the fire, he would tell his own story, and then, well, then tomorrow would come and everything would be different, and whatever it was, however it changed, it would be as it should be.

Phillip hadn't seen Anna for days. He had asked Raven where Anna had gone, if perhaps she was ill, and Raven had laughed and said not to worry, Anna was fine, she would be back in a few days.

"Will she be at the fire tonight, then?"

Raven nodded, she was busy. Phillip was nervous and fluttering around her like a deer fly, persistent and annoying.

"What troubles you? Be still!" she said turning on him. She put down her knife and wiped her hands on the grass.

"Me? Nothing! Not a thing. I…well, I want to know, could I, would it be allowed were I to tell a story at the fire tonight?"

Raven looked shocked, but then a broad smile took over her face.

"Yes, of course. Anyone may stand at the fire and tell their stories."

"How?" Phillip said.

"How?" She arched one brow, "Oh…I see. Well, when there is a pause, and no one else seems ready with their story, you just stand up and tell yours. And if you do it well… ah, everyone will help you anyway, so you don't have to be worried."

"What do you mean, if I do it well?" he asked.

She smiled a clear challenge. "If you do it poorly, everyone will start talking until you stop!" And she laughed and laughed until tears came and Phillip walked away chagrined.

Raven finished preparing the food with the help of her clan sisters, and everyone was wandering into the lodge to find their food and take a place around the fire. The children were settling at the breast, or sleeping soundly in soft bundled corners. Phillip was at his usual place, his rightful place, not close to the fire, but just behind where Raven would sit when she finished serving food to the elders. No one spoke to him, but everyone made room for him, expecting him to be exactly where he was doing exactly what he was doing. He had finished his meal and was working on his little wood carving. He was making a small raven fetish for her. When one of his neighbors would pass by and see the little bird coming to life in his hands, they would laugh and chuck him on the arm.

Everyone but the women who cooked and served the food had eaten, and still he hadn't seen Anna. Raven had told him that Anna would be there at the fire. Phillip didn't want to look worried, and he knew that he wasn't supposed to care about Anna, not in the society of the clan, Anna was a slave, he was a slave, he should only care about what his masters needed from him. Here Anna was not his. Not even his friend. Most of the Makah tolerated his connection to Anna as understandable, and they allowed them to speak to each other if they came upon one another by accident. But deliberate assignations would have been deeply suspect and dealt with fiercely.

Anna came in with Raven at the last, followed by four elder women that Phillip recognized as the women Anna worked beside at the fish drying racks. The fire had just been stoked with three huge cedar logs, sparks shooting to the roof blocked Phillip's view of them. When he saw her go around the fire to her place near Yutramaki, he gasped.

Her skin glowed red and glossy, her dark hair was loose and long with small braids here and there ornamented with tiny bells. She wore nothing but Yutramaki's blanket, wrapped and pinned at her shoulders in the Makah way. Before she had always clutched the blanket over her clothes in a manner that made her huddle in a lumpy bear-like mass. Now she stood straight, slim and calm. She reached Yutramaki and stopped, asking permission to sit, and Phillip noticed he too seemed stunned for a moment, and then he gave a quick nod of approval and she turned, looking across the fire toward Phillip, her face full in the firelight.

"Anna!" he shouted. He couldn't stop himself, he started to his feet but just as quickly, just as Yutramaki looked his way to find to source of the call, Raven pulled him down roughly and shushed him with a quick hard look. He opened his mouth to say something, but closed it at the firm look on her face. No good would come from making a scene, but something in his heart was jumping and he was at once terrified and shocked.

Across the fire, in the flickering light, Anna turned her face toward him, the bright clear image of a frog tattooed on her cheek.

9

Phillip's Tale

Yutramaki

The chief watched Anna make her entrance with benign interest and a stunned pride at how beautiful the woman looked. He had already seen her at his own lodge fire, already approved of her appearance. His mother and sister had done their work well. In fact, he was satisfied with Anna. The shaman had cleansed him of the unclean spirits who might take advantage of his vulnerability because he had touched her blood. The shaman railed at him, he should have known better, he was not a young boy, he knew the ways of women well enough, he at least should have been counting even if the white woman had been oblivious. At first he wondered if she really had not known, or if she had purposely contaminated him. Perhaps she was not as pliant a captive as he thought. She always seemed ready enough to lie with him, and had done her work well, if not particularly competently. He wondered, watching her, what she did for her work in her own homeland and for her own people. Her hands were a mass of cuts and rough worried areas, she surely had never worked very hard before this. Perhaps that was a part of what attracted him to her. He didn't need another bedmate, he had his pick of the very healthy women of his clan, any one of which his mother would happily make ready for him. No, something about Anna intrigued him—the paleness of her skin was a shock and yet the contrast, when he looked at her in the firelight, when she was waiting for him with legs bare, his own dark body looked fascinating against hers, it made him surge with power. And now that the women of his clan had tended to her, her scent had changed and he liked it better.

He rubbed a finger along his narrow nose as the thought of her scent made his senses react. Yes, he was satisfied. The shaman had been angry and unwilling at first but finally had blown smoke over him and chanted all of the appropriate banishing rituals. He had instructed the women to do the same over Anna. There was only half a moon phase left before the men would begin fasting in preparation for the whale hunt, he would make use of the time with pleasure.

Of course, if it happened again, he would kill her, or sell her. He shrugged, and refolding his long legs under him, he sat with his pipe, content, waiting for the storytelling to begin.

Phillip

Raven put her hand on his shoulder and pressed down. He felt her power surge through him like the wind, forcing him to relax back into his seated posture.

"Be still," she said in his ear.

"But"—

"No." And when he looked at her she gave her head a quick and incontestable shake.

Phillip raised his hand to his face, to the place where Anna's tattoo had been carved, high on the cheekbone. "But, is it…it's a frog?" He thought he could ask this question without making Raven angry. Anna's face was dominated, transformed by a strangely curving block form, almost a simple box design but he realized that it was indeed a frog, he could clearly see the frog's four legs depicted within the box, the tattoo was black and red, a simple and yet elegant design that covered the hollow beneath one cheekbone. Phillip wondered if it pained her. Her cheekbone was faintly swollen, the design outlined in pale red angry skin.

She smiled. "Yes, frog," she said.

"But I don't understand, are you not of the Raven clan?" Phillip had been so sure he had figured out the way it worked, that the women formed the basis of each clan group, bringing men from outside of their own clan for marriage. Yutramaki's mother was the Raven clan matriarch. Whoever she had chosen as her mate, they had produced a very unusual man in this Yutramaki.

"I still don't understand," he said. "If Anna lies with Yutramaki does she not become raven?"

"Oh, not at all!" she said, looking horrified. "Do you not

see, that would be as if he would lie with his sister! Aich." She made a growling noise in her throat and spat.

"Well then, who else is of this frog clan?"

Raven pointed out the other women in the room who seemed by nature to take a secondary role in the goings on of the lodge.

"They are not so important," Raven said and dismissed them with a flap of a hand.

Now that he saw them, he realized that their work parties were also defined by clan groups. Anna had been set to working with the fish catch alongside these other women, not the Ravens, who did other complementary work, including handling the small single and double cedar canoes.

"Hmm," how could he ask this simply? "So they offered to adopt Anna?"

Raven shrugged. "One of their young women died in childbirth last spring. They decided Anna should take her place."

When Phillip looked shocked, she continued in a placating voice. "It is our way, and it honors both the dead person and the adopted person, you see, that they think well enough of her to want to adopt her, that is a very great thing, indeed." Raven had started saying "indeed" at the end of nearly every sentence because Phillip used the word and she liked the way he seemed so certain after he said it, always puffing up like a little bird preening. "Indeed," she said again.

"But, Anna…" Phillip couldn't fathom the transformation.

Raven looked at him with sympathy, shrugged her shoulders and decided it was time to change the subject.

"Will you tell your story now?"

———

After a time, the lively conversation over food settled, the children were quiet, some leaning sleepily against their mothers sucking on pieces of jerky, others, the older ones, sitting with increased attention, knowing that stories would start and not wanting to risk being banished for talking or jostling just when they would begin.

Phillip stared into the fire for several minutes, lost in his own memories, memories of firelight on cold and snowy nights when they huddled in their wooden house on the island, listening to the wind tear at their thin buildings. He took a deep breath and stood, take three steps toward the fire to the space reserved for the story tellers. Murmurs of curiosity swept the room, some people looking sharply at Yutramaki for approval. Would he allow this slave to speak his tale?

Yutramaki looked Phillip up and down, looked briefly at Raven who steadfastly ignored her brother's gaze, and then nodded curtly. He folded his arms and sat back to watch.

"I am Phillip Kotel'nikov. This is my story to tell, and mine alone. It happened this way—"

Phillip felt the audience give way as if one being. Eager for a new story, ready to criticize, also ready to enjoy, they leaned forward, their faces gleaming in the firelight. He called up the image of Raven and how she used her whole body to tell her story, and he let his tale fill him, take control. He looked around the room, letting his eyes glaze out to that dreamy non-reality of one who is very tired and near sleep, his scan passing over Anna almost without recognition. He was filling himself with his old life, allowing his inner self to depart from the present, from this tribe of people who owned him now, back to the northern land of his birth. He wondered briefly how to begin the tale, but then the tale just took hold of him and he plunged ahead.

"My people are the hunters of the white north, where there is vast flat land covered in snow." Phillip made a sweeping gesture with his whole arm, turning his body so that the immenseness of the great land to the north would cover his audience. Then he made his fingers flicker like snow falling from the skies, and he realized none of these people before him would ever have seen snow except as the distant mountain tops of the great mountains to the east that would change from gray to white each winter. "My people are the sea hunters who live on the islands of the land where the sun journeys away in winter to see his children on the other side of the world. I am Alutiiq, born of my mother, the shaman of the people of my village." He splayed his fingers across his face in mock tattoos. His audience stayed with him, murmuring approval. "My clan is the whale, for no other clan may live on my island. When I was small, great sickness came to us from the white man and many people in my village died. Even my mother whom everyone said was the most powerful healer in memory could not save them. The Russian god could not save them." He choked suddenly with emotion.

Phillip felt torn in two. As if in the telling of his tale he had exposed his own faults. And yet he had not thought of his parents in this way. Suddenly he was drowning in his own memories and felt he might not be able to continue, and yet his audience were now leaning forward, as if he had finally come to the point.

Phillip became very quiet and the people before him waited while he overcame the tears and anger that threatened to make him mute.

"My mother feared I would die of the spotted sickness. She performed her rituals, asked the spirits for advice and protection, but she feared our spirits could not protect me and so she sent me away with my Russian father. She gave me up to their world." His voice split and choked, he realized his hands were balled into fists, as if more words and more tears might leak out through his fingers if he opened his hands. Those around the fire murmured their sadness at this news, and a sympathetic wave of quiet chatter surrounded him.

Raven jumped to her feet and stepped beside him, she lifted his fisted hands and held them together between her own, searching his eyes for complete understanding. She nodded and stood in front of him, then, her arms folded, her stance firm and secure.

She spoke to her clan members with rapid and deliberate phrases, too rapid for Phillip to catch the full meaning, but there was no question of her intent. Raven was claiming him as more than slave or conquest or lover, she was claiming him as her own.

Raven stepped back, standing shoulder to shoulder with Phillip, firm and quiet once her speech was finished, her eyes sweeping the little group but always returning to Yutramaki and her mother sitting opposite her at the fire. Yutramaki watched her, returning her gaze, but her mother talked, low and fast. Phillip couldn't tell from her demeanor what her opinion was of this sudden change in his station. And then there was silence. Everyone waited for Yutramaki to give his blessing.

Yutramaki stood, letting his blanket fall away. He reached at his side and pulled out a knife, the handle carved in a raven's form, and without a word he tossed the knife across the fire to Phillip, who instinctively caught it, and understood. He grinned, the last of his brief tears drying in the firelight.

The full moon came, and with the winter light being so short, the bright night sky lengthened the workday as the fishing and food preparing increased to maximum effect in the last days of their harvesting. Phillip noticed that Raven did little actual fish processing, leaving that to the slaves and less important clan members. Now that he understood more about her family and its complicated structure he saw how clearly marked the hierarchy was. That some men never spoke to him was not accidental. Phillip's status had increased now that Raven had aligned herself with him. *Are we married?* He still did not have words adequate to ask or explain that question to her. When he tried, she would fix him with her dark eyes, and say "Indeed." But it was clear she did not fully understand what he was saying. The family unit was fluid, one could, as Phillip surely had, achieve higher status through marriage, or actions of importance, and just as quickly lose it in disgrace. The clan mothers and the fearsome shaman—Phillip had only seen him twice and decided that was two times too many—were nominally in charge of daily and ritual activity, but the order of importance of the members of each clan was as complicated as the Russian royal family, which Phillip recalled Tarakanov trying to explain to him one evening when he was tired of learning mathematics.

The moon came up full on a cloudless night sky creeping to the tops of the cedars on the ridge line and then higher, and the river was full and calm. Raven found him stacking firewood and, pulling him by the hand, walked with him down to the sand where the small canoes were beached. Next to the smallest canoe was an even smaller boat, one that made Phillip's heart surge with excitement. A *baidarka*.

Thinner than the canoe, crafted of narrow bent wood frame with a skin body and almost no draft, Phillip knew these boats well. Raven grinned at him. She shoved the little boat off from the sand and jumped in, sliding her small body down through the oval hatch while pushing at the sand with her paddle. Phillip stood on shore and watched her. The kayak was swift and precarious. Raven had had some practice with it, but Phillip could immediately tell that she was more at home in the canoe. She was light and the kayak responded to her paddling as she gained the tidal current, shifted her weight, leaning slightly over the paddle and spun into the center, the moonlight flashed on the white skin body of the boat as she dashed along the shoreline. Phillip laughed out loud, and heard Raven give the piercing whistle that was her own private call of joy.

She maneuvered a turn across the weight of the outward flow and paddled hard back to the spot where Phillip stood grinning at her. She levered her body up out of the hatch, and tossed the paddle to Phillip.

"Yes? Really?" He didn't wait for her to answer. He shoved the boat deeper into the shallows until he had enough way, and then he slid his long body into the hatch in a single fluid movement.. His feet nearly touched the prow, he was a good foot taller than Raven and his body filled the hatch. He dug the paddle into the sand as she had, swung his whole weight into a fast turn and he was off, shooting across the easy water and into the carrying current. His heart sang with joy. He couldn't remember when he had first traveled in a kayak, surely he'd been a baby, nor could he recall when he first took up a paddle. Children on Kodiak Island played with toy kayaks until they learned to paddle their own. Kayaks and hunting were integral to life on Kodiak, and Phillip felt nearly as at home in this little skin boat as he did walking on two feet. He handled the boat with ease, taking several turns across the current back and forth in front of Raven, until he saw her wave and heard her whistle him in to shore.

He jumped from the boat and carried it clear of the water, thinking to store it away. The moon was high, and the river was quietly illuminated; they were alone. There was none of the activity on and off the water that there had been all day long.

Raven stopped him.

"No, wait," she said.

It took some time, and numerous exasperated breaths, and finally some seriously hilarious pantomiming, but at last Raven was able to show Phillip that she wished him to teach her how to tip over the little boat and right it again without getting out. From her pantomime, Phillip gathered she had tried only twice and both times had failed to bring the boat upright again, having to exit the little hatch and swim to the surface, letting the kayak find its own way, and then—and

Raven was much disgusted by this humiliation witnessed in front of her younger brothers and their friends—she had to swim for the boat that, caught by the tide, had been sailing fast out toward the open ocean.

Phillip tried not to laugh, tried not to even smile, but failed miserably, his joy at paddling still full inside him. He picked up Raven and swung her around, laughing.

"Of course!" he said. "'Tis easy once you know the way of it."

Now he understood why they were on the river in the middle of the night. Raven was a proud girl. She would not be one to share failures in public. Cold as the water was, Phillip didn't seem to notice as he waded out pushing the kayak with Raven onboard until they were at a depth where he could show her the simple movements, how to strike downward with her paddle and push, moving as forcefully as she could, thrusting her whole body into the curve, keeping the momentum of the turn going so that the boat wanted nothing more than to turn full over and pop to the surface.

She practiced over and over. Only twice did Phillip have to reach out and grab the kayak, saving her from having to swim clear, but bringing her sputtering to the surface mad as a snake at her failure. At last, they both began to notice the cold, and shivering, tired but elated, they made their way to shore, and then to their bed. It took a long while for Phillip's teeth to stop chattering, but the cold never removed the smile from his face, and eventually, Raven warmed him through.

The Navigator

Bulygin lay on his side, face to the rough hewn log wall, his knees pulled up toward his chest, his hands clasping the worn remains of his great coat, and panted while the coughing fit subsided. Short breaths, gasping, he felt drops of sweat chill across his face and shivered along his whole frame. He could just see through a small crack in the logs, a peephole of activity along the water's edge beyond their small foursquare fortification. He closed his eyes, trying to increase each breath just by a little, desperate for more air in his lungs.

"Let them come," he said to himself, "let them just come away now and end all this torment."

The Englishman crouched over him. "Ay, what, man? What did ye say?" he said.

"Doesn't matter." Bulygin waved the man off. "Leave me be."

"Ah, well, now, ye see, we canna do that." He tapped Bulygin's shoulder, "Hey, man, will ye attend me now? We're gonna speak wi' the chief."

Bulygin felt his chest constrict, another fit of coughing began as he rolled over facing the Englishman, fear and anticipation lighting his fevered eyes with a wild glow.

"Aye?"

The Englishman cuffed him on the shoulder.

"Right. Ye take care. Tarakanov will bring us outa this."

Bulygin could do nothing more than roll back toward the wall, coughing and close his eyes. *Surely, it is too late.*

He heard a shout come from outside, and peered through the crack in the logs to see Tarakanov, the Englishman, and two other Russians walk across the river ford. On the other side stood several Indians and...was it Phillip? *Dear Blessed Virgin!* It was Phillip. Bulygin couldn't hear their words, but he watched intently, straining his eyes to see each movement, the subtlest gesture—were they acting friendly? Accommodating? Who was speaking the most? It seemed to be Phillip. He watched as Phillip spoke, first to the chief, and then to the Russians, turning his body to each with respect and deliberate care. At one point he saw the chief gesture toward the musket that the Englishman held ready at his side, and he saw Tarakanov step back and shake his head vigorously. The chief folded his arms over his chest and stood firm. Words were not necessary. Bulygin could see that the treaty party had hit an impasse. He tried to call out, to beg Tarakanov to relent. *Just give them one bloody musket, what little good it'll do them, we're out of shot and barely have powder left at all.*

As if Tarakanov heard him, he turned to look toward the little fort, shrugged his shoulders in the first sign of weariness that Bulygin had seen in the man since the shipwreck.

Tarakanov turned back to the party of men and nodded. The chief stepped forward as if to take the musket from the Englishman right then and there, but Tarakanov stayed his hand with his own, and Bulygin knew what he said. *Anna.*

The chief stood eye to eye with Tarakanov and Phillip,

much taller than his men, who were short, powerfully made men. As they shook hands, Tarakanov taking the chief's hand in his and pumping it vigorously, the chief reluctantly acquiescing to being touched, Bulygin thought, from the way he pulled his hand back and looked at it for a moment as if it were now an alien thing instead of an integral part of his own body. He wiped his hand ostentatiously on his blanket before returning to Tarakanov speaking. He seemed to be asking a question. Phillip translated, and the chief held up his hand, thumb tucked down.

"Four days." Bulygin choked out the words. Relief flooded his body. Four days and he would see his Anna.

The treating party separated, the Russians making their way through the shallows at the ford talking excitedly. Bulygin watched as Phillip and the Indians disappeared out of sight down the river trail. He closed his eyes with a sigh, exhaustion covered his body like a veil of fog. In spite of his jubilation at what seemed certain to be the recovery of his dear wife, beneath the emotions of the day lurked the certainty that he was dying.

Tarakanov, Diary Entry
Queets River Treaty

Our attempts to negotiate assistance and recovery had reached an impasse whereupon with great reluctance I undertook to treat one last time with the Makah chief know as Yutramaki. He is firm in his refusal to help us without payment of muskets. I have yielded to his demands, and he will trade back our fellow shipmates, and Mrs. Bulygin, in four days time, in exchange for one musket. I have not mentioned that we are nearly out of shot and powder. They will find that out for themselves. Perhaps in the end, the trade necessity that this gesture will create may benefit us in our quest for suppliers of furs along this coast. For once they have guns, they will have no choice but to trade further for the means to use them.

We will exchange for Mrs. Bulygin and the others and decamp this place, before any of us becomes so weak they cannot travel. I fear we may have left it too long for poor Bulygin. But we cannot wait at this place forever as ships ply up and down the coast in ones and twos, passing us by. Yutramaki informed me that one such ship had already gone, surely this must have been our sailing partner. My heart sank at the news.

10

Guns for Brides

Anna

The lodge fire crackled sending sparks outward and a fine height of flame toward the ceiling. Anna sat close by, mending her clothes. The women of her clan had washed her clothes in the river and then returned them to her, but Anna wasn't sure whether that meant Yutramaki would want to see her in that foreign dress. Dressed in the fine blanket pinned with the ornately carved wooden pin she had felt a sense of freedom as she paraded before him and the rest of the clan at the nightly fire. She noticed his actions, the smallest flick of his eyes as she entered the lodge, framed in the hide covered doorway, the darkness behind her. The sense of naked ease made her attend to his responses in a way that she had not done before. Now she saw herself as wanting to please, to attract him, she wanted his eyes on her. It was more than a matter of survival, she decided. It was as if she had been bemused by the firelight and the exotic feel of her body so exposed. She watched the other young women, women like Raven, who she knew was attracted to Phillip. She watched how the women carried themselves, how they wore their blankets, how they twined their hair with decorations of bells and feathers and beads, and, most of all, how they looked at the men. Anna had spent most of her short adult life trying to avoid looking at men. This was new, this feeling. *No*, she corrected herself, *not entirely new*. As a girl only a few short years ago hadn't she felt the very same for Nikolai? Before they married, of course. She hadn't known, *oh, how little I had known*. She gave a small inner jibing laugh. *How little.*

She bent her head to her sewing. She had carefully pulled a single linen thread from the edge of her shift, and with a borrowed bone needle, she was mending the tears with short darning stitches that formed a crosshatch patch over the holes. Cloth was valuable and irreplaceable, whether she wore her shift again or not, it was now one of her only possessions.

What did she know now that was so different? She analyzed her life now. Marriage to Bulygin had become something of a war. She was rigid in her refusal of him, forcing him to take her when he wanted her, refusing to play either the sweet coquette, or the blatant whore, she had averted her eyes from his nakedness when he presented himself to her. And while she understood that her survival depended upon his grace, no differently than it did now depend upon Yutramaki's good will, she had not seen before that their union was a partnership that she had ignored. No, more so, she had played with it, deliberately found shelter in her girlishness, playing at tea and conventions instead of...what? Opening her body to her husband willingly? She shuddered. Could it have been that bad had she not made it so? Yutramaki had taught her something about her body, had shown her his appreciation for how she began to make herself available. Not overtly, she would still not play the whore, but in the firelight and the warm scents of his temporary lodge, had she not felt that warmth cover her skin with anticipation?

It was only a few days since her return from the women's lodge, from sanctuary. Anna lifted her arms and studied them, long and slender and golden in the firelight, glossy with scented oils. She pulled her blanket away from her legs and ran her hands along her thighs, down her calves to her slender ankles. And she laughed to think of the Hussars at the balls in Russia whose most daring wish would be a glimpse of one ankle encased in white silk stockings brush by as she whirled around the dance floor. Only a few days, and yet these changes she felt, they couldn't be mere survival. She carefully smoothed the blanket around her body, tucking and readjusting the shoulder pin. How shocked she had been, that first night of her return from the women, shocked when Yutramaki entered his lodge. He knew full well she would be there, aware at every moment of every movement of his clan, her presence in his lodge again was at his command. He had stopped for a moment in the doorway, then reaching behind him, pulled the hide covering closed, and there she stood, illuminated in the firelight feeling so foreign, so bare without her layers and layers of Russian clothes. She had steadied her gaze and watched him, some instinct telling her that he would disapprove of fear, of weakness now.

Yutramaki had walked up to her, pulled the pin from her blanket, and in an instant she was naked. The shock of it was the speed with which he took her down. The blanket at her feet became her bed. And in that instant before he took her, while he hesitated, lost in the enjoyment of his body, she had felt again a tiny moment of power. Now she knew how it would be. This was her life now, its parts becoming clear, fitting together like a child's puzzle.

The door flap shifted and Anna looked up from her sewing, shifting in embarrassment, caught as she was thinking about these things. She cried out in surprised delight.

"Phillip!"

He grinned at her and made a silly bow. "It is," he said. "It is, indeed."

"But, Phillip, should you be in here?" Suddenly Anna's voice registered panic, this was Yutramaki's private lodge. But Phillip waved her fear away with a laugh.

"Ay, I may be. I've come with news for ye."

"What…what news? Of my husband, surely? Is he well." As she said the word "husband" her thumb rubbed along her finger where her   should be, and she felt a rush of fear. It had been a whim, to remove those things, and yet, somehow she knew that removing her ring had meant something to Yutramaki, assured him something about who she would be for him that she had no words to convey. She knew without doubt that every detail of that night in the woman's hut had been retold to him. She was certain that the account of her behavior had led directly to being given more freedom.

She was allowed to be alone now, free to bathe in the river when she wished. The women had stopped watching her as if she were a rabbit about to bolt. She gulped.

"What news, Phillip, do not torture me!"

"Yutramaki has spoken to Tarakanov about a trade. Muskets for ourselves to be set free." Anna stared at him. Phillip didn't look terribly happy about this. She hadn't thought about him or how he was adapting since the night more than a month before when she had watched him across the fire. Watched him watching the girl Raven. At that moment she had ceased to worry on his behalf.

"But, Phillip…" Anna said, "trade to do what? Go where? How would…" Her questions trailed away in disbelief.

"And Bulygin, did you see him?"

Phillip shook his head looking sorry for her.

"Nay. But if he'd been dead, I don't think Tarakanov would have bothered with talk of a trade." He shrugged. "They would have left us long ago," he said.

Anna nodded seeing the truth in what he said.

"Rescued," she said, pronouncing the word flatly trying to imagine what that would mean for all of them. Was there hope, yet, then.

"Will… do you think, Phillip, will it matter?"

He stared at her, not comprehending. "Matter?" he said.

"Without the Makah to keep us alive. What will we do?"

"Why, hope for a ship, surely," said Phillip, but Anna saw that he looked at that possibility with the hopelessness of someone much attached to a far different outcome.

Anna looked down at her hands again. She had taken up her shift and had been pleating the corner over and over.

She dropped it with a sigh and smoothed the edges. She had no words with which to comfort Phillip, and it was not her place to suggest he take his fate into his own hands. That was for each of them to come to on their own. A part of Phillip belonged to Tarakanov in much the same way that she belonged to the navigator. They were commodities for trading. Brides for guns. Yutramaki knew this even better than Tarakanov, even better than she did. A deep chill replaced the warmth she had felt before and she chided herself silently. She thought through how events might proceed. The trade would take place. The little group of Russians would begin to make their way south, along the shore, once again embattled by various tribes, threatened, attacked, perhaps killed. Their only hope would be a passing ship stopping for fresh water or to establish trade rights for furs. How many ships would there be? Surely none until early summer. And then what were their chances? Perhaps four or five ships. If they built signal fires would the ships fly away, fearing trouble? And if Bulygin died, overtaken by his coughing sickness, what then? Would she be passed among the men or would one of them become her protector, defend her against the others? *The way Phillip had been.* Anna knew these were considerations and decisions she would not be a part of, Tarakanov would decide. She would merely be another mouth to feed, another person to protect, another point of bargaining. Tarakanov was a logical and resourceful man. Anna had confidence in him, but in this wilderness? Soon the bears would come, increasing the danger to all of them. Anna had seen the bear tooth necklaces worn by the shaman. These great bears would soon awaken from their winter lethargy, awaken hungry. They would follow the shoreline just as the Russians would, searching for the same food, digging clams and crabs along the beach, and fishing for chum and salmon in the rivers. Bears with claws the length of a digging hoe. Anna had listened carefully to the story tellers, watched as they told stories of the great bears, throwing shadows three and four times greater than a man onto the lodge walls, the story teller growled and prowled its lumbering self around the circle of listeners, terrifying the children so that they would not wander away alone, and reminding everyone at the fire of the might and fearsomeness of this honorable godlike creature.

"Anna?"

She looked at Phillip but her eyes were distant with wondering.

"I don't want to leave." Phillip said it so quietly that at first Anna wasn't sure she heard him right.

"You..?"

"Raven. I don't want to leave her."

Phillip

He said it out loud. The thing he had been thinking, screaming in his head all the way back down the trail after the meeting with the Russians. All he could think of was Raven. He had tried to argue with himself—that he was still a slave, that he had no freedom, that this was a dangerous life, that he would never see his mother's family again. The only image that came to mind was Raven. The power of her acceptance of him was a lure stronger than any bond beyond that of him to his mother. And he had long ago known that he might never see his mother again. Without this tether, life had little value.

"I don't want to leave Raven." He looked at Anna with a desperate cry. "Never."

"We'll have no choice, Phillip, you know that well, do you not?" Anna said. She rose and smoothed the blanket around her body as if feeling suddenly absurd in her costume. "Tarakanov, Bulygin, they want us back." She lifted her shoulders in a small shrug, and her hand went to her face where the tattoo lay vivid in the firelight.

Phillip turned to leave.

"I must go find Raven."

"Wait," Anna put a hand on his arm. The touch was enough, it lit a fire of emotion in Phillip that he could not contain and he turned like a child into her arms, bending over her small frame, laying his head gently on top of hers, crying great desperate sobs.

The door flap flipped open and Yutramaki stepped inside. Anna stepped back with a start and Phillip turned to the chief in fear. Yutramaki saw the emotion on his face, studied Anna quietly for a moment, and gestured to Phillip to leave.

Anna exhaled in relief. Yutramaki seemed amused at Phillip's emotion. She had explained in as few hurried words as possible that Phillip cared for Raven. Yutramaki just nodded his head and shrugged his shoulders.

———

Walking behind Yutramaki and the others as they headed inland to where the Russians camped, Phillip hadn't known what action either Yutramaki or Tarakanov would take. He had been surprised to be asked to translate. Previous visits to the opposite shoreline had been restricted to gestures and posturing of more that a little threatening nature. There had been times, early on, when Phillip had feared for his own life, thinking that at any moment Yutramaki might grab his long band of hair and lop off part of his skull just to make a point. The considering, even tempered side of the man was never in evidence during these visits. Phillip began to see that the chief was acting deliberately. Yutramaki had made it clear that he would not waver in his desire for guns. Phillip couldn't blame him for that. The neighboring tribes were divided. Some had a few muskets, others had none. A tribe as important as the Makah would require guns to preserve their status of strength amid the constant pestering between tribes. It was a recognized matter of salvation, and Phillip could see why Yutramaki was behaving in such a single minded fashion. Even, and Phillip had lately made a point of telling this to him hoping to alleviate some of the ferocity of his performance, allowing for the obvious fact that they would sooner rather than later run out of powder or shot, Yutramaki knew he could barter for or steal these things. These displays of intractable determination on Yutramaki's part, not only that he would not give up on muskets as the means of recovering the captives, but also the clear message that the Russians would not be left to their own devices. They were watched, limited in the territory they could safely mine for food. Yutramaki had shifted his pattern from random visits colored by much shouting and displays of knife wielding young men who would shout and gesture at the Russians as they gathered to watch on the far side of the river. Now he began to arrive at the same time. It was clear to Phillip that he intended to leave himself available in this way for Tarakanov to prepare a negotiating party. And so, at last, they had been ready. This visit had been quite different. Phillip, instead of being a clear slave and captive, mute by threat and meek by self-preservation, on this occasion Phillip stood beside the chief, and it was no coincidence now, Phillip noted, that Yutramaki had thrown him that knife, for here he was standing beside the chief, a knife in his own belt.

What must Tarakanov think of that?

Phillip had stood still and calm while Yutramaki made a long speech to Tarakanov. He spoke directly to him. He had asked Phillip the name of the man who was chief to these lost people and practiced saying it over and over until it came without hesitation, giving weight and strength to his meaning. Tarakanov, Phillip knew, had some Makah language, but Phillip did as he was asked and translated as best he could the full text of the speech. While he waited for Phillip to finish, Yutramaki stood with arms folded, clearly satisfied and in control. Phillip had kept his eyes on Tarakanov, trying to read any subtext in his features. But Tarakanov had not responded more than to say he would think it over, and turning to the Englishman who carried the musket that was the subject of such a dialog, he nodded curtly and stepped away. Phillip thought that would be the end of it, that they would leave, come back another day for Tarakanov's answer, but at that moment Yutramaki shouted at Tarakanov to stop. Phillip translated as quickly as the words came out. There would be no more time. They would trade, captives for musket (for they had at least agreed to only one of the two weapons, Tarakanov relying on their necessity to survive once the trade had been made). They would trade now because the Makah would be leaving their fishing village to return north to Ozette. Phillip was stunned.

Now as Phillip walked away from Anna's lodge wiping his face, that sense of irrevocable fate flooded his heart, a heavy weight. He remembered Tarakanov's startled face and yet Tarakanov had seemed to know this was coming for he barely hesitated. Turning back to Yutramaki, he stuck out his hand in total surrender. It would be so. And in that moment, Phillip realized what this meant for him. In just a few days, this new life that he had adapted to so completely would be turned upside down. And then what? What he wanted to do just at that moment was find Raven and hide in her arms, but in truth he wasn't sure what her response would be. What would she think of this news? Would she shrug as Anna had, and give Phillip up? He thought she loved him. He had seen other couples in the lodges express these feelings of affection, of devotion to each other, Raven wasn't a primitive being without heart or soul. Did she love him? And if she did, was it enough? Phillip felt as if his chest would burst. He made his way down to the shore and took off at a trot, and then a full run. He ran and ran until his lungs felt they would pop and his throat ached with the effort, and then he turned around and ran back.

When he reached the river, Raven was waiting for him. She was sitting on a huge log—something the river had spit out during a storm many years before—sitting quietly, patiently in a rare moment of complete focus on his approach. She watched intently as he came to her and did nothing as he threw himself down in the sand at her feet, unable to speak. She looked at him for a while, waiting while he caught his breath, and then very slowly she stood up and straddled his body.

The Navigator

Bulygin roused himself to a sitting position, clutching his ragged coat around his frail body. In the months that passed since the wreck of his ship his body seemed to have consumed itself until now his clothes hung about his frame in loose folds. While none of the survivors thrived, the navigator had fared the worst, his cough growing more dangerous sounding with the passing of every long damp night. And yet, now, with the news that Tarakanov had at long last made a deal, that he would recover his wife from the savages, well, and if he died then, so that would be the will of God, he would have done his best by his wife. He closed his eyes and waited to hear Tarakanov enter the fort and come to him.

"Three days time," Tarakanov said without prelude,

knowing this was all that Bulygin wanted to hear. "Three days. And then we will shift from this place and take our chances with the coast."

The Englishman stood beside Tarakanov looking thoughtful. There were times when he seemed the most trustworthy of them all. Certainly he had been the most useful. His skills at trapping hadn't been overtaken by any two of the other men combined, and in the moments when anyone had a sense of humor about them at all, much was made of this disparity, calling the sailors worthless eunuchs on land, which caused one young sailor to query Bulygin privately as to what was that thing called a "eunuch"?

The Englishman now wore a fur coat, the product of twelve mink that had made meals for them all and provided skins that he had sown with gut threads. Every so often the man was struck by a fit of itching, but otherwise, his warm coat was much envied by the others. He had kept himself busy and healthy and had become indispensable, but Tarakanov and the navigator both felt uneasy around him, instinctively fearing that the Englishman didn't need them as much as they obviously needed him. On days when the Englishman followed his trap lines far into the forest, the men waited nervously for his return. Anything could happen, mountain lion, bear, native attack, but most of all, the others wondered if he would just up and leave them, taking the musket with him.

Standing behind Tarakanov as the chief had laid out his terms, Tarakanov could feel the Englishman and some of the others resisting. Tarakanov himself had confided this to Bulygin at the same time that he let him know that there would be no choice but to make a deal. Clearly Phillip and the others could not, or would not escape, they'd had plenty of time in which to effect a run for it. No, Bulygin agreed, the actions of the Englishman now could ruin their last chance of survival. He would have to give up the musket, and then the others would have to watch him.

The idea of getting his wife back revived Bulygin and by evening he was sitting with the others around the fire chewing pieces of smoked fish and smoking pipes filled with Indian tobacco, a noxious smelling concoction offered around by the Englishman. He had carved a simple pipe, curing the bowl to hold a pinch of finely chopped leaves. This he packed tightly and lit with a rush from the fire, inhaling deeply as he did so. Once the pipe was lit, he smiled broadly and passed it to Bulygin.

"Good for yer cough, mate."

Bulygin took a long pull on the pipe and came away choking which made the others laugh.

"Give her here," said Tarakanov longing for a smoke. He held the pipe for a draught or two, feeling the smoke ease his chest. Soon the pipe had been passed among all the Russians. They ate without thought to storehouses. Now that they would be leaving they would only take small amounts of food with them. There would be food in plenty along the shore: clams, crabs, mussels and birds. The spirit of the day held them long past their usual time for sleep and they sat enjoying songs sung for them by the young Russian men who sang strong and clear tunes and occasionally leapt to their feet to dance in the Russian fashion, kicking out their legs, leaping up and down, slapping their thighs like drums, all the while the Englishman passed the pipe.

Bulygin slept deeply and well, thinking that the smoke had indeed been good.

Tarakanov, Diary Entry
Queets River

We have made a bargain with the Makah, guns for the woman and the others. We will make the exchange in three days time. There is no need to hide the extra powder and shot, or the extra musket, for the Englishman has disappeared and taken it all with him. He left us with enough to effect our barter. We should be grateful for that.

We will regain the captives and hope they are fit enough to travel. Bulygin seems revived in his joy at the news. I hope it does last. As the rivers begin to rise from winter rains and run-off, they become more difficult to cross. We will have a sorry time of it, but we must try to find our way south to Gray's Harbor. God keep us safe.

11

The Rag and Bone Man

Anna

Yutramaki had the habit now of holding her small body inside the warm cavern of his own, wrapping his legs with hers and folding his arms about her waist. In this position he would fall asleep, and it seemed to Anna that he did not move a single muscle until many hours later when he would wake, alert and friendly. She was grateful for his warmth and grew to accept that he would remove her blanket before taking her to him, and that it was his body that kept her warm at night. Later in the day, after he had left her by the lodge fire, she would notice that their smells had become joined as one. She wondered if he noticed that. They did talk, in their manner. And in the months of their captivity Anna had learned many words from Phillip as well as from the women who worked alongside her. Her clan women, she reminded herself with a small smile.

Anna thought a lot about Phillip and Raven and love. She didn't know love. But there was tenderness in the way Yutramaki dealt with her. She knew him for a just man, even a kind man. And while she never refused him, never would dare to refuse him, she noticed lately, since her time away being cleansed, that he would give her a moment's hesitation in which to what? Prepare herself? Refuse? Make some excuse? The only excuse acceptable, she knew, would be her blood. So what was he hesitating for? Was there something missing in their joining? She couldn't know, and there was no one to ask. He was more gentle than the navigator ever was, and his attention rarely varied. He would come to her, pull gently at her blanket, push his body against her back and begin to move, holding her to him.

She noticed Phillip and Raven doing other things. Small kisses and caresses. Once she had seen Phillip slip his hand inside Raven's blanket and cover her breast with his palm. Raven had smiled and leaned into him as if she had enjoyed that. Anna had experience of her husband pinching and slobbering at her breast, and was revolted by it. Since seeing Phillip with Raven, she wondered about that.

Anna went to the far end of river marsh at high tide, it was her special place to bathe, to be alone briefly. She knew that the clan mothers watched her go, knew that they allowed this little bit of privacy now. She was bonded to them, in blood, in ritual, and that manufactured a level of trust that at least extended to bathing alone. She left her blanket and the pouch containing her comb at the water's edge and walked into the shallows where she squatted in the water for a while, just letting the cold water numb her lower body, her arms crossed over her breasts. It was the contrast she longed for. Some measure of shock, something that would bring more feeling to her inside, for she feared she was without feeling now. Perhaps she had always been so.

She scrubbed with the moss and sand and rinsed in the water so cold now that her teeth chattered but she took pleasure in it, in forcing her body to withstand this as something inconsequential. At last she came ashore and sat on her blanket, still naked and no longer with even a thought to someone perhaps watching her. Those feelings of modesty were gone. She pulled the comb through her long hair, tangled as it always was in the early morning. She applied a small amount of whale oil and combed it through until the dark long hanks gleamed as she twined them into braids and wrapped each braid on either side of her head as the clan mother had shown her.

The wooden comb brushed against her breast and she felt the sting of her nipple respond. She covered her breast with her hand. "Ow." Softly she patted her breast, covering her nipple, remembering Phillip and his lover. Her nipple responded, and she felt a tugging deep in her belly, a tingle of response between her legs, something completely new, a damp sense of well being. *Was this love?* Anna didn't think so, and feeling the cold, she dressed with haste.

She spent the day helping the women of her clan pack up all of the smoked fish, carefully wrapping stacks of dried fish in the huge leaves of ferns, gathered green that morning. The men, she was told, would paddle the canoes north.

The women showed her with their hands the zigzag pattern they would make, working against the currents and the on-shore swells. The women, protected by the remaining men, would carry great baskets full of dried fish. Anna was told that many, many people lived in their permanent village. It was time to return and make ready for the whale hunt. The women became hushed and excited when they talked about the preparations for the whales. Anna worked hard and listened attentively. The women told her that in the next month the men would stay away from their beds. This made the women giggle and make jokes, but underneath there was a serious reverence about the task of hunting the whale and the ritual celibacy it required. The men needed their strength, they needed to fast, to pray to their spirit guides, and conserve their power in order to be ready for the honor of hunting the whale.

The idea that Yutramaki would leave her alone in her bed was disconcerting. Anna realized that her only real connection to him was the one they made together. And while she had not resisted, in fact, she felt she had made it clear she was malleable, otherwise, why would she have been adopted into the Frog clan? But she had not, she admitted to herself, had not participated. Not the way she had seen between Raven and Phillip. She longed to ask Phillip if....what....if it was different between them because of love? She couldn't form the words, it was out of the question. And now, she would be traded back to her husband, Bulygin, and Yutramaki and his band would move north back to their whaling village, the most permanent of their seasonal villages, and it would be done. At least for her. But what of Phillip? Would he refuse. Would love for Raven make him stay?

Anna realized all this was making her angry. Why had Yutramaki not told her? Why had he sent Phillip to say what would happen? And why hadn't he commented since then, given her any idea at all of what was going to happen. Was he planning to trick the Russians again? Trick them so that he could keep her? It was a romantic notion, a wild idea, and yet, he'd achieved just that already, so why not? He wanted her, so he would trick them again, and have her, and Phillip, and the musket. She spent the afternoon crafting the scene in her head. Of course, he wouldn't tell her that, for fear her loyalties remained with Bulygin and the others. And they should, shouldn't they? She was shocked at herself. She should be terrified that Yutramaki might well intend to do just that. Kill the others and steal what he wanted. Why not? He had the power to do it. Why wasn't she in a panic at the thought?

She sat alone at the end of the day, outside the ring of firelight, leaning against the lodge wall. Her mind was awash with ideas, she chewed her fingernails and addressed herself to each idea as it came. It was all she could do, try to reason with her fear. She didn't want Yutramaki to come in to the lodge and see her face, she knew he could read all of her emotions, he would know that she knew what he was planning. Or thought she knew. Two days time. Two more nights with him and then it would be done.

Anna hadn't seen Bulygin since her abduction, and the others only briefly in the drama Yutramaki performed using her as bait, but Phillip had told her how they did each time he returned with the watch. She knew that her husband was very ill. She knew that they were desperate for food, for rescue. Phillip described them to her in detail, she demanded to know exactly what state they were in. He had come back the day before and honestly reported that while Tarakanov said Bulygin was alive but ill, Phillip had not seen him this time at all. He could be dead.

She shivered, and stood to tend the fire, adding three new logs to the dwindling embers. Where was Yutramaki? Suddenly she realized it was far later than his usual time to come for food.

By the time the door flap opened and Yutramaki stepped in, three more logs had been added to the fire and Anna had begun pacing back and forth. He stepped in, and her fears disappeared. She flung herself into his arms, catching him off guard and off balance with her uncharacteristic action. Never before had she initiated any congress between them, not of speech or action, she had always responded, acquiesced, withstood. She had determined her place and found solace within it. Reactive, without passion.

Yutramaki held her by the arms, watching her face without showing any emotion of his own.

"Humph! Jesus!" he said.

"I want to ask you something…"she said.

He lifted one eyebrow and stepped back, waiting.

She was wringing her hands and resumed her pacing. As she paced she talked, and all of the things she feared, all of the scenarios she had conjured up in her mind about what might happen came tumbling out. She talked too fast and twice Yutramaki had to step in front of her to make her stop and slow down and repeat what she had said, until at last she had said everything she could think of to say. She had gambled, taken a chance that if she were completely honest with him about how frightened she was, that he would, in turn, be honest with her. But it was the last thing that she said, that made an impact on him and he grabbed her by the arm and made her come in front of him, and her face lit by the glow of the firelight, repeat exactly what she had just said.

"I don't want to go with them."

He looked surprised. She didn't think she'd ever seen him look surprised.

"I don't. There, I said it. Blessed Saint Anne save me, but I don't."

"Why?"

She shrugged at first, trying to find the right words.

"Safety, I could die, I probably will die, with them. Captured again by some other tribe, killed." She shivered, thinking of the torture she knew happened often.

"And?" he said.

"And?"

"Is that all?"

"Isn't it enough, then?"

He shrugged. "Could be."

He turned to face her. "Your man won't like it."

She blushed. Some part of her wished he didn't know that, know that she had a "man" as he put it.

"What if he is dead?"

He shrugged again. His complacence was beginning to annoy her. If she was willing to fight, shouldn't he be as well? He was making her force the issue, and he wasn't going to give her any help making this decision. It came as a shock…

the shock, the reality dawning on her, so her anger rose and burst.

"I want to stay with you." She said the words carefully and clearly and tinged with not a little anger, but controlled.

He smiled. "Good."

She exploded. "Good?! Is that all you can say? I risk my life, I give up all chance of my old life, my Russian life, to choose to stay with you, and all you can say is good?"

"You risk your life in leaving," he said. "You may stay."

"I *may* stay?!" She went for him, her hand raised. He caught it and pulled her to him, holding her still. She struggled but there was no point to it. He would hold her, pinioned, until she stopped struggling.

"I may stay," she repeated, her face muffled in his chest, changing the inflection just slightly, "but, how?"

It was late in the evening before they bedded down by the fire. They had talked, Anna with growing emotion and conviction, Yutramaki with acceptance and pragmatism. A plan was formed. Anna would accompany Yutramaki on the following day to confront her husband and the others. Phillip would come as well. Anna thought, but didn't say, that Phillip would be very glad of her plan. The Russians could choose to come to the Makah as slaves, or to go free; but Anna would stay, and Yutramaki would have the musket.

When she stopped talking and calmed, surrendering to fatigue and emotion, Yutramaki lay her down beside him and reached for the pin of her blanket. She stopped his hand with her own, and turned toward him, her hands pulling aside the blanket to expose her small breasts in the waning firelight.

She took his hand in hers and guided it to first one breast and then the other. She looked down at his hand and felt the frisson of warmth that she had felt before for herself sitting by the river. She sighed and moved closer, face to face, and while she wondered briefly if he knew the things to do, the smile on his face made it clear. For the first time, she closed her eyes.

He slept, but Anna stared at the fire. So much about this night had been different. He had made her feel wild inside, and full of power. And now, now she felt something shift low in her belly, and she ran her hands over her breasts and down, and felt she had become someone new.

Yutramaki

"Women are curious creatures, are they not?" Yutramaki said to Phillip the next day as they walked down to the canoes to begin the job of loading.

"Huh?" Phillip said, a wary expression on his face.

Yutramaki shrugged as he so often did when he was at a loss for words. And just as it seemed there was no more to be said on this subject, he spoke again.

"The woman wants to stay."

Phillip stopped dead and then had to hurry to catch up. Yutramaki had not hesitated and was striding out of earshot as if the conversation had just ended instead of just begun.

"Are you joking?" Phillip said, hesitantly touching Yutramaki's sleeve. "I mean no disrespect," the boy added.

Yutramaki wasn't used to being touched beyond the heat of battle or sex, but he granted the boy some cautious allowances for not truly knowing his place. He stopped and waited for Phillip to form his words.

"Anna you mean? She told you that? Did she really?" Phillip's face showed a cloud of both surprise flooded over by growing relief. "Did she really..." This time he spoke so softly that Yutramaki barely understood that he had merely repeated himself.

"She did," Yutramaki said without elaboration.

"But, what of....what of...of the others...and myself!"

"Anna says she will convince them." Yutramaki gave his usual indeterminate shrug and then grinned.

"And so I...?"

"Of course!" Yutramaki slapped Phillip a hearty clap on the back. "Sure and you're one of us already!" His accent fell into some faintly tinged Irish patois which startled Phillip into a huge grin that Yutramaki didn't understand, but he didn't allow the confusion to alter his good humor. This long negotiation was turning out exactly as he would have wanted. If Anna convinced the rest of her party to come under his protection he would win all the weapons and have slaves to trade for many months gathering even more honor for his clan.

"Of course," he said again and he laughed and laughed as he walked down to the beach.

Midday he went looking for Anna. He had agreed to take

her up to the Russian fort where they would exchange the new terms of the trade. He had absolute confidence in her decision and in her ability to convince her fellows. She was right, wasn't she, they would not survive a moon's passing before succumbing to death one way or another? He hid his approval and excitement as was befitting a chief, and entered his lodge with a serious countenance that made Anna jump.

"What is it?" she said.

"It?" He knew what she meant but didn't want her relaxed for this. He wanted the tension high. He grabbed her by the arm and held her tight until she cried out.

"You're hurting me!" Her voice registered shock.

"Yes," he said. "Do not forgot who you belong to today." Though he had no doubt whatever that she was his, not after last night, he needed her to remain frightened of most things in order to be convincing.

It hadn't been a question. Anna gave no response but he saw the fear in her face and knew he had achieved his goal.

"We go now," he said and strode out of the doorway knowing she would hurry at his heels like a pup. Several of the men were waiting near the trail, including Phillip who could not help grinning at Yutramaki as he came abreast. He hoped Phillip's elation would help the negotiation, not hinder it. He still felt that convincing his enemy to do things his way based on fear was the quickest means to success.

It took only a moment to gain the attention of the full company of Russians as the party approached the fort. Yutramaki had whistled a piercing call that was unmistakably human and irrevocably authoritative, gaining the active response of the exhausted watch who ran back inside the fort shouting.

This time it was Anna that Yutramaki pulled forward to speak. His manner remained indifferent, and while he was not gentle with her, neither was he cruel. He needed her to present her case not from any attraction to him or fear of him, but from a sense of practicality and safety.

"Do not look at me," he said firmly in her ear. "Do you hear?" He felt her fear rise up and was satisfied when she looked down rather than at him. If she understood his methods and motives, she didn't say so. It didn't matter to him, as long as she did as she was told.

Tarakanov approached them alone. Yutramaki instinctively knew something was already different. He searched the faces of the twenty odd men standing in front of the fort now. No Englishman.

All right then. Something to hunt.

To confirm he held out his hand palm up. "No English?" And he saw the surprise on Tarakanov's face. Surprise he'd paid that much attention. Or surprise that perhaps Anna and Phillip had been so talkative about their companions. *No matter, I'll deal with the English later.*

He gave Anna a gentle prodding at the back of her skirts. They had agreed the night before that she would wear her old clothes. She was dressed in her shift and skirt with her white linen shirt tucked into the high narrow waist of her gown. He found himself thinking that he liked her dressed like this, now that she was his, he liked that he could see her breasts through the thin cloth, liked that her waist was narrow and her buttocks defined beneath the soft gathers of her skirt.

He was enjoying these thoughts while he listened to Anna speak to Tarakanov. He knew she would not deflect from what they agreed she would say. He could tell simply by her tone of voice that she was doing as she was told. Thinking about her in this other way kept his face impassive and powerful.

"No!" Tarakanov's first words of response didn't surprise either Yutramaki or Anna though the vehemence of his tone made all the Russians jump, including Anna. Yutramaki let her continue to argue her point. She talked fast, her words sometimes too much of a jumble for him to comprehend exactly but he caught the important ones—bears, Hoh tribesmen, the Quileute to the south, the lack of opportunity to gain a ship in the near future, how a ship might as easily come here as anyplace else—and he heard her speak of his kindness to them all, pointing out that no one had been beaten or tortured and that, in fact, she and Phillip had been "adopted", this last causing a departure explaining "what in the devil" she meant by that.

Yutramaki realized Anna had deliberately kept her head scarf on, and had held her body so that her tattooed cheek was on the side away from Tarakanov's view. She chose this moment to turn to face him fully and he had the pleasure of seeing Tarakanov's shock at what he saw.

Tarakanov stepped back and ran his hands through his hair. He knew Anna at her word now. Yutramaki could see that. The two men looked at each other and Tarakanov spoke first.

"Will you kindly wait here and I'll speak to…to the men,"

he looked at Anna and nodded, "to Bulygin. He's inside. He isn't well, Mrs."

Yutramaki waved at him and sat down, pulling his blanket around him.

Tarakanov turned to cross the river and then turned back suddenly. "And you, Phillip? Are ye in with this scheme?"

"Ay, I am," Phillip said and sat down next to the chief.

Tarakanov shook his head. "Ay, well…"

They didn't have to wait long for a response. From the fort came explosive shouting, and then Bulygin crashed out of the doorway carrying the one remaining musket, Tarakanov hard on his heels also shouting, but it was Bulygin that Anna and Yutramaki understood first.

"I'll kill you before I let you stay with that bastard!" he said, screaming at Anna from the middle of the river. He was knee deep in water, staggering to hold himself upright against the flow and the slippery rocks, struggling to load the musket; but in his weakened state he wasn't faring well. His face went red, he went down on one knee in the icy water, waving the musket high over his head as he did so. Tarakanov caught up to him, grabbed his arm reaching for the musket and they struggled.

"Stop it, man! Ye'll get us all killed!" Tarakanov and Bulygin tussled over the musket each one trying to gain control but careful not to cast it into the river. "Stop!" Tarakanov cried again. By now the others gathered around, pulling Bulygin to dry ground on the rocky point. The man was crying pitifully now. No longer a threat.

Yutramaki never even stood up, but he noticed Anna

stagger as if she'd been struck. Phillip had instinctively changed position to cover Anna from gunfire, and now he led her back down the trail toward a safer range waiting for Yutramaki to tell him what to do. He stood, nodding to Phillip, and motioned to Tarakanov.

"We go. You will decide by tomorrow. Either way, Anna stays with me." He moved off toward where Anna stood, put his hand on her shoulder and led her down the path. He could tell by touching her that she was stunned.

Bulygin howled at the words, spitting with rage. "You whore!"

Anna

She sat by the fire, dazed and silent. Yutramaki left her alone, there was still much work to do before leaving their fishing village in the morning. Tomorrow would be a long hard day for everyone. She felt drained, used up. She knew Yutramaki was happy to be heading north back to their main village on the Cape. She had not allowed herself any uncertainty, and in doing so, had tried not to think about the changes ahead. She knew from his stories that the village was quite large; several hundred people lived there as four separate clans. Would they be as accepting of her or would there be trouble and regrets to come? She diverted her mind from these thoughts

214 • The Navigator's Wife

as best she could, first with the work of the moment, preparing food for the evening, and readying their belongings
for travel. She had little or nothing to pack for herself, but it
was left to her to collect his things and stow them carefully
in baskets and hide bags. The smoked fish and other items
that must stay dry would be carried north by the women.
And the Russians, she thought suddenly. It was only a half a
dozen leagues north, but it would be hard and fast walking
through enemy territory carrying heavy loads. Now that she
had made up her mind to follow Yutramaki, she found that
rather than easing her mind, an entirely new set of problems
and worries arose. Bulygin's hatred spilled over her again as
she replayed the scene in her mind. His spitting self-righ-
teous anger! What did he think had been happening to her
all this time? She felt ashamed and angry at the same time,
the anger flowed up from her belly. Struggling to keep back
tears—Yutramaki didn't like tears, *but then, did any man?*—
she forced herself to focus only on the task at hand. *If only I
didn't care a whit what happened to the others.*

Phillip's lean form standing in the doorway startled her.
Her mind had been lost in the red fog of anger. She straightened and went to him, her arms out, but he stopped her, taking her elbows and, with a backward look outside, moved in
by the fire. She looked at him in surprise. He'd never placed
distance between them before, he'd always welcomed her
friendship with a matter of fact complaisance, perhaps born
of his youth and his lack of motherly companionship.

"Phillip, what is it?" Anna said, and inside she thought
Now what? How much more can I bear?

"'Tis nothing. Just…well…" and Phillip blushed. He had

a diffidence that was so attractive, Anna could see why Raven had taken to him so easily, why the others accepted him.

"Nothing, is it?"

"Well, just, with tempers so frayed, I wouldn't want Yutramaki to get the wrong idea."

"The wrong…?" Anna shut her mouth, suddenly realizing what he meant, and then smiled broadly at the idea. "Oh, Phillip," and she started to laugh. He looked injured.

She held her hand over her mouth and tried not to laugh but something very like hysteria was building and she felt tears start down her cheeks. She flapped her hand at him.

"No, no, don't be embarrassed," she said, managing to choke out the words around near guffaws of inappropriate laughter. *Dear God, have I been that much on edge?*

Phillip stood watching her, arms folded, trying not to smile, trying to remain slightly insulted but failing at both. At last he turned as if to leave.

"But wait! Phillip, you haven't told me why you're here. What d'you need?" Anna wiped her face on her shirt sleeve and tried to calm herself.

"Yutramaki told me to come," Phillip said. "He says to be ready at first light. I'm to bring down what needs stowing in the canoes." Phillip cast a look around the lodge.

"Oh," Anna said. "Phillip? Are you, are you afraid? Have we made the right decision?"

Phillip held her gaze, weighing her question carefully.

"Aye. We have. Any other choice would be the death of us."

"And Raven?" Anna said. "Is she glad of the news?"

He grinned.

———

Anna stayed by the lodge fire all evening, sitting between great baskets of packed fish. Nerves kept her from joining the others in the family lodge, she would only be in the way, they would be busy themselves, arranging bundles, it would only heighten her tension. In the morning everything would change again, but tonight she wished Yutramaki would come to her. Whatever had been between them felt sullied by the events of the day and she felt a need to reassert her position, to look in his eyes and find where he placed her. She needed him to need her.

Whether by intent or by necessity, he did not come, and he did not come, and at last Anna ate a small portion of the food she set out for them to share, and curled up in her blanket by the fire. She could hear the chatter and laughter coming distantly from the family lodge, they were all up late preparing for the early departure. Their voices excited at the prospect of seeing their village, seeing their families, carried from lodge to lodge, merry and cheerful.

Long into the night, Anna lay quietly without sleep. All around her was darkness and quiet, and still sleep would not come to her. The constant replaying of the events of the day waned. She began to focus once again on Yutramaki. Perhaps he would not come to her at all? He had not spoken that afternoon, not once as they returned to the fishing village. He walked behind her, and this was unusual, it was his habit to walk in front, she supposed as chief, he felt that was where he belonged, and he relied on his lieutenants to watch her; but this time he walked behind her and it had made her jittery, made her walk faster. Several times she had lost her footing on the narrow concave path and stumbled. He had stopped and waited for her to regain her feet, but didn't give her a hand, didn't comment. It was left to Phillip to mind her, but even he seemed intimidated by Yutramaki behind them watching instead of striding off down the path assuming they would keep pace. Anna rubbed her arms. She felt bruised, but she knew the bruises were inside her skin, not great purple welts, badges of honor, but a sense of hurt that would not heal.

She thought about Phillip and Raven and about what love was. This was her calming device, her way of distracting herself from fear. She would conjure images of Phillip and Raven talking, engaging, making love and try to imagine what they felt for each other, and how that feeling had happened. The only time the word "love" had come up in her life directly had been during her marriage ceremony. And then it had seemed the priest had placed so much more emphasis on the word "obey" that followed hard on the heels of the sole romantic word, that she had barely time to consider—did Bulygin love her? No. She didn't think either of them knew the word for what it was.

Anna woke to a cold fire and an overwhelming stench of fish. She was curled in a ball, her face pressed against one of the baskets full of dried fish. Her stomach gave a lurch and as she came up on her knees she threw up violently into the fire pit.

Yutramaki was not there. She wondered if he had come into the lodge at all during the night. While it seemed as though she hadn't slept at all, clearly she had, and soundly so, for the fire to have turned to ash. Of course, Yutramaki would not have stoked the fire, not with the people decamping this morning. She could hear activity, sometimes someone with a load would brush against the lodge. Anna wiped her mouth, straightened her clothes into some sense of order, feeling for the first time in a long while a need for modesty, a need to portray a woman of respect. Was it because she would see her husband again?

My husband, my chief. She thought the words, and then she said them out loud.

"My husband. My chief." With each phrase she paused, exploring her inner response. *Do I feel nothing?*

She appeared in the lodge entry dressed as a Russian. Her Makah blanket was folded carefully and lay on the top of the basket that was to be her responsibility to carry. The basket held the strips of fish she herself had cut and dried, and while it was smaller than the baskets of the other women, it was heavy enough for someone unused to carrying such a weight supported solely by a strip of leather across her forehead. She stepped away from the basket as it sat at the ready and walked down to the river to wash. Alongside her clothes that morning when she woke was the jacket Yutramaki had taken to wearing. So he had been there, perhaps had not stayed. She wondered what he had thought, looking at her sleeping form. What had made him give back her jacket? Was it simply recognition that she might need the warmth? Or was there deeper implication. Now that the Russian negotiations had ended—any way it went today, the talks were over—perhaps he had only worn it to annoy Bulygin and Tarakanov. Or had he decided he didn't want her. The thought chilled her through. Goose bumps broke out along her arms and down her back. *Someone walking over my grave.* She smoothed her blouse, brushing bits of duff from the full sleeves, and straightened the black folds of her skirt. The pattern of tiny grey flowers and simple velvet binding on the bodice of her jacket was nearly worn away now.

She splashed water over her face, unplaited her hair and combed it through carefully winding it in a twist at the back of her neck and covered her head with her shawl, completing her transformation back to Russian wife. Her hand went to her cheek where the tattooed frog sat ready to leap.

"Well, not exactly all Russian," she said.

"What?"

She jumped, so lost in her thoughts she hadn't heard any-one come up behind her. It was Yutramaki. She turned with relief showing in high color on her cheek.

"Oh!" Anna's hand flew to her mouth and her rebellious stomach gave the second lurch of the morning.

"It is time," Yutramaki said. He motioned to her to follow him.

She fought her nausea, not able to respond beyond com-plying with his order. She thought he didn't look angry, or even distant. That was good. But what his thoughts really were, she had no notion. She was all at sea, a phrase she had come to know as a reality. Like one of those great birds float-ing on a vast ocean, entirely free of land. She'd hated the life on board Bulygin's ship. She had been hasty in her judgment, erecting a disagreeable wall of silence between herself and the navigator. She would like to have the chance to remedy the distance that had become manifest, to exchange this pelagic existence for the security of landfall.

These thoughts carried her along the path. Yutramaki was taking her back up to the Russian fort, taking her with him, she was sure, in case they needed more convincing, or more threats. Now that she was out in the air, bright and fresh as it was, her stomach settled and she felt more like herself, yet there was always a fierce edge of fear that she had no control over, fear that pushed her now to keep up with her chief, to focus on just one thing, surviving the day.

They reached the fort to find the party of twenty or so Russians standing uneasily together at the spit midstream. As they approached Tarakanov broke away from the others and crossed over for the first time to Yutramaki's side of the river, stepping carefully across the swift shallows.

Yutramaki stopped and Anna came alongside him.

"Surely, this is a good sign?" she said as much to herself as to those around her.

She searched the group of ragged and harried looking men for Bulygin, finding him at last standing between two of the Russian promyshlenniks, big powerful men, even hungry and bone weary as they clearly were. She realized they were holding him, one at each arm. Bulygin's face was pale and thin, the bones of his cheeks prominent with hunger and the threat of death, the two bright red spots of the coughing sickness seemed unreal, as if someone had painted them onto a white canvas, one on either cheek, high up. It looked as though he had gone mad, emptied himself, and what was left was this shell, this rag and bone man.

Anna felt sorry for him, nothing more. She felt guilt

that she didn't want to run to him, nurse him back to health, throw her arms about his thin frame and make him forget what had happened to her. No, nothing. She turned her attention to Tarakanov and what he was saying to Yutramaki.

"We'll take yer offer of safe shelter and hope you will treat us well," he said, "well as you've treated our young boy there, and our navigator's wife." Tarakanov motioned to a few of the men who, stood a bit apart from the others. "All's except those men there, they've decided to take their chances."

The men looked uneasy. Anna recognized them as the strongest of the Russians. Perhaps they would survive.

It seemed to Anna that he'd made the distinction deliberately, not using her name, but rather her position, reminding the chief that she was a woman of rank, at least as far as their little group went. She though Yutramaki didn't notice. In fact, it was clear he cared little for anything beyond the one remaining musket that Tarakanov now held draped over one arm.

Yutramaki shrugged at Tarakanov's words, a gesture neither respectful nor alien, merely accepting; as if the burden of ten instead of twenty more slaves should be enough compensation to the Russians as well as to himself. He stepped toward Tarakanov and took the musket in his hands, shouldered it as he had seen the Russian do, turned around and marched off down the path, Tarakanov and Anna close behind, the others stretching out along the narrow margin as best they could until at the end of the line came the navigator and his caretakers. No one looked back at the little group of remaining men, no one shouted last minute good-byes.

They were given no welcome and no time. Each man was shown to his burden and set on the way with the Indians. Anna swung her basket to her back and fitted the tumpline across her forehead, leaning her weight over to adjust her balance for the additional force. She found Phillip waiting for her. Yutramaki and his men launched their canoes and ferried everyone across the river, a process that took time, time in which Anna and Phillip were at last able to speak briefly with the new captives.

Anna said no, she hadn't been mistreated, truly. Phillip said she spoke the truth and chattered on excitedly explaining to the men where they were going, and what he knew of what they might find once they arrived at the big village. Then it was their turn to cross the river. There was much back slapping and congratulations for surviving. The men seemed pleased to relinquish control of their destinies for the time being. For a moment Anna became terribly frightened, recalling the scene months before when the Indians had tried to drown them, but no, not this time. Each canoe was heavily laden with baskets of precious food, the Makah themselves were chattering excitedly, happy to be heading home. The crossing was uneventful.

Anna rode in the canoe with her husband. Yutramaki paddled, sitting behind her at the back. She said nothing, terrified of insulting him, terrified that her husband would turn on her. Her husband didn't speak to her, didn't acknowledge her presence. *Ah, so you're angry still. Or is it the fever?* She looked at him thoughtfully and pursed her lips. *Just as well, for what is there to say?*

Tarakanov, Diary Entry
March, 1809

We depart our fortification with trepidation our party splitting into two groups, myself, Bulygin and nine others relying upon the convincing argument of Madame Bulygina that our purposes will be best served to offer ourselves into the care of these savages for whom we are now slaves. The others will take their chances, and try for Gray's Harbor. God grant all of us a ship soon.

Part III

Survival

12

The Month of No Women

Phillip

Yutramaki and the strongest paddlers had left the rest of the people on the north shore of the river and paddled out to sea. They would paddle the canoes home, navigating the familiar rock strewn waters and leave the others to carry the baskets of dried fish and make their way by land. Phillip was a little surprised the man would leave the Russians and the Makah women with just a few men to watch over them, but he observed that Yutramaki took it for granted that the situation they found themselves in reflected his good will, and therefore there was no reason to think anyone would bolt or cause trouble.

Raven was taking advantage of the relaxation of the sometimes grim and always pragmatic supervision of her chief, for though brother he may be, they had all felt the weight of his power and his agitation as the departure neared and she was no exception. The addition of Russian slaves gave everyone a greater part to play; ten or so new slaves was quite an undertaking for such a small band. In fact, some of the people had suggested trading off or even killing the weaker men—for they had all gathered round them as they came down from the fort, poking and prodding each one to see what there was to see, whether they had strength or carried valuable goods with them—they had been disappointed at the state the men were in and complained that they would just slow the group down, and require food, never mind the status possession of them incurred for Chief Yutramaki. And many of them shrank back in fear at the clear sickness that showed on Bulygin's face. Surely, they argued with Yutramaki, surely that one should be drowned.

But Yutramaki shook his head. Phillip heard him tell the others that he had not decided yet what would be done with so many slaves, but he would wait until they reached the cape and their village and counsel with the other clan chiefs. Without further talk, he had slipped into the prow of the massive ocean canoe and led his men away. Watching them shoot out the river's mouth and battle their way into the current, suddenly becoming so small against the great ocean swells, Phillip had been in awe of their skill and suddenly, surprisingly, longed to be with them, paddling a swift canoe instead of walking with the women.

Raven brought him back from his thoughts, clucking at him just like the bird for which she was named, a deep throated chuckling noise she made with her tongue. He smiled at the sound.

"You're not attending!" she said jabbing him playfully in the arm as she adjusted her baskets strap. "I was telling you all of the names of our year's moons."

"I heard you." Phillip grinned at her and proved his words by reciting what he could remember, for she was right, he had not exactly been attending. "Um, let's see, moon of picking salal berries, moon of strawberries, moon when the grey whale has babies, moon of salmon fishing…" He was ticking them off on his fingers as he spoke. She started to laugh, but kept pace with his recitation. "What comes after all the berries," he said, "I can't recall."

"Doing nothing!" She said it triumphantly with a big grin. "Well, almost nothing," and she poked him again.

He stole a quick kiss from her and succeeded in flustering the usually impenetrable façade of strength and control she wore. "And that sort of thing will stop this month entirely!" She was grinning hugely now, enjoying the look of complete bafflement on his face.

"Entirely?" he said, already feeling deprived. "But why? What have I done? You're not…"

"No! Oh indeed, no, no child here," she said patting her belly. "Not yet, anyway. No, it is our custom. The month before the great whale kill, men must not give away their power by sleeping with their women. They must fast, and counsel with their spirit guides. No women." She shook her finger at him.

Phillip was dismayed at her glee, wouldn't she feel the lack of him as keenly as he would—already did—just thinking about it, of her?

"But…"

"No. The shaman insists." Invoking the medicine man put an end to his amorous thoughts as well as the drift of the conversation.

"Oh, indeed." Phillip kept walking by her side but stayed quiet for a long while remembering the preparations his own people made for the whale harvest.

"And it begins tonight?" He was trying to recall where the moon had been last night and realized it hadn't been visible through a dense and damp fog.

She winked. "Tomorrow."

The Navigator

As it always is when one is retracing one's steps, the distances seemed shortened, the surroundings smaller, the world more manageable as the band made their way north toward Cape Alava. It seemed no time at all before the group of forty or so people came to the mouth of the Hoh river and the site of the dear ship, all but a skeleton by now, stripped by man and nature of every possible loose material: beam, board, sail, and rigging. When Bulygin saw it, he was stunned. His hopes for a profitable future had lain with her; and now he looked at her in dismay, her coppering stripped, her sheathing timbers struck off or floating nearby. Nothing was left. Tracks in the sand made it clear that parties of scavenging natives had made short work of dismantling the craft. He could see that they had built a sort of raft from the ship's timbers and float-ed it back and forth, off-loading whatever they could untie, unhinge, or rip free that wouldn't fit in a canoe. The raft itself was abandoned on the beach. He walked over to it and sat down with a heavy sigh.

"My God." He ran his hands over the raft's timbers. One of them was marked. *Sv. Nikolai*, it said in deeply cut and el-egant lettering. Perhaps it had been the cover of a gun locker or storage bay for coiled rigging. He traced the letters with his index finger. If he closed his eyes, he could remove the hell that was now his meager life, and by means of the regular caressing sounds of the ocean waves he could almost pretend he was onboard, taking his leisure on the quarterdeck.

"Nikolai?" Anna said. She was standing near. Not exactly in front of him, so that he was required to turn his head to see her full on.

What, was she afraid of me? he thought. *Perhaps she should be.* But he was too ill, too fatigued to bring the anger forth again.

"Aye." He looked up at her finally, pulling himself upright and smoothing his hands on his clothes as if to straighten them into some semblance of rank and propriety. He squint-ed. "Anna," he said. And then his eyes filled with tears.

He felt her hand on his shoulder, just resting there, not softening or restraining him in any way, just a weight on his shoulder that he couldn't acknowledge. He shook his head in shame and turned away, facing west toward the ocean, toward his past. He could tell that she remained where she stood for a while and then walked away.

One of the Makah women came toward him yelling, waving a stick. He got to his feet and shuffled off with a last look at his ship.

Phillip had told them they would only make camp one night as they went north before arriving at the village the natives called Ozette. The camp was set among the driftwood and boulders of the beach. The women set about collecting firewood immediately and settled into preparing food. They didn't rig any shelters for sleeping, and as evening came down so too did the fog. Soon everyone was wet with dew. The natives had cone shaped hats and capes fashioned of cedar bark that kept the damp off their heads and shoulders but the Russians were soaked through, huddled by the fire eating handfuls of dried salmon. Exhausted and feeling feverish, Bulygin ate what he could, curled up near the fire and fell asleep.

He dreamed of Anna and Yutramaki. The man was performing unspeakable acts against his wife's person while he watched, helpless to stop him. Yutramaki stood with his bare back toward Bulygin, pumping his strong gleaming body against Anna's small white frame. He looked over his shoulder at Bulygin and grinned as he pulled out, his member shining and rigid, and offered Anna's backside to him with a slap and a coarse gesture. Yutramaki's face was contorted into a leer, like an animal with a long red tongue. Bulygin was trying to move to help Anna or kill Yutramaki but he could do nothing, he couldn't even shout for the others to save her. He woke with a start to find Tarakanov shaking him.

"Wake up, man! God, Bulygin, ye must have been havin' some bad dream. Are ye all right then?" Tarakanov said.

Bulygin couldn't speak, but he nodded his assent. The dream stayed with him, as that sort of dream can so often do. He lay awake the rest of the dark night, and with the dawn stood near the Russians waiting for life to come to the camp, his eyes on Anna sleeping quietly across the way.

Anna

Their journey ended shortly after midday. The first signs of the village came in the arrival of a pack of five or six pale colored dogs who barked with enthusiastic welcome and no small amount of curiosity, sniffing first their familiar family members, and then, with more interest, the profoundly different smelling Russians. Anna had seen Raven hurrying Phillip along. She wanted to be the first to announce their approach and had quickly disappeared from sight in the morning. Now the dogs bounded back and forth between the approaching party and the village.

Ozette. The natives said Hosette, but the maps ignored the added "h". Anna said the word over. Yutramaki had described it to her. A few hundred people lived here. She looked around, surprised at how much it looked the way he had described it. Wooden houses perched on the edge of the land just above the beach. Plain rectangles, not fancy houses, but many of them had wild decorations painted on their exteriors. She could see whales, and bears, and wolves, all painted in black and red in the fancy way that she had seen them decorate their blankets and their woven mats so that the eyes and the mouths of the animals were huge and prominent. One of the largest houses was covered with these paintings and she saw that the doorway was the mouth opening of a bear painted on the exterior. She wondered if this was Yutramaki's own house. She looked for signs of him. She saw the canoes pulled up on shore and knew he would be nearby. She felt a sense of unease with Bulygin and the Russians behind her, a sense that she didn't want the new people she saw, the people of the village, to treat her as if she were just a slave like they were. She needed Yutramaki to make his possession of her known to everyone. She had already watched some of the villagers come down as if they were choosing among the others. Didn't they all belong to Yutramaki? She'd asked his mother this, and his mother had said yes, but Yutramaki would sell them for blankets.

"Blankets?" Anna said, shocked.

Yutramaki's mother had nodded. "More blankets, more power," she'd said.

Anna searched the crowds that were forming around the newcomers for Raven or Phillip or Yutramaki. She stayed as close by Yutramaki's mother as she could, following her with her burden basket, waiting to be told where to store it away. Yutramaki's mother was chattering affably with some of the other older women who came to welcome the woman home. She talked and laughed as if recounting a hilarious tale, sometimes pointing to Anna, sometimes to Raven and Phillip who had at last appeared and were helping to unload and store away the things they had carried.

Once the baskets had been properly stored, Anna was dismissed into the care of Raven who led her to Yutramaki's lodge.

"Wait 'til you see it, Anna," Phillip said. "It's beautiful, all carved and nothing at all like the fishing lodges. You have to crawl through the bear's mouth to get inside!"

Anna stood inside the great lodge letting her eyes adjust to the dark, for while there was a center smoke hole in the roof planks, and a good fire burning in the ring beneath it, as there were no windows in the lodge, the corners were darkly shadowed. Raven gave her a soft nudge forward and Anna collected herself, smoothing her skirts and brushing off her hands, wishing she had taken the time to wash and to change into her blanket. She felt out of place, alien, in the firelight and under the gaze of the men who sat talking and smoking at the end of the room. Raven nudged her again and she stepped forward toward Yutramaki who hadn't looked up, hadn't seen her yet, or had chosen to ignore them.

Anna was about to speak when her eyes caught the expression on the face of the man sitting with Yutramaki. He looked at her with hatred, with disdain. She stopped. He raised his arm, she saw he held a club perhaps as long as her forearm, carved with animal shapes. He shook the club at her and shouted something. His voice was harsh and strong, as though no one ever doubted him.

The shaman. Raven tugged at Anna's sleeve and stepped

up next to her. Anna didn't sense in Raven the fear she herself felt, but she saw that Raven was more than respectful. There was something about her demeanor, the carriage of her body, that changed in the presence of this powerful medicine man. Anna and Raven stood side by side, Phillip stopped behind them. Anna could feel his uneasiness as well, feel it seep into her own and begin to combine into panic. She had a feeling that Phillip was crafting an escape plan and would look out for her as well if he could.

Yutramaki looked up from the pipe the shaman had just passed to him and watched Anna impassively.

This is another test. Anna's agitation grew but she struggled to keep her fear controlled and unnoticeable. What did Yutramaki want her to do? If only Raven would give her some direction. Anna looked at the young woman, her eyes conveying her fears and questions. Raven gave a small smile and a quick tick of her head toward the platform where the men were seated. Anna's eyebrows lifted in disbelief.

"Watch and follow me," Raven said.

The girl turned to Phillip and took his hand, more the way a mother would lead an addled child than a woman would lead the man she bedded, but Phillip seemed willing enough. Anna watched the two approach the seated men. Raven seemed to introduce Phillip, and then Anna, whom she waved forward. As Phillip sat down, Raven and Anna stood before the men waiting permission. The shaman spoke. He seemed angry with Anna, or was it Yutramaki he was angry with? She wasn't sure. She couldn't understand enough of what he said. Phillip, however, had turned pale and was nervously fiddling with his knife. Anna opened her mouth to speak, but Raven, seeing her face, stayed her with a quick flap of the hand.

Just wait. She seemed to be saying. Anna looked at her feet and waited, letting the shaman's rage flow over her.

The shaman finished his rant with a shout and a gesture with his club, he stood abruptly and strode between Raven and Anna. Pushing passed Anna he struck at her with his club, just a glancing gesture but so full of anger, Anna had to step aside in order not to be forced down. She saw the look of distaste, of disgust in the shaman's eyes.

Yutramaki said something curtly to Raven, who took his words as orders not to be argued with. She took Anna by the hand and led her to the other end of the great house, deep in the shadows and behind a curtain of hides.

To her surprise, Anna found her personal belongings here, including Yutramaki's blanket, and a wooden bucket of clean water. Her things were piled carefully inside a square carved box. The top, when in place, became a table. Around the sides of the box were carved images in relief, again of animals, and again in the striking geometric way that the house paintings had been done. Raven gave Anna brief instructions. The girl was anxious for Phillip and not inclined to leave him to the mercy of Yutramaki and the after effects of an annoyed medicine man. Anna tried to ask what would happen next but Raven just shrugged. She really couldn't say.

Raven looked Anna over and sighed. She picked up the blanket and handed it to her along with the bone pin. And then she left.

Anna changed quickly, removing her Russian clothes, which she stored in the cedar box. She splashed water on her body, and rubbed herself all over with the soft young needle hemlock branches that sat in a pile next to the bucket. She combed and replaited her hair in the Makah style making two braids over her ears. Then she slipped the blanket over one shoulder and pinned it at the other. The transformation complete, she stood for a moment fighting the nerves that threatened her resolve.

Dear Saint Anne, let this be the right thing.

To her surprise she found Yutramaki sitting alone by the great fire. The other chiefs, if that was what they were, had retired to their family lodges. Raven and Phillip were nearby, she could hear them talking, but they were outside the entry performing some task at Yutramaki's bidding. Between them, at least, all was well. Anna stood before him and waited. He'd watched her all the while. Watched her walk toward him, she knew he saw she had left off her clothes for him, cleaned herself, and done over her hair. She stood close enough for him to touch her, and waited.

He looked at her, exhaling on the long pipe. At last he tapped the last of the tobacco out of the pipe bowl onto one of the fire ring stones, and with a sigh, he rose to his feet. He put out his hand and traced a finger along Anna's forehead. She put her hand up and followed his.

"Oh," she said, tracing the ridges made by the tumpline of the basket. She rubbed at them realizing she must look funny.

"Hmm," he said. And he sighed again.

Anna wondered at this. "What…" She wanted to ask what the shaman said. Was is about Anna herself, had he not forgiven her for the shame she had caused Yutramaki, or did he just not like foreigners, or foreign women, was it? She was at a loss for the words, though, there was not sufficient level of sophistication between them for what needed to be said.

"My mother," Yutramaki said, and Anna stopped dead and turned to him dropping her hands to her sides.

"Your mother…what?" Anna said gently.

"Loved the eeglishman. Very bad, the shaman says, very bad. So my father eeglish, bad, so I take you, eeglish, also bad, not big enough for a chief of the Makah." He took a breath and seemed to be thinking through his words before continuing. " Shaman says you will bring bad luck. He says I must trade you for blankets or make a present of you at potlatch."

"Potlatch? What…" Anna started to speak, to make a defense for herself, but he stopped her with his hand on her mouth.

"Not now," he said, and he led her back to the privacy of the dark corner.

She didn't want to join the group that congregated in the middle of the great lodge, but Yutramaki made her put her blanket on again and follow him back to the fire where there would be a welcome feast. He had made his ownership of her clear, laying her out on a pallet behind the skin curtain, he held her head fixed with his hand and watched her eyes as he moved inside her, and their sounds were ignored by the people she could hear coming and going about the business of the great lodge. Now, by the fire, some of the new people she had not seen before grinned at her, but somehow the dangerous attention that she had drawn at first had been diffused, at least for the time being. Without the shaman's menacing presence the villagers, both those who were now used to her, and those she was just meeting for the first time, seemed to take her presence as nothing unusual, treating her for the most part as a valued slave, perhaps more gently than most female slaves, she thought. They knew better than to bruise or otherwise abuse his mistress, but still she felt relieved that her status was clear to everyone.

Anna sighed. It was clear enough to herself as well. Her life meant little to anyone here, a pleasure thing to Yutramaki perhaps as insignificant as a child's toy, an insult to the shaman, another mouth to feed to the women of the village. She traced the patterns woven in her blanket studiously avoiding eye contact with those around her. She folded her hands tightly together and said a silent prayer. Surely she had been right in this. She must believe that. She must rely on his good will to see them finally to safety, to rescue.

Several of the clan chiefs entered the house followed by slaves carrying piles of blankets. Raven and Phillip came and sat with Anna. Phillip leaned toward her and cautioned her, "It will be for the others," he said with a hitch of his shoulder toward the piles of blankets.

The Russians were herded in as a group and held standing near the firelight to give the potential buyers the best view of their worth. Yutramaki and the other chiefs sat together as they had before on a raised platform at the north end of the house. One by one the Russian men were led forward, paraded before the dais and then returned to their group. Once or twice the group became agitated as someone resisted this process, and Anna heard clearly someone refuse to be bought and sold like a serf. It was Bulygin. She feared more than anything else now, that Bulygin would do something to bring attention to Anna, bring her into his pitiful influence and thus lower her own position. When it was his turn to be displayed, he balked. She could see him scanning the crowd, felt his eyes searching for hers.

"Anna!" His cry was choked with coughing, spittle flew, and those around him stepped back as they saw how very ill he was. He fell to his knees but two Makah warriors pulled him up again and dragged him from the lodge.

There was a sudden ruckus at the door and the sound of a drum so loud and fierce it sounded to Anna for a moment like thunder. The drumming rolled and rolled and came on into the room. It was the shaman, surrounded by boys, some beating on box drums, others blowing a heady smoke from long pipes, while still others held cups of scented water that they sipped and then spit out in a fine spray over anyone close enough to reach. She noticed that the people within reach of the smoke and the spray were glad of it, and seemed to try and capture the smoke and bring it over their faces like a mask.

"There must be more than a hundred people in here," Phillip said, "and those drums…"

"You like the drums?" Raven said. "Good thunder drum, he calls the spirits with them," she said pointing surreptitiously at the shaman. "Powerful thunderbird."

The entourage passed close by them. Anna looked down, hoping to avoid the shaman's attention, but it was not to be. Surely he had known where they were right from the start. She stiffened, waiting for him to beat her, or drag her out in front of the rest of the people to shame her in some other way. But he did not reach for her; instead, it was Phillip he touched lightly with his club.

At the sign, Raven instantly jumped to her feet, pulling Phillip with her. Phillip looked excited, but not frightened. Anna looked at the shaman and saw a placid face; no longer did the medicine man wear the fierce countenance of hatred.

Raven pushed Phillip forward until they stood in front of the shaman, side by side. The shaman spoke rapidly to Raven, repeating some words over and over as if trying to convince her of something. Raven responded with short but determined words.

She's claiming Phillip.

A shiver ran down Anna's arms and she crossed herself reflexively and then, embarrassed, looked around to see if anyone noticed her gesture. All eyes were on Raven, the drummers were increasing their tempo. They had taken themselves to the corners of the rooms and beat the drums in such a way that the sound rolled around the circle of villagers like thunder across a wide plain, over and over again, louder and louder. The drummers were waiting for a sign from the shaman to stop. He seemed to be waiting for the intensity around him to mount, for the people around him to be nearly insensible from the fury of the drums.

The medicine man lifted his club high over his head and spun in a circle, and the feathered cloak he wore over his shoulders swung out like wings. He gave a piercing whistle, bent low to the ground his cloak flowing out around him and then leapt high in the air as the crowd hissed in excitement and awe. It seemed to Anna that the shaman had become a great bird. He turned away and when she saw his face again, he wore a wooden mask carved with a huge long beak. She could just see his face beneath the mask, painted red. He swooped and dived again and again, twirling himself around and around never faltering, dodging his masked face up and down, and from side to side the way a raven would looking for prey.

Raven! Suddenly Anna understood. The shaman was calling Raven's spirit helper. She looked at the young woman and saw her face was passive, glazed with the constant drumming, captivated by the shaman's dance. Her hands hung loose at her sides, she seemed no longer aware that Phillip stood beside her. Her spirit animal had come for her. Anna thought that if the shaman told her at that moment to leap into the fire, she would go without question, go and be consumed by flames without a whimper. Anna shook herself, trying to stay free of the shaman's power. Everyone around her was entranced, she thought the shaman would keep dancing until he had each one of them completely in his power. She knew she should relent, give in to the flow of energy, of the thunder around her or risk the anger of the shaman. She let her eyes close, and her body instantly swayed with the drums, and she was his.

He screamed and the drumming shifted, the pounding coming from all corners of the house at once. Everyone present focused on the shaman and Raven standing before him. This wasn't about Raven and Phillip, Anna realized. This was about Raven alone. She was being honored in some way for her actions. Perhaps because of how she had helped kidnap the Russians? Suddenly Raven didn't look like a headstrong young Makah woman, flirting with Phillip, telling stories. Suddenly she looked like a high priestess, a queen. She stood as straight as the cedars in the forest, taut and ready, confident and in full power. She was aptly named, Raven, she loved the shiny things, the abalone shell beads and ear and nose rings. Tonight she had a circle of abalone through her nose, and her hair was bound loosely back with a dagger of colorful abalone shell. Small beads circled her arms. Her chest was bare, as was their custom, but her body glistened with a sheen of oil. Her short skirt of cedar rushes was decorated with bells and beads. She had known this would be her night and had taken great care with her dress.

As the whole village looked on, Raven stepped forward as the shaman spun his blanket of feathers out one last time, and disappeared into his feathered arms.

Phillip

He was stunned. One moment Raven had been standing confidently by his side and the next she was gone, it was as if the shaman had become the great thunderbird and taking her under his wing had fled the house with her. The whole village roared their approval. It seemed to him that they understood what had happened, in fact weren't surprised by it. They were proud of the power of their shaman to shape-shift, to control the people around him. They nodded and talked among themselves about the good omen that this was. It seemed to Phillip that the Russians were forgotten entirely.

This hadn't been just a slave auction. Selling the Russians to various clan chiefs was just the preliminary. The stacks of blankets around the hall had shifted. Some were great tall piles of blankets made of many different fibers, the beautiful feather ones on top of fine dog hair and mountain goat like the one Anna wore. There were stacks of cedar boxes, drums, and mats. The potlatch would begin once the meal was brought in and laid out for everyone to admire, and then to share.

But Raven had been the main event. He realized this now. He had thought that she planned to ask the shaman's blessing on them. But that hadn't happened. Now he realized she was merely claiming him publicly because she knew what the shaman was about to do. Phillip was being studiously ignored by everyone around him. Politely, but studiously ignored. He moved off toward Anna and sat down with her, shrugging his shoulders.

"Where?" Anna started to ask, but he shrugged again.

"Damned if I know," he said. What little he did know, he told her. "This is what they call a potlatch. They gather all their wealth and lay it out for everyone to see, and then they give it away," Phillip said.

"They do what?"

"They give it all away: slaves, blankets, boxes, everything. Of course, they're giving it to each other, so there's something of an equal exchange, but it's a notion, isn't it? To stockpile all this with the express intention of making a gift of it. This one tonight must be to honor to beginning of the fasting season. You know, Anna, the men will fast this month so that they have all their strength for the whaling come next month."

"Fasting doesn't seem like it will make them strong," Anna said, shaking her head. "I didn't know."

"Er, fasting, um, ye know, from their women." Phillip blushed furiously, but as understanding slowly came to Anna's incredulous face he couldn't help but laugh at her.

"Yup, all month. And Raven seemed right glad of it too." Phillip was chagrined but became philosophical. "I suppose it'll do no harm, eh?"

"I don't know," Anna said, feeling her own security shift again. "And Raven, what of Raven and the shaman?"

"She was chosen, was all she'd say," Phillip said. "But she seemed proud of it. She told me she'll help with the whale hunt, the kill, and the distribution of the meat. It's a particular honor, done to her and to Yutramaki, for a woman to go along. It's 'cause of her skill with the paddle too, of course."

As the atmosphere of drama shifted to one of cheerful dining around them, Phillip waited for Raven to reappear by wandering among the people, some of whom slapped him on the back in congratulations for belonging to such a powerful woman, some ignored him—those were mostly the new people he had not formally met—and others, the women, smiled shyly at him and turned away. He sought out the Russians who were eating a hearty offering of venison cooked in a soup with roots dug from the marsh inland, a welcome change from the fish diet of the past months. The men were nervous, clinging together in a corner of the hall, knowing soon they would be separated and sent to the houses of their new owners. Tarakanov had spent all day with Yutramaki. He was explaining now how it would be as Phillip came into the group.

"Ah, Phillip, ye'll help me explain, ay?" Tarakanov rarely deferred to anyone; but Phillip supposed him right in thinking he'd need all the force of his personality to keep the other men from bolting in fear and no doubt being slaughtered as a result.

Phillip rubbed his nose. "Ay. Well. You've been sold off by the chief, Yutramaki, there. For blankets." He looked at the men, gauging the impact of his words. They looked appropriately insulted. Phillip reminded himself not to tease; his own position was far more stable and comfortable that theirs. There was still a likelihood that some of the men would be sold out of the tribe, or worse, tortured. They needed to behave like slaves, and not all of them understood that. Phillip looked at Bulygin. The man looked dreadfully ill, but also angry, it was a dangerous combination.

Tarakanov held up his hand. "Here's the thing," he said, "ye must be useful to them…to stay alive, do ye see? Ye can hunt, fish, and carry as well as any of them, right? Mind yer work and they'll do right enough by ye…and soon enough, surely, a ship'll come and take us out o' here. Soon enough." He repeated the words, his eyes searching for comprehension and agreement among the men. "They'll keep ye alive as yer no good to them dead."

Phillip saw that the men understood, but the truth was that many of them were too weary to care, perhaps had even given up hope. He wondered if that was why Tarakanov had agreed to Anna's suggestion so easily.

With the meal ended, the villagers, satiated, had removed themselves from the central area around the fire, forming a wide open space in the middle of the room. Around the four sides of the hall it appeared that each clan group settled down among themselves for the evening's events. Someone from each clan had come to the little crowd of Russians and in ones and twos led the men off to join their new owners with only a little persuasion needed. Bulygin had been allowed to rejoin the men for his meal, had looked confused and needed to be helped along by Tarakanov who seemed to take pity on the man.

Phillip returned to Anna's side and sat with Yutramaki and his mother's clan. Yutramaki gave him a quick look, but then nodded. Anna sat next to Yutramaki who had one hand on her thigh. Phillip thought he was making a statement to the other clan chiefs before the festivities of gift giving began. She would not be one of the gifts. He thought she looked beautiful in the firelight; her dark hair bound back from her face made the tattoo show prominently. He wondered what Anna would look like with a ring through her nose.

Yutramaki

His anger at the shaman waned as the evening grew long. Tempered by time and the comfortable feeling of being well fed, he had to admit that the shaman's displeasure was righteous enough. The shaman hadn't forgotten the shame of Anna's blood. Well neither had Yutramaki, and while most of the time he had sloughed it off as not Anna's fault, not with deliberate intent to harm him or his spirit guides, still, there were times when he cringed inside at the thought. Perhaps he should have killed her, right then when it happened. The shaman would have approved, in fact, the shaman had reproached him for not doing just that. Sliced through her with his knife and cast her into the woods for the mountain lions. The shaman had had his say, and while he could go further, could make life for Anna a misery if he wished, Yutramaki did not want her harmed. He was, in fact, a little sorry about this new moon proscription. He would like to continue to lie with Anna as he had been. The novelty of joining with her face to face, and the sense that he was teaching her something in the doing of it. He liked that.

He sat with his pipe in one hand, the other resting casually on Anna's knee, sometimes stroking the soft blanket under his fingers, but for the most part, just resting there as if she were the arm of a chair, or a convenient tree trunk. When the shaman reentered the great lodge, it was without fanfare. No drums or acolytes preceded his entry. But still the medicine man swept into the room like the bird that he was, striding around the open fire one complete circuit before coming to sit in the place of honor just behind Yutramaki and Anna.

He felt Anna stiffen and tapped her knee gently to relax, thinking it was the shaman's reappearance that worried her, but he followed her gaze and saw she was looking at Bulygin, her husband, and he too stiffened, for Bulygin was leering at

Anna with sharp wild eyes, hatred for her spilling out of him, a bright poison.

"He dies soon enough," he said to Anna, and felt her give a start under his hand.

"He is ill. I should give him care," she said.

Yutramaki shrugged and made a sound of disgust.

"You will not. He will not let you," Yutramaki turned her face to his, "and neither will I."

Yutramaki stood and the crowd instantly quieted. He spoke to them about the fish harvest, and about the month of abstinence to come. He walked around the fire as he spoke, a fine strong voice that captured each person's attention as if he spoke only to them. Then he motioned to the shaman who gave a signal wave of his club, and twelve men leapt into the center of the room wearing all manner of carved masks. The drummers took up their drumming as the masked dancers began the dance that brought whale and whalers together in the hunt. The dancers mimicked the lift and dive of the whale, the thrust of the whaler's harpoon, the frantic paddling that would come. And at last, the prayer for the whale's gift of life, for their ancestor, the whale, who was the blood of their tribe. Yutramaki was pleased with the dancers and rewarded them with blankets pulled from the pile at his feet.

"Will Raven come back?" Anna said.

"Not this night. She spends tonight in the lodge of the shaman, tending his fire while the shaman seeks his spirit helpers."

Yutramaki sent Anna away with the women of her clan as the evening celebrations came to an end. He wished he could retreat with her behind the curtain of hides and lie down with her on the cedar mats. He had grown used to her body, and wondered at its softness. He shook himself. For a month, that would not be. The honor of the whale that they hunted demanded serious preparation and focus. It was dangerous work. Men who did not prepare died. The whale would not give himself up to those who would not make themselves ready with fasting and long journeys of the mind to commune with the spirits.

Yutramaki had sold off all of the Russians but Anna, Phillip, and Tarakanov and Bulygin whom he reluctantly kept as being a danger to them all and thus his personal responsibility. He found something in the man, Tarakanov, that heightened his curiosity. He felt instinctively that Tarakanov would be of value. And Phillip, well, Phillip would soon be a member of the tribe, of that he was certain. Raven would make sure of it. The girl was stubborn and clever. She knew how to get her way. Yutramaki smiled as he sat on his sleeping mat and reached for the bear skin fur, the night was cold, and the warmth of the house, full as it had been of so many bodies, was beginning to cool now that most had gone home to their own lodges.

He heard coughing in the distance. Bulygin. Yutramaki wished the man would die, but in deference to Anna he would let him be, for now. He had sent him to a small lean-to on the beach, away from the people who were justifiably fearful of his sickness. He knew they would not allow the man to remain in the village for long. Useless and sick, what good was he to anyone, least of all Anna? Yutramaki grew angry if he thought of Anna in connection to Bulygin. He had not wanted his first real woman to have belonged to someone else before him. And while he could tell in the way Anna lay with him, that Bulygin was nothing special, he had been with her before him, and that rankled. He closed his eyes, putting thoughts of Anna and her husband out of his mind by reciting his personal spirit chant, calling on his spirit guides to come and people his dreams with the excitement of the hunt, and calling on the great whale to meet him far out in the sea.

Tarakanov, Diary Entry
Ozette Village – Spring 1809

Now that we are established as various servants and slaves, for there is a distinct difference among these people, I find I must agree with Anna Petrovna Bulygina that we have made the right decision in placing ourselves under the protection of this chief Yutramaki and his people. I find they are a sophisticated people with a fine level of art, and leisure time enough to produce vast quantities of beautifully woven blankets, some made of feathers, some skins, but many made from the hair of light colored dogs that they raise for the purpose, and who range among the village lodges in friendly packs, much cosseted by the children. I have had occasion to inspect the great sea going canoes and find them crafted of a single cedar log, singed and decorated, and with a sense of shame see the bailing plugs in the hull that were our own undoing so many months ago.

Our life in the village is hard but satisfactory. We are given work to do alongside the Makah and rewarded with a warm blanket and plenty of food. Bulygin has responded to the good food and isolation to the extent that I doubt he is near death, but also doubt he will survive his sickness in the end. The Makah wisely put him apart from themselves, and only Anna brings him food and Indian tea to drink.

I find myself looking for things to make or suggest that would make life easier for he Makah, and some of these ideas Yutramaki has seemed grateful to have. Most mornings I have spent teaching the chief to shoot the musket. We are now out of bullets, but as the villagers salvaged nearly every bit of iron our ship contained—cauldrons, fittings, lamps and the like—we may be able to fashion bullets for ourselves. As for powder, that will have to come with trade, but I have no doubt that a ship will come once the weather turns fair and the winter squalls pass. In that event, I will hope this chief will trade ourselves for the powder he so desires.

With the Englishman run off, and one of our company dead in a curious and unexplained fall while trapping mere days after our arrival at Ozette, we are now eleven souls under the eyes of God and the Makah. Each day one of us sets up to watch for sail while at the same time accomplishing his assigned task. We live in dread of missing an opportunity of rescue and long for our families at home and in New Archangel.

13

Whale Hunting

Phillip

The month could not have been longer, nor passed so slowly had he been tied to a stock in the hold of a ship. Or so he thought. Raven had left him at the ceremony and it seemed literally had flown away with the shaman, a man who seemed perpetually angry with everyone and was much feared as a result. Phillip had barely spoken to Raven since that night. When he had seen her, he had been shocked that he was not allowed to touch her. He had laughed when she stepped back shaking her head in what seemed to him sheer terror.

"What? Now I canna even touch ye?" He'd laughed and stepped toward her but she stepped back again and yelled at him to stop. She'd never raised her voice to him before, and it brought him up short.

"You may not touch me, no. We should not even talk.

I am the shaman's helper for this month. Preparing for the whale hunt is the most important thing we do of all the seasons of the year. The whale will not give us his life if we have not honored him with our greatest respect. Go away." And she turned away from him and went back to her duties.

Release from Raven's pleasure had not been all bad. He had learned how to shape and sharpen deadly knives to attach to the throwing spears. Making the harpoons brought back memories of his childhood, and he had impressed the Makah men by showing them his own particular skill of tying the points to the wooden spear. He had a way of wrapping the thin strong cordage, binding it around the indentation in the wooden shaft just so, making the point rigid and strong. He knew from experience on Kodiak that the spear point would have to pierce flesh so strong many points would simply bounce away, the thrust and great force of the throw required practice as well as good fortune, and while one might hit home, there was still the danger its shaft would shear off leaving the wound bloody, the point intact, but the shaft and its long tail of rope floating away on the sea.

Phillip took Tarakanov's admonishments to heart, taking every opportunity to help the Makah men prepare for the whale hunt. Secretly, he hoped they would ask him to come along in the great sea canoes. He spent time down at the beach admiring the boats, and had found the time to begin carving his own paddle. Each man had his own, fitted to his particular grip and decorated with his personal spirit animals. Phillip carved his with a raven, of course, but felt something else was needed, some totem that was his alone. He wondered if the shaman would assist him in finding his own spirit animal, and resolved to ask Raven when next he saw her.

At night Phillip divided his time between the Makah men, Anna, and the Russians. Often the Russians would not be allowed to congregate either by orders or simply by being compelled to tasks that kept them busy their whole waking day. Anna too had tasks given to her by her clan mothers. They were treating her well enough. Phillip knew Bulygin was living in a hut on the beach, nominally kept alive by Yutramaki who allowed Anna to take food to the man as long as she left it outside and had no interaction with him, rightly worried as he was that the sickness not spread, particularly not to the chief himself. Phillip had heard Yutramaki and the shaman argue about this. The shaman wanted Bulygin dead and predicted terrible things for the village if he were not dispatched immediately. Phillip wondered why Yutramaki bothered to keep the man alive. Certainly there was no love lost. There was no doubt in Phillip's mind that Bulygin would never be well again, and logic would say therefore that he would never make a useful slave.

Tarakanov and Phillip spent most days together, both men having been singled out as being clever and having knowledge of things Yutramaki desired to learn. They grew healthy and strong, and became comfortable around the Makah, learning more and more of the language. Tarakanov showed Phillip and the others a genuinely friendly and in-quisitive side of himself that hitherto he had kept apart, per-haps thinking his station prohibited his genuine personality from being displayed. Tarakanov and Phillip made toys for the children and played with them on the beach, much to the surprise of the women, both men laughing as the children squealed with delight at each new toy.

Each evening Phillip and Tarakanov would join Yutramaki at his fire in the great hall. Yutramaki had a quick mind and his knack for languages meant that each evening he would have better and better command of their tongue, sometimes combining Makah, Russian, and English words all in the same sentence to such an extent that often Phillip would have to raise his hands and ask the chief to slow down so that he could make the necessary translations in his own head. Yutramaki asked them about the Russian sailing ships, and they explained the quest for fur that had brought them south in the first place. Tarakanov told Yutramaki that many more ships would come. Many more. And promised that if they were treated well, that Yutramaki would be rewarded with more guns and powder than he could use in a lifetime. Phillip noticed that Tarakanov brought the conversation back to furs as often as possible, emphasizing the vast and hungry market that existed in a world so great that Yutramaki could not possible imagine the wealth involved. Once, when Tarakanov was explaining about western exploration and expansion, he spoke with such vivid enthusiasm that when Tarakanov gestured to the East and said to Yutramaki that people were coming, Yutramaki turned in alarm, reaching for his knife. Phillip had fallen back on his blankets laughing, and such was the ease between the men, that the chief, though momentarily startled, soon was laughing as well.

The Russians were not the only ones keeping watch from the high rocks out to sea. Each day teams of Makah took up stations up and down the cape, strategically positioned at high points and land spits reaching far out into the ocean. They weren't looking for ships. They were looking for the whales. At night the same men gathered around their fire and danced the whale dance, calling upon the great whales to come easily to their shores, to allow themselves to be hunted and killed, and the honor of feeding the people of the Cape.

The whaling crews began to form and outfit the canoes so that they would be ready at a moment's signal. Runners moved back and forth between the lookouts making sure no one fell asleep or went hungry.

On one particularly clear day, Phillip had been sent into the lodge to bring down cordage that had been taken from his ship and stored there. Tarakanov had thought to bring it to Yutramaki's attention for it was a length much greater than any the Makah had spun. Yutramaki had directed Phillip to a large cedar box in the corner of the lodge.

To his surprise, the box contained more than rope. Among a jumble of iron spikes, strips of copper flashing, bolts and rivets from the rigging, down at the bottom of the box lay a treasure: Bulygin's glass, its usually gleaming brass beginning to green with patina. It had clearly been discarded without anyone knowing what it was for.

"Sir! Sir!" Phillip caught up with Tarakanov first, fairly hopping with excitement. "Look what I've found, sir," he said, and he pulled the glass to its full extension and put it up to his eye with a grin.

Yutramaki noticed their excitement and was fast approaching. Tarakanov grabbed the glass and motioned to him. He showed him how to open it and put it up to his eye, closing the other one. Yutramaki gasped, looked, put the glass down, looked, put it to his eye and looked again this time searching for some landmark. He smiled widely at Phillip, clapped him on the back, and took off at a run. Phillip watched him run up the beach toward the watchman at the north end of the cape.

"Well done, Phillip," Tarakanov said. "Well done, indeed."

Yutramaki

Yutramaki did not return. Instead he sent a runner down for blankets and food, saying he would stay with the lookout. He sat on the sheltered side of a rock sheer huddled in his bear skin blanket, the glass up to his eye, scanning, always scanning.

On the northward passage of the great gray whales the mothers traveled with their newly born young, keeping closer to shore than in their southing in the fall when they stayed far out at sea traveling fast. The first whales to return north would not be the mothers and calves, but were the young bulls, strong and hungry, and the older males, slower but wiser, more cautious. They traveled in small groups, searching for food which they often found at the river inlets. As they moved north, sounding and then cresting the surface with a great exhale of water, they would pause amid schools of small fish and create a turmoil of ocean water while they satisfied their hunger. And then they were gone again.

The first whale blow came only a day into the new month following their days and days of ritual fasting, and followed a storm that had chased all of the lookouts back into the lodge to huddle by the fire; no point watching when there was no chance of detecting a whale's blow out in the churn of ocean. The day the storm cleared, Yutramaki resumed his position as lookout, and there they were. Almost impossible to see with the naked eye, and oh how he regretted all the whales that had passed by without notice in all the years before! Yet here they were, a small pod of feeding whales, circling around each other in a frenzy of feeding just west of the sea stacks in open ocean. He leapt to his feet, sent the runner ahead to call the men to the canoes, and loped down the sands toward Ozette.

Three canoes launched in quick succession, everyone having been well prepared for the call. Yutramaki called to Phillip who stood excitedly by, hoping to be allowed on-board. He didn't hesitate, but jumped to the offered position and readied himself to push the canoe off the sand and into the shallows. Yutramaki nodded his approval, and yet wait-ed, holding off the launch, watching across the beach to the lodges. Phillip followed his gaze and saw Raven running fast toward them. In her hand she carried a harpoon.

Raven stood in the prow of the canoe just behind the tall carved prominence, herself a figurehead to admire. Yutramaki's sister was a beautiful woman, no longer a girl, and he was proud of the honor bestowed on her by the sha-man. While her status and her presence were a part of the ritual required for the whale kill, every member of each canoe was strategically important, any one of them could strike the killing blow and take on the medicine of the whale as theirs forever.

They shoved the great canoes off the sand and took their places paddling hard against the surf. Yutramaki put Phillip in the back of the canoe, handing him the glass. Without the years of practice maneuvering the sea canoes working in cadence with his fellow paddlers, Phillip paddling would be a hindrance if not dangerous, but with the glass he could direct them as he kept up with the whale's progress.

Paddling hard and sure, they covered the westward distance quickly, growing smaller and smaller to the villagers gathered on shore. They had preparations to make as well, assembling the great cauldrons to hold the whale oil and laying out huge planks on which to cut and distribute the meat. Everyone was confident of a good kill. Yutramaki had said he would bring them a whale, the shaman had cast his magic, and they would not let the people down.

Phillip shouted directions, Yutramaki called out instructions and the whole crew worked as one as they singled out a strong young male. Yutramaki studied the whale's actions, watching him dive and surface with regular cadence. He nodded to the others and they reached for their harpoons, coiling the length of line free and loose behind them. Each of them focused on that one whale alone. Raven had begun the ritual chant, and while Yutramaki and Phillip in the back of the canoe couldn't hear the words—swept away as they were by the wind and sea, away across the ocean as she sang— Yutramaki knew the song well and heard it in his head, a cadenced prayer that he knew was accompanied by the drums of the shaman back on shore. Everything depended upon a successful whale hunt, everything, including his own status within the tribe. He looked across to Phillip who closed the glass and stuck it safely in his trousers. Phillip was watching Raven as if she alone mattered and not the whale.

They were near the feeding zone and could easily count five or so whales circling the surface, sometimes diving deep. They were all males, no mothers, no young, and they had not yet noticed the great canoes approach. Yutramaki gave another shout of orders and his canoe raced into the middle of the feeding party of whales, the water thrashing with foam and chop as the whales dove, sounding one after the other. The hunters stood, harpoons ready, choosing the right moment to strike. A sense of the exact present timing gripped each of them and they reacted as one body with a shout.

At that moment, the canoe lifted, the prow rising straight out of the water on the powerful back of a surging huge male gray rising and rising. Phillip screamed a warning to Raven, Yutramaki called orders to his hunters but all any of them could do was reach for the gunnels and hold on.

As Yutramaki watched in horror, Raven lost her hold on the canoe's figurehead. The gray gave another great lurch toward the sky, his mouth coming clear of the surface of the ocean followed by his long dark body, and with a kick of his tail that Yutramaki could feel just under him, the canoe jolted upwards and back from the thrust, and in disbelief he saw Raven, hair streaming out behind her, fly over him and disappear into the blue deep followed by the gliding body of the whale.

14

All is Lost

Anna

The village went into deep mourning, the whaling equipment abandoned on the shoreline. The sounds of the shaman chanting blanketed the quiet sadness with an ominous monotony.

For five days, Phillip had walked along the shoreline, pacing and watching. Every few steps he would pull out the glass and search the water. Anna watched him, but left him alone, knowing there were no words that would comfort him. On the morning of the fifth day when Anna rose and went to search for Phillip, hoping this time to convince him to eat a little food, she found his half carved paddle stuck upright in the sand. He was gone. A search in his sleeping place revealed he had packed up his few belongings, including the glass, and slipped away during the night. Anna felt bereft, but relieved that Phillip at least had not drowned himself.

The shaman railed at Yutramaki for taking Phillip along, blaming Phillip for the bad luck. Yutramaki had told Anna it was as well that the boy had gone. He shook his head and she saw how sorry he was, sorry for the loss of his sister, the loss of the whale kill, and the loss of his friend, for he and Phillip had grown close.

The events of Raven's death were shared and recounted in whispers around the fire. Anna knew Phillip would not have been able to bear hearing the story of how Raven flew. Raven's flight would become a tale told for generations, embellished and enlarged until it became a part of their whaling mythology. But for Anna and Phillip, Raven was an emblem of heartbreak from which Phillip fled, and Anna faltered.

The month of the gray whale passed in quiet. The shaman would not sanction another kill attempt. The whale, he said, had decreed that the people would suffer. The shaman took himself off into the mountains to fast and journey with his spirit guides searching for the healing that would bring luck back to the village of Ozette. No one bothered to hunt after Phillip, and most privately hoped he had taken the bad luck with him.

Anna felt Yutramaki pull away. While there was nothing overt about his distance, he still came to her bed and claimed her obedience, he was not unkind or cruel. But he seemed, most of the time, not to see her. He didn't watch her as he used to do, watch her in a way that made her feel protected and desired, a way that she had come to welcome. She passed this off as grief at first, but as the weeks went by, she began to see that he was quite simply uninterested in her. She applied herself to her work, asking permission to assist with the collecting and spinning of the fine dog fibers. She spent more time with the women of the village, careful to dress and behave as they did. She went along on several trips into the forest to collect herbs and search for valuable mountain goat hair that the spring weather caused the goats to rub off onto the rough bark of trees. She attended the elder women, watching and learning from them. After only a few short weeks she could spin a consistent fine fiber, mixing dog hair with a little mountain goat wool for strength. She spent hours pounding dried herbs into powders and grinding the yellow and red stones of ochre into the powders that made paints.

Bulygin stayed quietly away from the village center but hovered at its edges watching for her. When he could, he tried to talk with her. Sometimes she took pity on him and brought him extra food—for Yutramaki ignored his needs and the Russian men often forgot him in their worry to keep themselves safe and well fed. Anna felt sorry for her husband, but she didn't look for opportunities to speak to him. He had grown well enough, thanks in part to constant generous consumption of Indian tea, to be allowed at the lodge fire when the village gathered together, but the people mistrusted him and moved away when he approached, sometimes striking out at him with a stick or a club if it seemed he took too much interest in their work, in consequence he was nearly always bruised and had formed a demeanor that anticipated trouble. In isolating him, they had assumed he would die. Now that he hadn't, they suspected him of at least some of the bad luck that had fallen on the village, and their dislike of him would surely have resulted in his death had not Yutramaki insisted on his protection for Anna's sake.

To Anna this seemed a test, though she had no words with which to convince her owner that she was loyal, she did what she could to make her obligations clear. And as it seemed the only place where she could reach out to Yutramaki was within the confines of her bed, that was what she did. She had observed other young women, just as she had watched Raven with Phillip, and within the lodge there was very little privacy should one wish to learn by the intimacies exchanged around her, Anna could and did watch and listen. She listened to the women moan as the men moved over them. She heard the women talk and laugh about their men. She found them exchanging recipes for salves that they said would make the task more enjoyable, and she took some to use for herself. She began to move with him and make small sounds on the occasions when he did come to her, and it shocked her when the smallest movement on her part incited a groan and a desperate lunge on his. A moment of power shift that surprised and pleased her. Eventually, perhaps his mourning healing, Yutramaki began to come longer to her bed, and while he never slept the night through with her as he had done in the fishing lodge, she counted on him coming late in the evening with the fire bright, and again in the early dawn, waking her with his warmth and weight.

In late May the evenings became fine, and as the moon waxed the villagers spilled out of their dark and smoky lodges to build driftwood fires on the beach. The lengthening day meant more time for work, but more time for visiting and entertainment as well. The Russians had used their extra time creating a liquor drink from the spring sap run, and this night they had decided to celebrate by sharing the drink around.

Anna was walking back to the plank house, the sound of the Russians who were singing old country songs at the tops of their voices seemed so strange, but they had brought back memories, memories of her homeland, the sweet fields of grain in summer, light muslin dresses and brightly painted shawls. She had left the circle and light of the fire wanting a few moments on her own before retiring to her bed with Yutramaki. She walked slowly up the path in the moonlight, her thoughts taken many miles away.

Out of the shadows stepped Bulygin. He had clearly drunk his share of the mead. He blundered onto the path in front of her, causing her to stumble. She could see the dark intent of madness in his eyes.

"Nikolai!" She took a step to the side but the path was narrow on the embankment walk way toward the house, she had nowhere to go but turn around.

He caught at her wrist, missed his grip and caught her blanket instead, lurching backward with a fistful of blanket in his hand he pulled and she fell.

He stood for a moment looking down at her naked body in shock, the blanket limp in his hands, and then he fell on her.

"No!" She gasped as her head struck the ground, and he came down on top of her.

All of her rough memories of him came flooding back as he shoved between her legs, biting and licking at her bare breasts repeating vile threats all the while. She struggled, but only for an instant, her first attempt at pushing him away brought him up roiling over her, his fist pounding into her nose.

When he had finished with her he staggered away cursing, her blanket fisted in one hand, fumbling with the buttons of his trousers with the other. He left her lying on the path stunned, naked, and bleeding, with three other drunken Russians coming up fast, hunger in their faces.

Yutramaki

Yutramaki was sitting by the great fire on the beach drinking with Tarakanov. Tarakanov was telling him an idea for making the houses warmer, more protected in winter, and he was trying to catch his meaning but the strong drink was muddling his senses and he felt sick. Looking back toward the plank house he saw Bulygin staggering toward his hut on the beach dragging a blanket. In the evening firelight, Yutramaki couldn't make out any details, but something about the man, slinking off, made him leave the fire. When he stood, the blood drained from his head and he felt he might fall down.

"Are ye well, man?" Tarakanov took his arm and helped him straighten. "Ah, it's just the drink, I expect. Ye'll not be used to our stuff. 'Tis strong, that's sure. It's what makes us such good singers!" Tarakanov slapped him on the back and sent him on his way. "Ye just go and sleep it off with that woman of yours."

Yutramaki found Anna on the path, her face bloody, her naked body limp and splayed open on the ground, showing clear signs of having been used. He looked at her for a long time. She hadn't looked up at him and seemed as though she was waiting for him to react.

He turned from her speechless with rage, and then suddenly turned back. He picked her up and slung her over his shoulders, his powerful arms made her seem inconsequential, as if he had shouldered his paddle or the musket.

Tarakanov came running up to him as he emerged onto the beach but Yutramaki brushed passed him. No one dared follow as he pushed his way into Bulygin's miserable hut. He dumped Anna on the floor in front of the dazed man, turned on his heels and without a word, left her there.

Yutramaki made his way to the far side of the village and broke loudly into the lodge of one of his clan chiefs, a man he knew had been watching Anna. This man was known to be cruel to his slaves.

"I trade you the woman and her sick man for that," Yutramaki said, pointing to a small cedar chest. His words were slurred and he wavered as he stood inside the lodge door.

"Humph," said the clan chief, considering Yutramaki briefly before nodding.

And it was done.

In the morning, Yutramaki's head ached miserably but his

anger had not waned. He refused to see Anna though he could hear her crying outside his door until a woman came and with a loud smack that produced a shocked cry, Anna grew silent. Shortly, he could hear the women move off across the village, the one prodding and cajoling the other punctuated occasionally by more strikes with a stick that the woman smacked against the lodge walls as they walked, pacing a cadence. Late in the day he smelled the fire that was Bulygin's shack burning. Their new owner would not feed him, nor house him. They would survive or no, it no longer mattered.

Tarakanov, Diary Entry
Ozette Village – June 1809

The men took to drink and in a rage, Bulygin and several others insulted his wife's body, exposing her to humiliation before Yutramaki who, taking this as a personal insult, has abandoned them both. I dare not intervene for fear he turn on the rest of us. Bulygin has taken ill again and will not live the week out, having suffered a beating by his new master and being cast into the woods as he is. Anna Petrovna sits huddled in the tatters of her blanket outside the clan lodge, scullery to the old chief within. When I can, I slip her bits of food. Everyone else ignores her, and she too, seems to have relinquished any will to survive, and sits waiting on her fate.

Still, daily I wait and pray for young Phillip to return, imagining somehow that he, surely, must survive. I wish he had not taken the spyglass with him, for my eyes are sore with straining as I watch daily for a ship to bring us away from here.

Afterword

The skeleton of this story that we know to be true is the product in large part of the research of Professor Emeritus Kenneth N. Owens, whose book *The Wreck of the Sv. Nikolai* and subsequent research into the life of Timofei Tarakanov and the Russian American fur trade was the inspiration and certainly the outline for my story. While I have not altered the fate of the story's players in any way, I have certainly fictionalized the events, motives, and details of how they came to the end that they did. Professor Owens has kindly allow me to reprint an article in the following appendix that he wrote for Montana Magazine which gives greater detail on this event.

Briefly, what we know to be true is that the navigator Nikolai Bulygin set sail on the Sv. Nikolai, a Hawaiian built sloop, as her captain, taking with him his young wife, Anna

Petrovna, several Alutiiq natives, an Englishman, and about twenty Russians including Timofei Tarakanov who was on-board to direct the process of procuring and soliciting furs as the ship made its way south in search of a good southern place for colonization. This place would become Fort Ross in central California, but its discovery and development comes after our story is done. From diary entries by Tarakanov we know that Captain Bulygin was a poor captain and a bad shot. We don't know anything about his wife except that she was young. It is possible that she was half Russian, half na-tive, that being a common habit among all the fur traders whether English, French or Russian to take what they called "country" wives whether they had actual wives at home or not. But there is no proof of this so far, and I have chosen to ignore the speculation and consider that she, Anna Petrovna, with such a proper Russian name, should be Russian.

We know that the party of Russians were initially set upon and harassed frequently by the Hoh Indians, and that the Makah cleverly tricked them by deliberately sink-ing one of their canoes. It is true that negotiations went on for months during which time the Makah chief steadfastly refused to give up his desire for muskets. And by the time the Russians were worn down in their purpose, Anna, for whatever reasons of her own, refused to be saved. I have tried to understand her motivations, and to speak to the issue of survival from her point of view.

There is some likelihood that chief Yutramaki was the son of a Makah woman and an Irishman, John Mackay, an assistant surgeon aboard an English ship, who had been left with the natives of Cape Alava to study their habits and form alliances for the English fur trade. MacKay lasted a year before catching the next ship to stop. Most people cite the similarities between the two names as good evidence of a connection, and the dates are certainly amenable. We can't know for sure. MacKay's rescuers, Capt. Charles Barkley and his wife, said to have been the first European woman to set foot on the Olympic shores, though it remains to be proved that she left the ship at all, remarked that MacKay was dressed like a wild man and desperate to be saved. Mrs. Barkley's diary of her own travels in the same waters that Anna would follow some twenty years later is a valuable resource.

We also know that Phillip disappears from the Makah village, and until recently, we didn't know what happened to him. The character of Raven is entirely fictitious. During research for the writing of this story I came across a footnote in a small book about Kodiak Island's inhabitants that told me Filip [sic] Kotel'nikov had survived. Somehow Phillip had made his way back to Alaska, and there taken ship to the new colony of Fort Ross where he married a Pomo woman and had two children. He died back on his home island of Kodiak where his details have been counted and preserved in an informal census tally.

Timofei Tarakanov made himself useful to the Makah and in return they treated him well, and when a ship did pass Cape Alava and stop, Yutramaki traded him off to safety. He too spent time in Alaska as well as at Fort Ross, and was a high ranking official in the Russian Fur Trade Company by the time of his death.

Bulygin never recovered from his illness which we can only speculate must surely have been tuberculosis.

Once Anna was traded off, she was badly mistreated, and within a year had fallen ill herself and died. There are rumors that her death went unremarked, her body being thrown into the woods, but they are only rumors.

There is a collection of petroglyphs just south of what remains of Ozette, many of which are abstract symbols sometimes known to be fertility symbols in many cultures. One stone, though, carries an image of a sailing ship. We can only wonder who carved that little ship. I think it was Phillip.

Acknowledgments

Ken Owens mentored me through my graduate degree some twenty years ago, and it was from him that I learned this story. I owe him thanks, for allowing me to run off with this tale and make it my own, and for teaching me the fine points of research and writing. Anyone can have a teacher, few of us are so fortunate as to have a mentor, and rarely one of his caliber.

Thanks also to my editor at Long Nights Press, Diane Reynolds, who brought me back to task whenever I tried to stray; and to Scott Hutchins at Stanford and my writing class friends who bolstered my confidence with their praise. And to Medea Isphording Bern, my writing partner/cheering squad who kept me at my work for the critical period needed to get this story finished. Thank you.

Whoever Anna Petrovna really was, for me she stands as an emblem of what is possible when we take strength from our own internal core. Each of us survives or thrives in our own manner, and it is the way we present ourselves to each day that counts, not the last day.

Appendix

Frontiersman for the Tsar:
Timofei Tarakanov and the
Expansion of Russian America

Kenneth N. Owens*

Abstract: Born into serfdom in Kursk, Timofei Tarakanov sailed
to Russian America at the beginning of the nineteenth century as a contract employee, a *promyshlennik*, in the service of the
Russian-American Company (RAC). Before the founding of
Ross Colony he led many of the first RAC sea-otter hunting expeditions to California and the Oregon Country. He also took a
leading role in closing out a brief, ill-considered RAC adventure
in the Hawaiian Islands. His adventurous career offers a unique
case study concerning the life of ordinary working people in early
Russian America.

In late October 1803, the Massachusetts trading ship *O'Cain*
slipped away from St. Paul harbor at the small Russian settlement on Kodiak Island off the Alaska coast, edged passed
the headlands into open water, and set a course southward
toward Spanish California. If the weather was typical for

282 • THE NAVIGATOR'S WIFE

that time of year, the day would have been cool and overcast, with a steady wind from the northwest to fill the sails and rain squalls to drench everyone on deck. At the helm was Captain Joseph O'Cain, an American-born Irishman who had made four previous trading voyages from New England to the west coast of North America. Crowded onto the ship were forty natives of western Alaska, principally Alutiiqs from Kodiak Island. These men were expert sea otter hunters who had brought aboard their hunting gear and light, skin-covered two-man *baidarkas*. Also on board were two contract employees of the Russian-American Company (RAC), appointed to supervise the Alutiiq hunters and serve as intermediaries with Captain O'Cain and his sailors. The senior Russian, Afanasii Shvestov, had worked in the Alaskan fur business for at least nine years. His junior companion was Timofei Tarakanov, born into serfdom in European Russia and now, at age twenty-nine, just beginning a career with the RAC that would involve him in a series of extraordinary adventures in California, the Oregon Country, and Hawaii.

From his humble origins as a serf, Timofei Tarakanov would rise by virtue of his exceptional accomplishments to positions of unusual trust in Russian America. His personal history, filled with high adventure, forms a small but significant chapter in the history of imperial rivalries over trade and national power in western North America at the beginning of the nineteenth century, at the very time that the Louisiana Purchase and the Lewis and Clark Expedition were bringing the United States into the Far West. Tarakanov must have entered the service of the newly formed RAC as a contract employee about 1801, presumably with the encouragement of his legal owner, a landowner and merchant from Kursk who apparently took a strong interest in his education and career success.[1] Company records identify him as a *promyshlennik,* a fur hunter, a vague, all-purpose job description applied to all Russian-born RAC contract workers regardless of their duties or their standing in the tsarist social system. Obviously intelligent and more or less literate, he could keep accounts, making him a valuable RAC recruit. Soon he would earn as well a reputation for trustworthiness, sobriety (no small matter in that time and place), good judgment, and resourcefulness.

Starting with the 1803 *O'Cain* voyage to California, Tarakanov gained unusual distinction among the Russian workers in the Company's service. Despite his legal status as a serf, which meant that his master had ownership rights to his labor, he became a key figure in RAC efforts to expand Russian hunting and trading activities southward from Alaska, and to establish colonial outposts both on the northern California coast and, briefly, on the Hawaiian island of Kauai. His superiors came to rely on his leadership abilities. Other Company workers, Russians and Native Alaskans alike, learned to trust him for his skills, prudence, and good fortune in escaping danger. Despite the failure of many of his hazardous ventures for the RAC, Tarakanov survived and even flourished on the farthest, most dangerous border areas of early Russian America. He was a frontiersman for the Tsar, promoting the expansion of a Russian imperial presence amid the competing efforts of Hispanic, British, and Anglo-American traders and settlers.

Eventually his services for the RAC gained Tarakanov

legal manumission from serfdom and the opportunity to retire and return to Kursk as a free townsman. With him came
his Alutiiq wife and their young son. Since the fragmentary
documentary record tells us nothing more, we are left to
wonder whether he found it possible to enjoy a respectable
and comfortable old age back in his homeland, far from the
scenes of his daring American exploits.

The *O'Cain's* 1803 voyage to Spanish California was a novel
and risky enterprise. Behind it was more than two centuries of Russian expansion eastward across Siberia and into
the North Pacific, primarily to gain wealth from furs. The
conquest of Siberia, begun in the 1580s, was a starkly predatory business. Bands of mounted Cossack raiders, closely
followed by traders and government tax officials, plundered
Native settlements, imposed arbitrary levies (*iasak*) collect-
ible in furs, and forced Native Siberian hunters to slaughter
the prized sables and other fur-bearing land mammals to
the point of extinction. Then in the 1740s, as Siberia's sable
population was at the point of collapse, the explorers Vitus
Bering and Alexei Chirikov led the way from Kamchatka and
eastern Siberia across the dangerous North Pacific to Alaska.
Their expeditions started a reckless new maritime fur rush
for the pelts of sea otters and fur seals that could be found in
abundance in the Aleutian Islands and the maritime districts
of western Alaska. Here too, greed and unregulated competition between rival hunting companies hastened the rapid
destruction of the animals, a problem consistently denied by
Russian merchants and government authorities who claimed
that the once abundant sea otter had simply been frightened

away by the hunters, and that further explorations would be sure to discover the refuges of these errant, extremely valuable creatures.[2]

Irkutsk in east central Siberia was the commercial capital for the North Pacific fur business, while the primitive port facilities of Okhotsk, 2,400 miles farther east, provided the Russian merchants and fur hunters their access to the North Pacific. A few merchants made great fortunes from the business, principally by exchanging Siberian and North Pacific furs for Chinese trade goods like tea, silks, and fine cotton fabrics, which were in high demand in European Russia and Western Europe. One of the most successful of these merchants, Grigorii Shelikhov, in the late 1780s proposed to Empress Catherine II, Catherine the Great, that her government should put an end to the costly rivalries among private companies by chartering a single organization with monopoly rights to hunt, trade, and administer all Russian territories in North America. The Empress rejected the proposal because of her principled opposition to business monopolies; but her successor, Tsar Paul I, established the Russian-American Company in 1799 with the type of exclusive authority that Shelikhov had advocated a decade earlier.[3] By 1803 the RAC's operations in North America were being directed by Chief Manager Alexander Baranov, a rugged and shrewd commercial genius who originally went to Kodiak in 1790 to take charge of Shelikhov's business operations.

Baranov's interest in California sea otters reflected not only the destruction of the population stocks in western Alaska, but also the hostility of powerful Tlingit and Haida Native clans in southeastern Alaska. Equipped with guns and gunpowder from their trade with British and Yankee shipmasters, the Tlingits posed a danger to the forays of Company hunting crews from Prince William Sound as far south as the Queen Charlotte Islands. Just the previous year, 1802, Tlingit attackers had destroyed St. Michael, Baranov's small new outpost on Sitka Sound, killing most of its meager garrison and giving forceful emphasis to the Chief Manager's need to seek other sea otter hunting grounds. Even though the RAC lacked sturdy vessels and competent sailors of its own, the arrangement with Captain O'Cain enabled Baranov to set in motion a low-cost exploratory project, with Shvestov and Tarakanov assigned to supervise the hunt and safeguard the Company's interests throughout the voyage.

Fortuitously for Baranov, Captain O'Cain had arrived at Kodiak a month earlier, bringing a cargo of trade goods and promoting a hunting partnership in California waters. After selling his cargo to Baranov, O'Cain described a supposed newly discovered sea otter breeding ground on an island off the coast of Baja California. He offered Baranov an arrangement that would open these waters to the Russians. His ship would carry Alutiiq hunters and their Russian crew chiefs to California for the winter hunting season. On their return to Kodiak, he would divide the fur catch equally with Baranov. In fact, O'Cain must have known that an abundance of sea otters could be found all along the California coastline, virtually untouched by the Spanish. Even though Spain's imperial policy prohibited contact with foreigners in its overseas colonies, O'Cain also knew that California's small, isolated cadre of military officials and Franciscan missionaries usually welcomed the opportunity for surreptitious trade with visiting Yankee and British ships, particularly if the trading arrangements were aided by appropriate gifts from the merchant captains to local authorities.[4]

From Kodiak harbor Captain O'Cain sailed directly to San Diego, then continued south to San Quintín Bay. Claiming falsely that his ship had been badly storm damaged, O'Cain received official permission to remain a few days to make repairs and secure supplies. He actually stayed for three months, anchoring in San Quintín Bay while Tarakanov, Shvestov, and the Alutiiq hunters in their baidarkas ranged along the Baja California coast between Mission Rosario and Santo Domingo. A catastrophe for the sea otters, this voyage was an outstanding success for the RAC and for Captain O'Cain and his ship owners, the Winship brothers of Brighton, Massachusetts. The *O'Cain* returned to Kodiak in June 1804 with no casualties, bringing 1,100 sea otter skins that were worth approximately $35,000 in trade at Canton, China, along with an additional 700 skins that the captain had secured on his own account in trade with the Spanish.[5]

The profits from this venture heartened Baranov at a low period in the RAC's history. Like Joseph O'Cain and the Winship family, he was encouraged to undertake similar operations regularly during the next few years. Not only a great financial success, the 1803 *O'Cain* voyage started Chief Manager Baranov on a course of expansion to bypass the Tlingit barrier and advance Russian sea otter hunting, trade, and the Tsar's territorial claims in North America well south of Alaska.

Soon after the *O'Cain's* return, Baranov's spirits were raised further by the reconquest of the St. Michael site on Sitka Sound, aided by the arrival of the Russian navy's warship *Neva* on the first of many so-called round-the-world voyages meant to connect Russian America with St. Petersburg. Following the victory, Baranov directed the construction nearby of a new, strongly fortified outpost, which he named New Archangel. Over the next few years the Chief Manager transferred the RAC's headquarters to this site, relocating the capital of Russian America into the heartland of the still powerful Tlingit clans. Baranov's move to Sitka Sound made good sense in terms of improved harbor facilities and potential access to southeast Alaska's sea otter population. But it had one extreme drawback. It greatly magnified the problem of keeping the RAC's Russian and Alutiiq employees adequately fed. Continued Tlingit hostility made it dangerous for Baranov's men to hunt deer or other game in the surrounding countryside, or even to fish at any distance from their fort. In times of shortage, moreover, the demands made by the officers and crew of visiting Russian ships could place a further strain on Baranov's slim stock of provisions.

In late August 1805, immediately after the *Neva's* departure, the arrival of the RAC ship *Sv. Mariia Magdelena* ushered in a season of severe hardship. On board was Nikolai P. Rezanov, a high-ranking official in Tsar Alexander I's government and an influential leading member of the RAC's board of directors. Rezanov was conducting a leisurely tour of inspection on behalf of the company and the Crown.

During an extended stay at New Archangel, he eased the immediate food crisis by purchasing the Yankee ship *Juno* from John D'Wolf, its captain and owner, with D'Wolf's full cargo of foodstuffs and trade goods.[6] But this was merely a stopgap measure. To secure a more certain supply of flour, beef, and other provisions, Rezanov decided to take the *Juno* to Spanish California.

Under the command of Navy Lieutenant Nikolai Khvostov, the *Juno* departed from Sitka in February 1806. The crew numbered thirty-three men, quite possibly including Timofei Tarakanov, all of them badly disabled by scurvy. On the way south, at Rezanov's behest Lieutenant Khvostov tried to enter the Columbia River. Rezanov hoped to find there a site for a new Russian post that might preempt British or American occupation of the lower Columbia basin. Had Lieutenant Khvostov and his men succeeded, the Russians might conceivably have encountered the Lewis and Clark Expedition, which left their winter encampment at Fort Clatsop to start their return to St. Louis in mid March of 1806. But a winter storm and the incapacity of the ailing crew frustrated the Russian attempt, so the *Juno* proceeded south, arriving at San Francisco Bay in late March.

To impress California's Spanish officials, Rezanov claimed authority as the Russian government's minister plenipotentiary. Although in fact he had no such specific commission, he negotiated in the Tsar's name with Governor José Arrillaga for trading rights and other privileges. Meanwhile he did his utmost to ingratiate himself with the household of Don José Arguëllo, commandant of the San Francisco presidio. When the *Juno* headed back to Sitka Sound early

290 • THE NAVIGATOR'S WIFE

in June, their California diet had fully restored the health of its crew and the ship carried a full cargo of mission-raised foodstuffs. But despite Rezanov's best efforts—including an intense romantic dalliance with the teenage eldest daughter of the Arguëllo family—he had gained only vague promises from California's provincial rulers that they would request authority from Mexico City and Madrid to trade with the Russians on a regular basis.[7] But he could report to Baranov the significant information that the Spanish had established no outposts farther north than San Francisco Bay.

During Rezanov's absence, the Winship brothers had arrived at New Archangel with three ships including the *O'Cain*, now under the command of Jonathan Winship. Baranov eagerly entered into a more ambitious partnership with the Winships, supplying them with Russian-led Alutiiq hunting crews under essentially the same terms negotiated for the *O'Cain's* first California voyage. After Rezanov returned from San Francisco with the *Juno*, a fourth Winship-owned vessel, the *Peacock* commanded by Captain Oliver Kimball, a Winship brother-in-law, also arrived at the Russian headquarters. Kimball too was keen to contract for an RAC hunting crew. If Tarakanov had been aboard the *Juno*, as seems likely, he must have been in port only a few days before Baranov assigned him to head the hunting crew he put aboard the *Peacock* for a return to California with Captain Kimball.[8]

Having had three men captured by soldiers near Mission San Juan Capistrano on his way to Alaska, Captain Kimball was anxious that Tarakanov's hunters should avoid contact with the Spanish settlements. After first anchoring in

Trinidad Bay on California's isolated north coast, Kimball made Bodega Bay, about sixty sea miles north of San Francisco Bay, his base of operations during the spring of 1807. From this secure harbor, Tarakanov and his hunters made a raid on northern California sea otter populations from the Farallon Islands on the south to the Mendocino coast on the north. Spanish records indicate that Tarakanov's hunters also entered San Francisco Bay, where they worked along the northern shore, avoiding the Spanish presidio (fort) on the southern shore. Exasperated by this incursion, in mid-March the acting presidio commander, Luis Antonio Arguëllo, ordered his men to fire a cannon at five baidarkas as they were leaving the bay. This surprise attack created enough of a panic that the hunters abandoned two baidarkas in their haste to escape.[9] Captain Kimball left Bodega Bay two months later, sailed south to San Quintin Bay to meet Captain Winship, then returned to New Archangel in August 1807. Tarakanov's men came ashore with 753 prime adult sea otter skins, 258 yearling skins, and the pelts of 250 pups, worth approximately $30,000 in trade at Canton.[10] More important for the future, Timofei Tarakanov now impressed Chief Manager Baranov with his expert knowledge of the geography and resources of Bodega Bay and the adjacent coastline, including the access routes to San Francisco Bay from the north.

At this point Tarakanov emerges as a central figure in Baranov's developing plans for extending the Russian presence southward. The Chief Manager evaluated both the reports from the California hunting voyages and the information gained by Rezanov about potential trade connections with the Hispanic missionaries and officials. Encouraged by Rezanov, he now determined to establish a Russian post north of San Francisco Bay that might serve as a permanent base both for fur hunting and for a covert trade in foodstuffs and other items available from the Franciscan missions. Also with Rezanov's encouragement, he intended to explore further the coastline near the mouth of the Columbia River—an area called New Albion by both the English and the Russians—to locate a possible site for another RAC post. Taking advantage of wartime conditions in Europe that were keeping British, Spanish, and American shipping away from the Pacific Coast, he was right to think that a window of opportunity had opened that might enable the RAC to increase its profits and widen its influence on North America's Pacific rim. And to accomplish his goals, Baranov made Timofei Tarakanov the leader of a small shipboard command with responsibilities as the ship's supercargo and crew manager (*prikashchik*) for an 1808 voyage that would sail first to New Albion and then proceed to northern California.

Baranov had two RAC ships available for this mission, neither built by the Russians. The smaller of the two was the *Sv. Nikolai*, a schooner originally constructed in Hawaii by Yankee craftsmen for King Kamehameha I. Purchased from its American owners for 150 sea otter skins, the ship had arrived at New Archangel in May 1807 under the command of *promyshlennik* Pavl Slobodchikov, who also brought from the Hawaiian king a regal feather cloak as a gift to Baranov.[11] With his limited maritime resources, the Chief Manager must have been pleased to secure the schooner and perhaps regarded its small size an advantage for the coastal surveying tasks he was assigning to Timofei Tarakanov.

Like the American president Thomas Jefferson when he dispatched the Lewis and Clark expedition, Chief Manager Baranov drafted detailed instructions for the *Sv. Nikolai's* 1808 voyage. The ship's captain was Nikolai Bulygin, a junior navy officer who had come from Russia in 1801 to sail for the RAC.[12] Baranov instructed both Tarakanov and Bulygin to complete a detailed survey of the coastline from the Strait of Juan de Fuca southward to the mouth of the Columbia River. In addition, the Chief Manager directed Tarakanov to investigate trade possibilities with the native peoples of this scarcely known region, and to prepare a detailed description of their manners and customs. "You are to find out if they are disposed to develop either exchange or trading relations with us," he directed, and also to learn "what kind what special goods and different animals living in the sea and on the dry land one can find there." In short, he concluded, "You are to notice, remember and record all those local peculiarities."[13]

To prepare Tarakanov for dealing with the New Albion natives, Baranov cited the example of Yankee shipmasters along the Northwest Coast. "Follow my instructions," he wrote, "and take some small and cheap items such as buttons, jewelry, beads, mirrors and knives of various kinds to give to natives of the region in exchange for various items. It is quite typical of all American seafarers to do so, and Captain [Thomas] Brown showed us a whole sack of such things he was going to exchange for various local goods in the area at the mouth of the Columbia River."[14]

Once these assignments were completed, according to

the Chief Manager's instructions, the *Sv. Nikolai* should sail to the protected anchorage at Gray's Harbor and meet the British-built *Kad'iak*, the second RAC ship he was dispatching to California. Aboard the *Kad'iak* would be Ivan Kuskov, Baranov's principal lieutenant and the general commander of this 1808 expedition. The *Sv. Nikolai* and the *Kad'iak* would then continue southward together and establish a Russian post at Bodega Bay or some other suitable site near San Francisco Bay. Because Tarakanov had been there and could be trusted to guide local explorations, Baranov regarded him as essential to the expedition's success. "Try to be a good manager," Baranov instructed him, "for I am determined to extend the period you will remain there and direct all those workers."

Unfortunately for the Chief Manager's plans, four weeks into the *Sv. Nikolai's* voyage a combination of bad luck, faulty gear, and Captain Bulygin's poor judgment found the ship drifting dangerously toward the rugged New Albion coastline, its foreyard broken and all anchors lost. While the ill-trained crew stood by helplessly, high waves and a brisk northwest gale pushed the schooner towards a rocky, tree-lined shore. Fearing the worst, all hands piously invoked divine aid. As if in answer to their prayers, the *Sv. Nikolai* floated safely passed looming rocks, drifted aground, heeled over, and settled firmly on a sandy, gently sloping beach.

The site of the wreck was Rialto Beach on the Olympic Peninsula in modern Washington State, just north of the mouth of the Hoh River, a location inaccessible for sailing ships.[15] The *Sv. Nikolai's* people were marooned in the rainiest region of the Northwest Coast just as winter set in, in an area cut off from the interior by the snow-covered Olympic range and covered by dense, virtually impenetrable rain forest. With minimal supplies and few tools except for an axe or two and their flintlock muskets, they would be on their own, with no ready means to communicate their plight to any ships that might be sailing offshore. Moreover, as they quickly discovered, the rumored hostility of the region's Native peoples toward strangers was no unfounded seaman's tale. The Hoh and their near neighbors—the Quinalts to the south, the Quileutes and the wealthy, aristocratic Makahs to the north—fiercely guarded their territories against intruders. Like other Northwest Coast peoples, they were accustomed to violent combat. Theirs was a culture of competition and conflict involving raids and counter-raids, in which the seizure of captives for enslavement was a primary motive for warfare. While they remained at large, the *Sv. Nikolai's* armed survivors could only be viewed as dangerous intruders by these peoples. If, on the other hand, the Russians and their Alutiiq comrades were taken captive, they could be regarded as highly prized human property, to be exploited for labor or traded from one owner to another as a prime commodity.[16]

Twenty-two people were stranded when the ship went aground. In addition to Tarakanov and Captain Bulygin, the roster included ten Russians and one Englishman working as *promyshlenniks*. The *Sv. Nikolai* had also carried four Alutiiq men and three women who were categorized as Native workers (*kaiury*) by RAC administrators. The remaining two passengers were Anna Petrovna Bulygina, the Russian wife of Captain Bulygin, and a Creole (Russian and Alutiiq) youngster named Phillip Kotel'nikov, identified as an "apprentice of mathematics."[17]

As they abandoned ship, the *Sv. Nikolai's* people loaded everything useful they could salvage into the ship's skiff and rowed it ashore through the surf. Trouble started immediately. Brazenly, as the Russians thought, a few Hoh men began pilfering from the growing pile of supplies and equipment on the beach. When the Russians attempted to drive them away, the clash escalated into a pitched battle. The Hohs used well-aimed rocks and spears as their weapons and, after Tarakanov and a few others were slightly wounded, the Russians replied with gunfire, killing three of the attackers. As more Hoh fighters came to join the fray, the beleaguered Russians were forced to flee. Taking two flintlocks each and a small reserve of powder and lead, along with a tent for shelter and a few trade items, they destroyed the rest of their armaments, burned most of the supplies they had salvaged, and headed south, using the skiff to ferry across the mouth of the river. Pursued and occasionally attacked by the Hohs, for six days the Russian party followed a faint trail that led through the rain forest and along the shoreline. As Captain Bulygin explained, by trekking southward close to the coast they would reach Gray's Harbor, where the *Kad'iak* should soon arrive for the expected rendezvous with the *Sv. Nikolai.* This, everyone agreed, was their best prospect for rescue.[18]

But under Captain Bulygin's guidance, the situation of the *Sv. Nikolai* castaways rapidly turned from difficult to desperate. Eighteen months later, when Timofei Tarakanov returned to New Archangel aboard a Yankee ship with twelve other survivors, he described what had happened, drawing on a diary of events that has since disappeared. Fortunately for the historical record, a navy officer with literary interests, Vasilii M. Golovnin, was visiting Russian America at the time. He interviewed Tarakanov and his companions, took down their account, and subsequently published it in *Severnyi Archiv*, the Russian naval journal. Golovnin later republished the story in a volume with reports on other Russian shipwrecks. Now translated and edited in a scholarly edition titled *The Wreck of the Sv. Nikolai*, Golovnin's rendition of Tarakanov's narrative is a unique frontier adventure story, replete with dramatic incident and considerable insight concerning the Native people among whom the Russians in time came to live.

In summary, the southward trek of the Russians was halted at the Queets River, where a group of Natives by a clever ruse captured Anna Petrovna and three others while taking them across the river under guise of friendship. The loss of his wife completely devastated Captain Bulygin who, with the consent of all the others, turned over command of the shipwrecked expedition to Tarakanov. After fending off another attack, the Russians retreated upriver, where they built a fort-like log structure, meanwhile subsisting on salmon they secured by raiding, trading with a nearby Native village, and catching fish on their own. For the next two months, Tarakanov would recall, they remained "the sole inhabitants of our realm of land and water. There we lived quietly and had plenty of food."[19]

From this upriver refuge, Tarakanov planned to lead his comrades southward across the mountains in the spring, hoping to reach the Columbia River and find there a trading vessel that might return them to New Archangel. But when the time came to depart, Bulygin refused to leave the region, insisting that the expedition return downriver to locate and rescue Anna Petrovna. As they neared the coast, the Russians were able to seize as a hostage one of the women who had captured Anna Petrovna and her companions by trickery three months earlier. A few days later this woman's brother appeared at the head of a large delegation, appealing for her release. Anna Petrovna was by his side and, astonishingly, she too demanded the release of the Russians' captive. She and her brother, said Anna Petrovna, were eminent personages "widely known along this coast. They had been quite good to her. Most astounding, she told Tarakanov that she was quite satisfied with her own condition and had no wish to rejoin the Russians. Instead, she urged all the other *Sv. Nikolai* survivors to surrender themselves to this "upright and virtuous man." A man of honor, she declared, he promised to free them and set them aboard one of the European ships then cruising in the Strait of Juan de Fuca.

Captain Bulygin refused to believe his wife, and even ordered Tarakanov to threaten to kill her since she did not want to rejoin him. "I do not fear death," she replied according to Tarakanov's account. "It is better for me to die than to wander about with you in the forest, where we might fall into the hands of a cruel and barbarous people." Her present situation was far better. "Now I am living with a kind and humane people," she stated. "Tell my husband that I scorn his threats."[20] In the end, Tarakanov and Bulygin were convinced by her argument. Along with one Russian hunter and two Alutiiq, they did surrender to Anna Petrovna's captor, a remarkable Makah personage named Yutramaki or Ulatillah Makee—quite possibly the son of a Makah woman of good lineage and John Mackay or McKey, an Irish ship's surgeon who in 1786 had been the first European to live among the Nootka people.[21] The remaining *Sv. Nikolai* survivors determined they would try to escape in their dugout canoe to the open sea, but they quickly wrecked in the surf and were subsequently taken prisoner, all of them coming to live as captives in various Native settlements along the coast.

The Makah people made their home in the most northwesterly corner of the Olympic peninsula, with principal village sites at Neah Bay and Mukkaw Bay. Closely related by culture and kinship to the Nootka people across the Strait of Juan de Fuca, they were renowned as hardy and brave seagoers, fishing for immense halibut and hunting whale long miles out in Pacific in their large cedar canoes. Like the Nootkas, they were feared and respected by their neighbors for their success in the trading, raiding, and the slaving practices that dominated relations between Northwest Coast societies.

When he surrendered, Tarakanov began a residence among the Makahs that lasted more than a year. Enjoying Yutramaki's friendship and support, Tarakanov soon distinguished himself, gaining recognition as a man of renown, a *starshina* or *toyon*. "By taking advantage of their simplicity," he later ingenuously explained, "I was able to make them love and even honor me." Among other devices that, to the Makah, proved Tarakanov's brilliance, was a kite constructed of paper with a string from animal tendons that sailed high in the brisk coastal breezes. His contributions to Makah culture included more practical items as well. He fashioned rudimentary tools from nails, carved wooden dishes that became prized articles, and constructed a large fortified lodge with gun ports facing the sea that the Makahs regarded as an architectural marvel. He also fashioned a "war-rattle" that seems to have been an adaptation of the bosun's rattle familiar to all European sailors. This device he introduced as a means to give signals to war parties. "Everyone was amazed at my intelligence," Tarakanov related, "and thought that few such geniuses could be left in Russia."

By contrast, the Natives were amazed that Captain Bulygin could ever have been a leader among the Russians. He could not shoot birds; he had no skill with an axe, nor did he excel in any other practical matter. Bulygin too benefited from Yutramaki's protection for a short time. But then he reconciled with Anna Petrovna, who was now living with another master, and persuaded Yutramaki to allow him to rejoin his wife. In the sequel, as Tarakanov declared, they suffered the bitterest fate of all the *Sv. Nikolai* castaways. Mistreated by her new master, the realistic, strong-willed Anna Petrovna perished during her captivity. Grieving her death and afflicted with a severe illness, most likely influenza, Bulygin died soon after.[22]

"At long last," Tarakanov declared, "merciful God heard our prayers and delivered us."[23] In early May 1810 the American brig *Lydia*, Captain Thomas Brown, came into view. Taking Tarakanov along, Yutramaki went aboard. They found that Captain Brown had already ransomed another Russian from his Chinook owner on the Columbia River. After talking with Tarakanov, Brown told Yutramaki to order his countrymen to bring all the *Sv. Nikolai* captives to the *Lydia*, and Brown would purchase them for a good price. The next day, after some haggling, the Natives generally agreed to a standard rate in trade goods for each Russian captive, including Tarakanov: five patterned blankets, a thirty-five foot length of woolen cloth, a locksmith's file, two steel knives, a mirror, five packets of gunpowder, and five packets of small shot. But the owner of two Russians demanded a much higher price, and the master of a third was absent on a whale hunt and could not be reached.

Proficient in the strong arm tactics commonly employed by all parties, Native and European, on the Northwest Coast, Captain Brown seized as a hostage the brother of the man who wanted a higher price for his two Russians. He would not release him, Brown announced, until the three remaining captives had been traded back to him. The hostage's brother delivered his two captives the next day. The third was brought to the *Lydia* by dugout canoe a day later, when the ship was already at sea fifteen miles off shore. Brown then freed the Native hostage. For these last three captives he paid the same amount as he had given for each of the others.

Of the twenty-two people who had sailed on the *Sv. Nikolai*, Captain Brown was able to rescue thirteen. Seven others including Anna Petrovna and Captain Bulygin had died either from battle injuries or from illness and misadventure during their captivity. One of the Alutiiq workers had been found living with the Chinook people on the Columbia River in 1809 by another Yankee sea captain, who ransomed him and carried him to Baranov at Sitka. According to Tarakanov, the young apprentice Phillip Kotel'nikov had been sold to a distant people, perhaps also on the Columbia River, and at that point he vanishes from the historical record. Captain Brown arrived at New Archangel on June 9 to deliver Tarakanov and the dozen other RAC workers to Baranov, who was pleased to reimburse the trader for his expenses and services.[24]

The report brought back from the Olympic peninsula by Tarakanov and his comrades must have convinced Baranov to abandon his efforts to establish a Russian outpost in the Pacific Northwest. Meanwhile, RAC hunting activity continued in northern California in partnership with American shipmasters. Handicapped more than ever by a shortage of RAC ships and skilled sailors, between 1808 and 1813 Chief Manager Baranov entered into seven additional partnership agreements for California expeditions, most of them with the Winship brothers and their associates. In addition, after failing to make the 1808 rendezvous with the *Sv. Nikolai* at Gray's Harbor, Ivan Kuskov directed the *Kad'iak* to the northern California hunting grounds at Trinidad Bay, Bodega Bay, and San Francisco Bay that Tarakanov had scouted aboard the *Peacock* two years earlier.

According to an abstract prepared by RAC historian Kyrill Khlebnikov in 1819, the Company's returns from California hunts aboard American ships totaled over 6,000 pelts, with Kuskov adding another 3,000 from his 1808-1810 expedition. These were by far the largest profit-making operations for the RAC during this period. Since the Russian and Alutiiq hunters were indiscriminately killing female sea otters as well as males, and yearlings and pups as well as mature animals, Baranov and his Yankee partners obviously had no intent to conserve California's sea otter populations or to follow sustained yield hunting practices. As had been true earlier in Alaskan waters, the predatory nature of these hunting expeditions was evident, the more understandable since the Russians were intruding in waters where they had no pretense of a territorial claim.[25]

Soon after his safe return to New Archangel with Captain Brown, Timofei Tarakanov again sailed southward as part of this onslaught against California sea otters. In the winter of 1810-1811 he headed a hunting crew with forty-eight baidarkas aboard the *Isabella*, Captain William Heath Davis who dropped off Tarakanov and his men to make camp on the north side of San Francisco Bay. They were joined by another hunting party of sixty baidarkas carried aboard the *Albatross* by Captain Nathan Winship. Subsequently, in February or March of 1811, yet another hunting crew of twenty-two baidarkas came from Bodega Bay, where Ivan Kuskov had arrived with the RAC ship *Chirikov* but found the hunting very poor. Together, these three groups must have wiped out the entire remaining sea otter population of San Francisco Bay. Kuskov returned to Sitka after three months with more than 1,200 pelts, which probably represented the combined returns for the season's campaign.

In the fall of 1811 Chief Manager Baranov revived his project to establish an RAC outpost in northern California, now with the explicit approval of Tsar Alexander.[26] Once again he placed Ivan Kuskov in charge, organizing an expedition that included sixty Alutiiq hunters in forty baidarkas along with twenty-five Russian *promyshlenniks*. Unfortunately, no documents regarding this voyage have come to light. Largely on the basis of Baranov's earlier desire that Tarakanov take a major role in the similar 1808 expedition, we may surmise that he was included in Kuskov's party. If so, he served as one of the founders of the small Russian settlement at Bodega Bay and perhaps also had a hand in the construction of Fort Ross, established in June of 1812 on a headland twelve miles north of the mouth of the Russian (*Slavianka*) River, adjacent to plentiful forest for building materials and land that might be developed for farming and grazing.

Tarakanov was back in New Archangel at least briefly in 1813, for in January of 1814 he headed a crew of fifty-nine Alutiiq hunters sent to California aboard the brig *Il'mena* (formerly Captain Brown's *Lydia*, purchased by the RAC a few months earlier), under Captain William Wadsworth, who had joined the service of the RAC.[27] Apparently he remained at Bodega Bay or Fort Ross until April 1816. He then he boarded the *Il'mena* with his hunting crew for a return trip to New Archangel, leaving California for the last time.[28] Once at sea, however, Captain Wadsworth discovered his ship leaking dangerously. Needing repairs, Wadsworth made the shorter, safer voyage to the Hawaiian Islands, arriving at Honolulu in May.

Reaching Hawaii by accident, Timofei Tarakanov found himself a part of yet another episode that called on his leadership abilities. For a year and a half he was involved in disengaging the RAC from an ambitious empire-building scheme launched by Dr. Georg Schäffer, a German fortune-seeker who had been acting as Baranov's agent, but who had far overreached his commission from the Chief Manager. This episode has been well documented in Richard A. Pierce's excellent study, *Russia's Hawaiian Adventure, 1815-1818*, which emphasizes Dr. Schäffer's maladroit efforts to profit from the enmity between King Kamehameha and his Kauai-based rival King Kaumualii.[29] Tarakanov's role is less fully described. He soon became Schäffer's trusted deputy on Kauai, taking charge of a Russian and Alutiiq work force at Waimea while Schäffer busied himself with expanding his claims and authority at Hanalei and elsewhere. With Kaumualii's approval, Tarakanov and his men began construction of a stone fort they called Fort Elizabeth. When Kaumualii bestowed land grants and other privileges on a select few Russians, prominent among these gifts was a grant to Tarakanov of a village with eleven families alongside the Hanapepe River.[30]

Early in 1817, apparently by way of the ship *Cossack*, Baranov sent a message from Sitka that repudiated Dr. Schäffer's various business transactions. He demanded the return of two Russian ships already in the Hawaiian Islands, as well as the funds he had earlier entrusted to Schäffer. The Chief Manager also sent a direct order to Tarakanov to return to Sitka with his Alutiiq hunters. "It is better for you to hunt beavers [sea otter] than to till the soil," he wrote to Tarakanov.[31] However, according Tarakanov's later report, Schäffer ignored Baranov's commands and refused to let him and his crew depart. "I will hold you," Tarakanov remembered him stating, "until Alexander Andreevich [Baranov] sends an intelligent, sober, and experienced man in your place."

Compelled to disobey Baranov's order, Tarakanov was sorely distressed. His conduct to that point, he believed, had been exemplary, but now he was placed in a situation "from which, with my simple soul, I could not find any way out." How," he asked rhetorically, "was I to escape this pig-headedness?" Indeed, he declared, "Life was very hard." He went to his residence, asked for a glass of vodka, then another, and took to bed. The next day he did the same, and so it went for more than a week. Whenever Schäffer asked for him, he received the answer that Tarakanov was drunk. At first the other Russians made excuses for him. He was not a young man, they declared, and should not be ashamed of "a little relaxation" after having served the Company for such a long time. But then, as Tarakanov later candidly reported, everyone started to wonder at his prolonged drinking bout, "knowing that I had always considered drunkenness as one of the worst vices." His excuse, he later explained, was his feeling that "everything I undertook [in the interest of the Company] was done in vain."

While these events were unfolding, another Russian navy ship brought the welcome news that the Tsar's government had approved Tarakanov's manumission from serfdom. He had petitioned for emancipation a few years earlier, presumably with Alexander Baranov's encouragement, so this was not entirely an unexpected event.[32] The necessary emancipation ceremony could not be performed in Hawaii because of the lack of the appropriate official; but the notice of his legal freedom must have been immensely satisfying, a reward be-yond price for his faithful service to the Tsar and the RAC.

In May 1817 King Kaumualii finally forced the Russians to leave Waimea and Fort Elizabeth. At Hanalei Dr. Schäffer declared he would remain on Kauai and await the two war ships and other reinforcements that he still claimed would be arriving soon from Sitka. In June he issued a most remarkable document, a manifesto of sorts meant to bolster the spirits of the small Russian and Alutiiq force, declaring his resolve to stay at Hanalei and his vainglorious determination to "show these Indian bandits what Russian honor is and that it can-not be treated lightly." Particularly, the German boasted, "I will show these barbarians that a Russian staff officer can put down rebellion." First among those who joined in signing this bombastic pronouncement was Timofei Tarakanov, now restored to duty.[33]

In the face of Kaumualii's continued militant opposition, however, Schäffer left Kauai a month later and took Tarakanov and most of his beleaguered command to Honolulu. There Kamehameha and a cabal of Yankee sea captains advising the king were likewise anxious to end the Russian bid for trade and influence in the islands. By this time the RAC employ-ees apparently also had decided that Schäffer's meddling in Hawaii's royal politics had made him a liability. In July 1817, Tarakanov headed a council that convinced Schäffer—like-ly against his wishes—to board a Yankee ship heading for Canton, with the understanding that he would proceed to St. Petersburg and report on the Hawaiian situation to the RAC directors and the Russian government.[34]

With Dr. Schäffer gone, Tarakanov took charge of efforts

to salvage a difficult situation for the RAC. He was on good terms with most of the American captains who had urged Kamehameha to banish the German\. His own goal was simply to retrieve the remaining Company assets on Kauai and return to New Archangel. He prepared an inventory of RAC property, including the plantations on Kauai presented or promised to the Russians by Kaumualii. In October, assisted by his old friend Captain William Heath Davis, Tarakanov arranged with Captain Myrick of the *Cossack* to take back to Sitka two Russians and the Alutiiq hunters who had accompanied him from California aboard the *Il'mena*. To pay their way, they would first sail back to California with Myrick for a sea otter hunt under the customary share arrangement.[35] A short time later Tarakanov, most likely sailing with Davis on his new ship the *Eagle*, also departed for New Archangel, reaching the RAC headquarters a few days before Christmas, 1817.[36]

On his arrival, Tarakanov learned that Captain-Lieutenant L. A. Hagemeister, a naval officer dispatched by the RAC directors, had come to New Archangel to review Alexander Baranov's administration of Russian America. A month later Hagemeister formally took command, allowing Baranov to retire, as the aging Chief Manager had so long desired.[37] Among other concerns, Hagemeister was anxious to clear up the tangled situation left by Dr. Schäffer in Hawaii. And he was not at all pleased with Tarakanov's initiative in sending his hunting crew to California with Captain Myrick. He believed Tarakanov did not have the necessary authority to make this agreement which, Hagemeister stated, "was contrary to instructions from superiors."[38]

The new General Manager, schooled in navy discipline, believed in strict rules and a meticulously businesslike management of the RAC colonies. While he apparently maintained a cordial relationship with Baranov so long as the veteran manager remained at New Archangel, within weeks Hagemeister was urging him to return to Russia "for the good of the colonies."[39] Concerning RAC affairs in Hawaii, he ordered Fleet Lieutenant I. A. Podushkin, captain of the RAC ship *Otkrytie*, to sail to the islands, reestablish cordial relations with King Kamehameha, and bargain with him for all the Company property that could possibly be retrieved. Tarakanov accompanied Podushkin, although Hagemeister cautioned the Captain to monitor the behavior of the veteran employee "which according to rumors reaching me were not so advantageous for the company because of carelessness regarding property, and prejudicial to his character because of licentiousness."[40] Hagemeister added that Podushkin should give Tarakanov all possible assistance in collecting the Company's property so that later he could not claim that any sort of obstacle had been put in his way.

The following August Hagemeister reported the disappointing results of this expedition. Captain Podushkin had succeeded in returning the RAC people left in Hawaii except for fugitives who were determined to remain in the islands. But "none of the property squandered by the Doctor was recovered. The plantations are desolate, and not being returned; the vessel *Kad'iak* has been abandoned because it is unfit. The tackle and several sails and whatever could be dismantled from the vessel [have] been brought back."[41] In other words, despite the best efforts of Tarakanov and Podushkin, the RAC's Hawaiian adventure ended as a complete fiasco. K. T. Khlebnikov, Hagemeister's assistant in auditing Baranov's accounts, later stated that the monetary loss amounted to more than 200,000 rubles.[42]

Baranov's retirement marked the end of an era in Russian America, bringing a change in administration that replaced his intensely personal management style and the crude ways of the fur hunting and trading era with a highly formal, punctilious, and class-conscious supervision by naval officers, trained in tsarist Russia's most elite service. The fragmentary records that have survived from this period contain but little further information on Timofei Tarakanov. We know that he had married. His wife, fifteen years his junior, was Alexandra, daughter of Ignat—a Alutiiq woman baptized with a Russian name. In February 1819 the couple's son was born at Sitka.[43] At that time Tarakanov would have been 45, his wife 30. So far as we know, this son, named Alexei, was their only child.

We have one more scrap of information about his American career. In 1819 Tarakanov had charge of a hunting crew with eighty baidarkas aboard Captain Young's *Finlandia*, which conducted a hunt in the highly dangerous and hostile Tlingit waters of Cross Sound adjoining Glacier Bay. The total return for this expedition was a mere 296 pelts, demonstrating emphatically the disaster that unrestrained commercial hunting had brought to Alaska's sea otter populations.[44] It may also have demonstrated to Tarakanov that the time had come for him also to retire from his long, hard years of service for the RAC. Governor S. I. Ianovskii, Hagemeister's successor in command at New Archangel, ordered him to sail for Russia and report to the RAC directors about the miscarried affair in the Hawaiian islands. "He is of no use to us here," Ianovskii tersely commented in his official dispatch.[45]

Tarakanov subsequently returned to Kursk with his small family. An 1834 entry in local census records states that "Timofei Nikitin, son of Tarakanov" along with his son Alexei and his wife Alexandra had been added to the Kursk class of townsmen.[46] This entry is the last appearance of Tarakanov and his family in the historical record.

Knowing nothing more, we can conclude that Timofei Tarakanov's remarkable career demonstrates that Russian America was not bereft of talented and enterprising frontiersmen. Particularly from his account of the *Sv. Nikolai's* shipwreck, it is clear also that despite the legalisms of rank and status, no sharp divisions of class, caste, or racial distinction divided the common society of Russian Alaska early in the nineteenth century. In ways that were encouraged by Alexander Baranov's personal example—though certainly not by his autocratic successors—Tarakanov flourished in a society leveled by the rough equality of shared risks, where status derived in large part from personal attainments.

Timofei Tarakanov was born into a role that could not bring him great rewards. While he did gain his legal freedom, his humble origins within the tsarist social system did not allow him to achieve renown beyond the small circle of his peers and comrades in Russian North America. Yet his reputation survived in oral tradition, and his name deserves to be retrieved from obscurity. He is surely eligible to be counted among those notable figures in western American history we honor for their daring, their skills, and their epic accomplishments.

Notes

* This article is part of a larger study of Alexander Baranov and the development of Russian America, with research funding from the National Endowment for the Humanities. The author would like to thank his colleague and friend Dr. Alexander Yu. Petrov, a senior fellow in North American history at the Russian Institute of Science, Moscow, for research assistance and translation expertise. It was originally published in Montana The Magazine of Western History, Volume 56, number 3 (Autumn 2006), where it received the Vivian Paladin Award as the best article to appear in 2006.

1. For Tarakanov's origins, see Aleksandr Zorin, Kurskie Teradi, Tetrad' Pervaia (Kursk: Kurskii Gosudarsvennyi Pedagogocheskii Institut, 1997), 22-33.

2. For the conquest of Siberia and Russian expansion into the North Pacific, the premier English language source publication is Basil Dmytryshyn, E. A. P. Crownhart-Vaughan, and Thomas Vaughn, trans. and ed., Russia's Conquest of Siberia: 1558-1700, and Russia's Penetration of the North Pacific Ocean: 1700-1797, volumes one and two in To Siberia and Russian America: Three Centuries of Russian Eastward Expansion, 1798-1867, A Documentary Record (3 vols., Portland: Oregon Historical Society Press, 1985-1989). An admirable summary appears in Lydia T. Black, Russians in Alaska, 1732-1867 (Fairbanks: University of Alaska Press, 2004).

3. The introduction to Dmytryshyn, Crownhart-Vaughan, and Vaughn, The Russian American Colonies, 1798-1867, provides a succinct account, as does Black, Russians in Alaska.

4. Mary Malloy, "Boston Men" on the Northwest Coast: The American Maritime Fur Trade, 1788-1844 (Kingston, ONT: Limestone Press, 1998), 137-38; Elton

Engstrom, Joseph O'Cain: Adventurer on the Northwest Coast (Juneau, AK: Alaska Litho Printers, 2003).

5. K. T. Khlebnikov, Baranov, Chief Manager of the Russian Colonies in America, trans. Colin Bearne, ed. Richard A. Pierce (Kingston, ONT: Limestone Press, 1973), 41-42; Adele Ogden, The California Sea-Otter Trade, 1784-1848 (Berkeley: University of California Press, 1941), 46-47.

6. John D'Wolf, A Voyage to the North Pacific (Cambridge, MA: Welch, Bigelow and Company, 1861; reprint Fairfield, WA: Ye Galleon Press, 1968), 25-34.

7. A modern translation of Rezanov's confidential report of June 17, 1806, appears in Dmytryshyn, Crownhart-Vaughan, and Vaughn, The Russian American Colonies, 112-48. The often-embellished story of Rezanov's relationship with the headstrong teenager Doña Concepcion de Arguello is reviewed in Eve Iversen, The Romance of Nikolai Rezanov: A Literary Legend and Its Effect on California History (Kingston, ONT: Limestone Press. 1998).

8. Khlebnikov, Baranov, 67-68.

9. Ogden, The California Sea Otter Trade, 50, 196 n. 16, citing Luis Antonio Arguëllo to Arrillaga, San Francisco, March 31 and May 15, 1807, Californias, Vol. 51, No. 12, Bancroft Library.

10. Malloy, Boston Men, 93; Ogden, California Sea Otter Trade, 50; Khlebnikov, Notes on Russian America: Part I: Novo-Archangelsk, 9.

11. Kenneth N. Owens, ed., Alton S. Donnelly, trans., The Wreck of the Sv. Nikolai: Two Narratives of the First Russian Expedition to the Oregon Country, 1808-1810 (Portland: Oregon Historical Society Press, 1985; reprint ed., Lincoln: Nebraska University Press, 2002), 28-29.

12. Pierce, Russian America, 75-76.

13. Alexander Baranov to Timofei Tarakanov, September 18, 1808, New Archangel. This document is located in the Otdel Rukopisei Rossiiskoi Gosudarstvennoi Biblioteki [Manuscript Division of the Russian State Library], F. 204. K. 32. Ed. hr. 7, ll. 1-2. Baranov's confidence in Tarakanov is evident also in his subsequent instructions to Ivan Kuskov, departing on the Kad'iak with orders to rendezvous with the Sv. Nikolai: Baranov to Kuskov, October 14 [26], 1808, in Nina N. Bashkina et al., ed., The United States and Russia: The Beginning of Relations, 1765-1815 (Washington, DC: U.S. Department of State, 1980), 545.

14. Captain Thomas Brown had carried out two previous trading voyages to the Northwest Coast in the Vancouver, the first in 1802-1804, and the second in 1805-1806: Malloy, Boston Men,168-69.

15. Owens, Wreck of the Sv. Nikolai, 4. In preparing Tarakanov's narrative for publication, V. M. Golovnin mistakenly identified the shipwreck site as Destruction Island, a prominent feature approximately fifteen miles south and three miles offshore, named by Captain George Vancouver. Many authors have repeated this misidentification.

16. Erna Gunther, Indian Life on the Northwest Coast of North America, as seen by the Early Explorers and Fur Traders during the Last Decades of the Eighteenth Century (Chicago: University of Chicago Press, 1972), 55-90; Robert H. Ruby and John A. Brown, Indian Slavery in the Pacific Northwest (Spokane, WA: Arthur H. Clark Company, 1993), 117-29 et passim.

17. Baranov's roster for the voyage is contained in his instructions to Captain Bulygin, September 22, 1808, Otdel Rukopisei Rossiiskoi Gosudarstvennoi Biblioteki

[Manuscript Division of the Russian State Library],
F. 204, K. 32, Ed. hr. 8, ll. 1-4. This may be compared
with Tarakanov's list of the survivors in Owens, ed., Sv.
Nikolai, 65.

18. As it happened, strong winds and high seas kept the
Kad'iak from entering Gray's Harbor to make the
expected rendezvous. At Kuskov's direction, the ship
sailed southward to Trinidad Bay and Bodega Bay,
where it remained until August, 1809: Khlebnikov,
Baranov, 71.

19. Owens, ed., Wreck of the Sv. Nikolai, 57.

20. Owens, ed., Wreck of the Sv. Nikolai, 60.

21. On Yutramaki and his parentage, see Owens, ed., Wreck
of the Sv. Nikolai, 22-25, and 94, notes 21, 22.

22. Tarakanov ascribes Bulygin's death to consumption,
a general nineteenth century term for diseases of the
respiratory system including both influenza and tuberculosis. Because Bulygin's illness was severe and quickly
led to his death, influenza is the most reasonable
diagnosis. Despite many efforts, no researcher has been
able to locate further information concerning Anna
Petrovna Bulygina.

23. Owens, ed., Wreck of the Sv. Nikolai, 64.

24. In April 1809 Captain Brown had taken command of
the Lydia, traded along the Northwest Coast during the
1810 season, and thus was in a position to rescue the
Sv. Nikolai's survivors: Malloy, Boston Men, 127; Pierce,
Russian America, 72, sv. Thomas Brown.

25. Altogether, well over 21,000 sea otters were killed
in California by Alaskan-based hunting expeditions
between 1803 and 1817. Kuskov's 1809 hunt aboard
the Kad'iak marked an effective end to the abundance
of these animals in the coastal waters of northern

California: Khlebnikov, Baranov, 71; Khlebnikov, Novo-Archangelsk, 9-10.

26. Between 1807 and 1809 Baranov had urged the RAC board of directors to secure Tsar Alexander I's permission to establish a Russian settlement in California. Chancellor Nikolai Rumiantsev recommended this proposal to the Tsar, who approved it in November 1809. The text of Rumiantsev's recommendation is in Bashkina et al., ed., The United States and Russia, 618-21. This approval may not have reached New Archangel until late 1810.

27. Regarding Captain Wadsworth, see Pierce, Russian America: A Biographical Dictionary, 537.

28. Ogden reports the supposed capture by the Spanish of Tarakanov and eleven Aleuts when they went ashore near San Pedro. This totally erroneous report comes from a patently forged document, a pencil-written manuscript in English found in the Bancroft Library with the title "Statement of My Captivity among the Californians by a Russian Fur-Hunter," supposedly by one Vasilii Petrovich Tarakanov, who is a fictitious figure loosely modeled after Timofei Tarakanov. Written by Ivan Petrov, a translator, researcher, and writer for Hubert Howe Bancroft in the 1870s, this fraudulent document is one among a substantial number of forgeries Petrov passed off on the Bancroft. See Owens, "Ivan Petrov's Fraudulent Tarakanov Document," pages 77-87 in Owens, ed., Wreck of the Sv. Nikolai, and works by other scholars cited there.

29. Russia's Hawaiian Adventure, 1815-1817 (Berkeley: University of California Press, 1965).

30. Report of Tarakanov to Lieutenant-Captain Hagemeister, received at Sitka, February 12, 1818, in Pierce, Russia's Hawaiian Adventure, 97.

31. Baranov's instructions were repeated by Tarakanov in

his report to Lieutenant-Captain Hagemeister, February 12, 1818, in Pierce, Russia's Hawaiian Adventure, 99.

32. Tarakanov's manumission is noted in Hagemeister, Report to the Main Office, March 7, 1818, in Pierce, ed., RAC Correspondence of the Governors, 43-44.

33. Declaration, Schäffer et al., June 1, 1817, of Decision to Make a Stand at Hanalei, in Pierce, Russia's Hawaiian Adventure, 93-94.

34. Tarakanov et al., Report to the Main Office, July 7, 1817, on Events up to the Departure of Schäffer, Pierce, Russia's Hawaiian Adventure, 105.

35. Hagemeister, Instructions to Mr. Skipper [Kh. M.] Benseman, January 17, 1818; Hagemeister, Proposal to the NA Office, 17 January 1818; Translation of a letter to the Governor of New California, Don Pablo Vicente De Sala, January 18, 1818, all in Pierce, ed., RAC Correspondence of the Governors, 3-6.

36. George Young et al. to Schäffer, December 1816, in Pierce, Russia's Hawaiian Adventure, has the notation "Delivered by Tarakanov at Novo-Archangel'sk, December 20, 1817. For William Heath Davis and the Eagle, see Molloy, Boston Men, 97.

37. Hagemeister. Report, NA Office [of the RAC] to the Main Office, January 11, 1818, in Pierce, ed., RAC Correspondence of the Governors, 1. The circumstances of Baranov's retirement, his departure from Sitka, and his death at sea are summarized in Khlebnikov, Baranov, 96-100. On Hagemeister's American career, see Pierce, Russian America, 185-87.

38. Hagemeister, Instructions to Mr. Skipper [Kh. M.] Benseman, 17 January 1818; Hagemeister, Proposal to the NA Office, January 17, 1818; Translation of a letter to the Governor of New California, Don Pablo Vicente De Sala, January 18, 1818, all in Pierce, ed., RAC Correspondence of the Governors, 3-6.

39. Pierce, Russian America, 186.

40. Hagemeister, Instructions to the Commander of the RAC vessel OTKRYTIE, Fleet-Lieutenant and Cavalier Iakov Anikeevich Podushkin, February 9, 1818, in Pierce, ed., RAC Correspondence of the Governors, 27-28.

41. Hagemeister, undated letter to the Main Office [July 13/18], 1818; Hagemeister the Main Office, August 18, 1818, both in Pierce, ed., RAC Correspondence of the Governors, 121-22.

42. Khlebnikov, Baranov, 94.

43. Pierce, Russian America, 499.

44. Khlebnikov, Notes on Russian America: Part I: Novo-Archangelsk, p. 94.

45. Pierce, Russian America, 499.

46. GAKO [State Archive of Kursk Region], Auxiliary list, Revizki Skazkii, eighth revision (1834): F. 184. Op. 2, D. 532, ll. 112 ob-113; F. 184. Op. 2, D. 593, ll. 241-42.

A specialist in the history of the American West, Dr. Ken Owens is Emeritus Professor of History at California State University, Sacramento. He has published extensively on the history of the gold rushes in California and Montana, and on the career of the pioneer California promoter John Sutter. Concerning Russian America, he is the author and editor of The Wreck of Sv. Nikolai: Two Narratives of the First Russian Expedition to the Oregon Country, 1808-1810 (Oregon History Society Press, 1985; Nebraska University Press, 2002). Ken's most recent book is Gold Rush Saints: California Mormons and the Great Rush for Riches (Arthur H. Clark Company and the University of Oklahoma Press, 2004).

Author's Biography

Jane Galer holds a BA in philosophy and religion from Colorado Woman's College, an MA in material culture specializing in Native American beadwork and basketry and a Certificate in Museum Curation for Anthropologists from California State University, Sacramento. She is a member of Lambda Alpha National Anthropology Honor Society.

An award winning poet, Jane Galer has published two books of poetry, *Too Deep for Tears* (2006 out of print) and *The Spirit Birds* (2012 Poiêsis Press), the memoir *How I Learned to Smoke: An American Girl in Iran* eBook, (2011 Poiêsis Press), and the non-fiction work *Becoming Hummingbird: Charting Your Life Journey the Shaman's Way* (2011 Poiêsis Press). Galer trained as a shaman with the Q'ero of the high Andes in Peru and has studied with The Four Winds Society in indigenous shamanic healing techniques. Writing as Galer Britton Barnes, she has published numerous articles on textile history and museums for Interweave Press. She is currently working on a joint project documenting the traditional ceremonies of the Q'ero people funded by a grant from the Lipton Trust. She lives in northern California with her family.

www.janegaler.com

CPSIA information can be obtained at www.ICGtesting.com
Printed in the USA
LVOW050140230612

287346LV00002B/2/P

9 780984 569731